THE FATE OF ANGELS AND DEMONS

MARIA A LEVATO

THE FATE OF ANGELS AND DEMONS

CONTENTS

Dedication
ix
Trigger Warning
xi

— Loathing Incarnate
1

one — The Transition of Power
7

two — Out of the Shadows and Into the Fire
19

three — Mother Fiercest
36

four — War, She Greets Us
48

five — Wastelands and Watchtowers
55

six — At the End of Everything
70

seven — When Tragedy Strikes
84

eight — The Queen-To-Be, Long Live She
99

nine — Mine
111

ten — Treason, Torture, Love
125

eleven — Helscape Be the Home of my Mother
141

twelve — Pleas and Bargains
156

thirteen — A Match Made in Jubilee
171

fourteen — A Matter of Honor
185

fifteen — Disrupting the System
200

sixteen — Between a Fire and a Hot Place
216

seventeen — The Art of Deception
230

eighteen — The Secret to Secrets
246

nineteen — Near Death
259

twenty — Father and Son, Reunited
274

twenty one — Homecoming
289

twenty two — Call of Freedom
304

twenty three — Allies Rising
318

twenty four — A Bittersweet Symphony
333

twenty five — Deranged, Debauched, Depraved
347

— A Shift in Perspective
361

About the Author
375

Copyright © 2025 by Maria A Levato
All rights reserved. No part of this book may be reproduced in any manner whatsoever without written permission except in the case of brief quotations embodied in critical articles and reviews.
Maria Levato explicitly forbids the use of this book and its contents being fed into AI models for any purpose, doing so will result in legal action.
First Printing, 2026
LCCN: 2026902442

*To the psycho bitches,
and the switches...
Here's a couple of MC's that will fulfill even
your kinkiest wishes.*

TRIGGER WARNING

The Fate of Angels and Demons is a fantasy book with a central romance that has dark-romance-esque elements to it. Please take care of your mental health and be aware of the following triggers:

Graphic sex scenes,
Kink/BDSM,
Degradation,
Praise/Worship kink,
Humiliation,
Obsession,
Choking,
Spanking,
Pyrophillia, kinda? (I KNOW! Don't ask; just read. LOL.)
Pegging,
Switch Dynamics,
Torturing prisoners as a form of foreplay (In my defense, please ref. The Cell Block Tango.),
Kidnapping,
War,
Murder,

TRIGGER WARNING

Death,
PTSD,
References to Abuse/SA/Rape (off page, remembered),
Attempted SA,
Stressed family dynamics,
Forced labor, child labor, starving populous (brief and in the context of highlighting important issues),
etc.

LOATHING INCARNATE

LILLY

It's been a year since I last went home, a full year since I last looked my mother in the eye. For most of that time, I've been on the remote island of Pallentine. Full of beautiful forests and inhabited by a tribal people that has allied themselves with my mother, I've come to use this land as a respite from the turbulence that plagues my relationship with her. As I look at yet another letter where she's barked orders at me without so much as asking about my well-being, I sigh, crumbling it and lying back in the pile of soft leaves I've created for myself.

"She really doesn't get why I won't come home, huh?" I mutter to myself, knowing there's no ears around to receive my words. "How could she save me from the nightmare I was born into only to become a gilded cage herself?"

Thinking back, things have been bad between us for much longer than I'm sure she would say. For me, it started just before Callian was born. For her, though, this tension probably took hold when I took the title of peacemaker, the centerpiece of the grand alliance between the islands from her. Frustrated as I think back on it, I keep my gaze on the gentle rays of sunlight peeking at me from between the treetops, staying in focus perhaps the only thing keeping me from losing it here and now.

She wanted me to take that title, then resented me for doing as she asked. I remember her exact words. "*You've grown, Lilly, and you're at least my equal.*" She swore I was ready, and that she trusted me. I thought she believed in me. As it turns out, it never mattered if I was ready. *She* wasn't ready. For years she's clung to that role, forgetting that she still has ample power of her own from the throne of Oceanica. It's not like going from peacemaker to queen is all that big of a difference. I feel like a puppet, taking only the actions she directs me to. I do no more and no less than I'm told. Mom loves to call it guidance but never accepts no for an answer. Like a wolf in sheep's clothing, her guidance camouflages any sense of free will I once had. The anger and resentment are growing, stirring within me more violently with each passing day, even the safe haven I've found in this peaceful land no longer masks it. I've become a cheap copy of her former greatness, rather than a leader formed from the rays of her own successes. For that, I hate her.

I had to stop going back. If all I'm going to do is take orders anyway, I can do that via letters while I live my life with semi-freedom, away from her. I love being around the Chief and his people. They're so open-minded and free. I sit up, looking at the village in the distance. Laughter rings through the air as children play and warriors' train. There's an uninterrupted since of community among them. Even the Chief interacts with them all. Unlike my parents, he's on the ground talking to his people every day rather than being huddled up in some palace where he can hide from the harm his mistakes have caused.

Here, I don't have to deal with the sort of rigid belief system my mother holds. It's like when we were trying to resurrect Kai and Cal. She didn't take Pastel's life to make it happen. Her morals wouldn't allow her to. Instead, she turned away while I did what needed to be done to give her the love I thought she deserved. I was eight. Even back then, I couldn't hold myself to that impossible moral standard she's always clung to.

I stand up and walk back towards the village. One woman runs over to greet me. "Lady Peacemaker, hello. Did you enjoy your walk?"

I nod. "Yes, I did. Thank you for asking."

The Chief interrupts. "Are you on your way out to fulfill the orders from your mother's letter, Lillianna?"

Even though I find some peace in Pallentine, it's still limited by the watchful eye of the Chief. He may believe in the type of freedom I want, but he's also a good friend to my mother, and I know that he'd tell her if I wandered too far off the path she so meticulously planned for me. Aside from a few messy late-night hookups with men I don't care to remember, I'm still restricted in many ways. The expectations that shackle me are just easier to ignore if I'm not at her side in Oceanica. "Yes, Chief. I'll get it taken care of. It shouldn't take long. It's merely a missing trade ship. I'll be back in a few hours."

In the end, I still believe my mother loves me. I love her too. She just needs to see that I'm Lilly. I'm not her. Nor should I have to be. It's not fair to expect me to be the hero everyone saw her as when she wasn't even that person herself. She made so many mistakes, many of which I still resent her for. Part of me still wonders if resurrecting Kai was a mistake, especially given the prophecy I had around that time. It still haunts my dreams every night, a recurring dream that I just can't seem to escape. Its terror doesn't end with daybreak, though. Lately, it's invaded my mind every time I call upon my power. Even now, as I call on it to levitate, the images invade my mind, chipping away at my sanity. The world engulfed by the flames of Michael, Malachi's son, who Johanna, Malachi's wife, raised to hate us because she blames my mother for her husband's eternal servitude to Myrkr, the first demon. The dream's always the same. I stand with the fire in the background, rubble piled beneath my feet as my little brother, Callian, now grown, faces off against Michael. One of them will die.

That's where I prefer to stop. I don't tell people what I see beyond that. While there are a multitude of reasons for that decision, the primary one is that I'm not sure what my role is in it. I'm only ever standing there, not trying to save Callian, not even sure which of them I want to live. The thought of either of them dying bothers me. For all that's happened between Michael's family and my own, I understand why he might want revenge. Hel, there's a part of me that wants my mother dead, too. "Oh, wait... No, I shouldn't think that." I try to self-correct as I hover over the seas, looking for the trade ship. It's useless, though. Trying to suppress my feelings about it only makes them rage louder. Once again, I correct my thoughts. "No, but I do. It's the truth. I may love her, but I hate her just as much. She already controls my actions. She doesn't get to stop me from thinking and feeling the way I do about it."

The feeling subsides and I continue mulling over my original thought at I search. I get Michael, and I believe that if we ever had a conversation, he might get me too. This goes deeper than the relationship I once had with his parents. It's a sort of connection I feel to him; one I often wonder if he senses. It's like we're mirrors, watching each other from different sides of an imaginary line our parents have drawn for us. My curiosity about that man might be the death of me, and if the prophecy unfolds, my brother too. Yet, I'm not sure I care, nor am I sure that I should.

From my understanding, Callian, my younger brother, has been away from home too. If the rumors are true, he's off somewhere training. He's recently come of age to be named the official heir to Oceanica, so I imagine that there's a lot he has to go through. That sweet kid I remember, the one I swore I'd do anything to protect once upon a time, is likely disappearing with each passing day. In time, he'll become more and more like my parents. He's always been desperate for their approval.

By the time the prophecy unfolds, I don't think protecting him will make sense for me. I won't be trying to save the boy I remember, but the man they've made of him. There's reason for me to believe that it benefits me more for Michael to live than the cog in the system they'll inevitably turn Callian into. After all, it's better to spare the one who might get me than the one who would undoubtedly have my head if I ever dared to speak these things that are buried so deep within my troubled mind.

CHAPTER
One

THE TRANSITION OF POWER

KAI

A knock at the door draws the attention of my husband and I as we lie cuddling on the small, lumpy bed in the ship's cabin. It's the captain. "Your Majesties, we'll be docking shortly."

All the joy seeps from the room when we realize the time has come for us to face all of our worst fears.

My usual seriousness once again lurks into my voice as I reply, "We're coming."

Jameson and I both understand that this isn't a game. While we steal moments of joy, we would never allow it to overshadow the severity of this situation. We both prepare ourselves, then emerge onto the deck. Unsure of how Tendu will take to our presence, he and I know that a fight is a possibility. A lot has happened these past years. The only good among the many events has been the joy of watching our beloved son grow into a man. We hope to thwart the foreseen threat directed at Oceanica's heir by our ex-allies in Tendu before it's realized.

That's why we're here. We must meet with Johanna and make her see reason before her son, Michael, our son, Callian, and our daughter, Lilly, are all consumed by her hatred.

The sound of metal unraveling causes my jaw to clench as the crew drops the anchor. I've always hated that sound. Honestly, I'm more comfortable in the volcanoes of Tendu than I am near any sort of water. As someone with a rock-based rune type, I suppose that makes sense. My home, Nollent, isn't too different from Tendu in terms of landscape. Our mountains don't have lava; the ones here do.

Good thing for me, though, I have a beautiful angel and his water runes at my side. His touch soothes my queasiness as he takes my hand. I roll my eyes a bit as Johanna's guards block our way off the ship.

"State your names and what business you have here," an assertive, stone-faced guard snapped.

I assume he's the one in charge of this group of testosterone-driven idiots. It takes everything in me not to laugh. Johanna had to have known that this wasn't a sound strategy for intimidating us. She sent them out here knowing they'd shoot their mouths off and end up dead. Yet, here I go, attempting to be peaceful anyway. "My name is Kai." I tilt my head toward Jameson a bit. "This is my husband, Jameson, but I'm sure you already knew that. We need only to speak with Johanna. Step aside."

The irrationally infuriating bark of laughter that shoots from this fool's mouth grates my nerves. "As if! Listen here, you filthy son-of-a..."

And there goes Jameson's patience... Mine typically folds first, except for instances like this. Jameson doesn't take well to people insulting our wife, Josie, and me. What is that? About fifty feet in the air? I should stop him. I don't feel like it though. Josie won't be too mad at us if we kill them, will she?

I shake my head. "Jameson, put him down."

The look he gives me could rival any puppy's adorable manipulation tactics. I may bottom him, but he's the brat. He knows it, too. He'll still do it for her. For her, we'd both do anything. In this marriage, Josie always gets the final say. She's our glue, our goddess, our reason for being, and our reason for being here right now. "Oh, fine." He huffs as he flies back down, placing the man on the ground. "Forget about them, then. Come on."

He doesn't wait for my reply before scooping me off the ground, bridal style, and flying toward Tendu's palace. If nothing else, this will save some time. I holler into the distance as we fly off, hoping Johanna's men will hear us. "Touch our crew and I'll let him drop you next time!"

Truth is, we didn't need the crew, or the boat for that matter, but we use it because it offers employment for sailors of Oceanica. They're our citizens, so I'm proud to protect them.

As he flies, I'm comfortable in his arms. I look down at the beauty that is Tendu. It's a shame that Johanna has tainted this kingdom's magnificence. For miles, the peaks and slopes of volcanoes cover the land as if they can recognize the wonder of imperfection. Vibrant cacti blooms surround the base of each, alongside other flora and fauna that compliments everything there is to love about this place.

Heartbreak follows the awe when I notice that the citizens all look like they're suffering. I witness thin, uncovered bodies of children whose ribs are entirely too visible, forced into labor by men who wear their gluttony like a badge of honor. The pathetic sight brings back memories of my childhood in the oppressed half of Nollent. I can't help but tense up. Jameson, trying to ease me, says, "We'll save my cousin's kingdom, even if it means we must kill his psychotic bride."

"Not soon enough," I reply. "Many of them won't make it."

"I know, my love. We'll mourn the losses. I won't allow it to go unseen."

I try to compose myself as we arrive at the palace. Johanna is already at the gates, awaiting our arrival. Her expression is fierce. She's ready to fight us on this. For Josie's sake, we try anyway.

"Johanna," Jameson begins, "We must speak."

She scoffs, well aware that this will go poorly for her if she resorts to violence right now. "Follow me."

She turns and walks inside, leaving little room for objection. We follow her through the elaborate décor of the palace halls. I once enjoyed viewing the grandiosity of it, but that was when Malachi ruled, and the people weren't suffering to maintain the lavish lifestyles of the royals. Now, it just disgusts me. She's driven this place to the economic brink by cutting it off from the alliance. Yet, she won't give up her comforts to accommodate change.

She leads us to the throne room where she sits, looking at us as we stand side-by-side prepared to face her down. I start off, hoping to remind her of a time when we were friends. "Johanna, it's been years. We've hardly spoken since I came back."

"Your life cost my husband his freedom. That's not a simple thing to move past."

She's right, but is this really the only path forward she can see? "I know that, Jo. I don't expect you to forgive me, or Josie and Jameson. However, the citizens, ours and yours, don't deserve to suffer for this."

"But they are, and they will continue to so long as the three of you still roam free whilst my husband is suffering in servitude."

Jameson pipes in. "How do you even know he's suffering? Josie and I had time to get to know Myrkr before everything happened. He's not that bad. I don't think he'd mistreat Malachi. In fact, he seemed quite fond of him."

She looks at Jameson as if he's a total idiot. I suppose she struggles to see why she would have to explain. "You don't know that any more than I know he's suffering. All any of us can do is theorize based on what we know. That's not good enough. Hypotheticals and possibilities aren't good enough for the safety of my husband, the father of my son, who, by the way, is heir to one of the most powerful nations on the planet."

Once again, she's right. I just don't see what starting a war that our children will have to fight fixes. I answer before Jameson can. "You aren't wrong about that, Johanna. We don't deny that. Your fate, and your son's, and Lilly's, and Callian's are all going to be grim though. If you don't alter your course, you'll doom everyone. Not just us."

She stands from the throne, moving toward us until she's mere inches away. The seething expression on her face could send chills to the bones of even the fiercest warriors. "Get out! Get your asses out of my throne room, out of my palace, and off my fucking island! Now, or the war will begin at this very moment and, in the name of every goddess from here to Rallem, I will destroy you all."

I look at Jameson. He nods, then looks at her. "Fine, Johanna, have it your way."

With that, we depart. Our boat arrives back in Oceanica in the evening. We call a meeting between us, Josie, Lilly, and Callian. It's set for the next morning since everyone else has been busy with work of their own.

Lilly has been working tirelessly to strengthen our other allies so that they, too, can resist Tendu should war break out. Callian still has quite a long way to go to master his abilities, so Jameson has been training him. He needs to be strong enough to defend himself, especially since it was him Lilly saw in the prophecy as being in the most danger. With all that going on, Josie, of course, has been the one looking out for our people. It's nice having three ruling royals here. It's easier to break up the work and make sure there's room to tag team issues that require more than one person's attention. Still, with everyone being this busy, things can get rough when we need to get ourselves in the same place. We make it work, though.

Michael

"Ugh!" I groan to myself from the hall when I hear arguing coming from the direction of Mom's study. It sounds like she's bickering with that one general again. He seems to have trouble following orders. The damn coward doesn't want war with the other islands. I'm tired of him talking back to my mother about her decisions. He understands how monarchies work, right? It's impossible for me to understand why she continues to let him live. She doesn't even give me, her own son, that much leniency.

I make my way down the hall to shut him up when suddenly, it all goes quiet. My instincts go on edge, and I realize that something is very wrong. I run and bust through the heavy wooden door with ease. Upon entering, I see my mother lying on the ground in a pool of blood with his sword in her chest. The general's eyes meet mine and he knows his life has already ended. I don't allow a single word to pass between us before I set the eternal flames of my Helfire upon him and toss him from the window into the lava below. After, I rush to Mom's side, but it's too late. She's gone.

My screams ring through my kingdom, attracting every guard in the palace. When they see what's happened, they pledge their loyalty to me even though I'm too distraught to pay them any mind. I only realize when they're done because one among them says, "Your orders, King Michael?"

King... Are they calling me king? I'm the king. Mom is dead. Dad is gone. I have to rule. I stuff my emotions down and meet their eyes, making damn sure that my expression goes soulless and cold. "My orders..." I glare. "My orders are as my mother's orders were. As they always have been. My orders are to prepare for war against the islands. We shall make them pay for all they have cost me."

The men surrounding me salute as I rise to my feet, taking my rightful place among them. "And clean this mess up!"

They look at me, almost heartbroken, as they realize I'm referring to my mother's corpse. Yet, they obey. I may be a new king, but none present are quite foolish enough to believe my authority is up for debate. They've all witnessed my power, and they'll avoid irritating me while I'm still fuming over this.

I glance down at the body again, fury and disappointment overshadowing the pain I feel in the moment. "What a fucking embarrassment... How weak must a queen be to allow herself to be murdered by cowardly scum? She was never a real queen anyway, I suppose. Just a regent, a placeholder until I became old enough to take my rightful place on my father's throne."

I notice one guard wince at my words, a subtle sign that he isn't wholehearted in his dedication to my rule. I kill him on the spot. "Consider that a warning to any others having doubts. Resolve yourselves to supporting me without reservations or die."

My eyes meet each pair of theirs. My methods seem to have been effective; there's no more hesitation in this group. They get moving, following my orders to clean this disgusting flesh off the floors of my palace.

As I leave, I have one of the court advisors summon me a noble girl to make into a whore. I need to blow off some steam before I lose it and someone ends up witnessing my true feelings, and no, I don't care whose reputation I have to ruin to accomplish it.

About an hour later, the whore gets tossed into my bedroom by the advisor. She stumbles to her knees and looks up at me. An eager one, huh? Must be looking for favor with her new king. I hate to break it to her, but this won't go her way. Still, I'll indulge her pathetic attempt at taking advantage of me.

I approach, towering above her. "You're here of your own volition?"

"Yes, sire." Her voice is a whimper.

"That's right." I grab her chin and force her to meet my gaze. "Such a filthy little slut, you are. You'll ruin your family's good name just to choke on your king's cock, won't you?"

She gulps. "Yes." Contrary to the fear in her voice and eyes, the way she leans toward me and the subtle grind of her hips as she seeks friction indicate that she is truly willing.

"You better get to work, bitch."

Pulling my robes open, she frees my dick. Her eyes widen at the sight of it. I assume it's the size that brought the shock to them. Little does the whore know, she's about to swallow it whole. "Open wide, little bitch."

She does, and I ram my cock straight down her worthless throat. As she gags and chokes, I fantasize about the day Josella and that pretty little daughter of hers, Lilly, are on their knees serving me this way in some vain attempt to keep me from ripping their hearts out. I force her head deeper as I imagine it. This whore is just a filler for my true fantasy, and I make sure she knows it. With each punishing thrust, I take into that tight throat; I degrade her as I would them. "I fucking hate you."

Another bruising thrust. "I hope you die sucking my dick."

And another. "You took everything from me. My mother hated me because of you goddess-damned priestesses."

I can't take it anymore. Ramming into her esophagus, I convulse, then send cum down her throat. I yank her off me and drag her up by her hair. My hand flies across her face and sends her back to the ground, crying. Even in tears, the lustful slut continues begging for more, but I'm done with her.

I summon the advisor back and have him escort her back to her family's estate with a warning never to speak of this day. I can't afford to have vicious rumors spreading through the kingdom about my sex life right now. It's preemptive and cruel, I know that, but my instincts have never been wrong before. I've learned to trust them. That girl had every intention of leveraging our interaction against me and I simply don't have the time to deal with it. That would most certainly hinder my plans for war against Oceanica and the other allies, a mission I've now inherited from my mother, and one I intend to continue in her honor. I need my people cooperating. I need them blaming the allies for the suffering they've endured all these years. It's the only way to avenge my parents. No matter what I've said out loud, I owe them that much.

CHAPTER

Two

OUT OF THE SHADOWS AND INTO THE FIRE

LILLY

My brother and I stand beside one another, looking toward the center of the room where the sources of our ever-growing fear sit. We love them so much, and they love us, but it feels impossible to thrive in a world where they are our parents. We dubbed them the Triad of Shame. Mostly as a joke, but also semi-serious because, like, how does one cope with having three parents who are the pinnacle of perfection? It's no wonder Mom tries so hard to control me. Every time I look at her, I'm reminded of how useless I am.

At least Callian has the genetics of two out of three of them. I don't even have that miniscule thing to cling to because I'm adopted. As much as I loathe my mother for not trusting me, I love her. Admire her, even. I just wish she didn't cast such an enormous shadow. Those dark thoughts I have when I'm away might diminish some if I wasn't constantly trying to be good enough. My mind bounces between thinking I wouldn't want it any other way and I'd derail the entire planet to change it. I guess in those moments where I feel invisible, I forget just how lucky I am to have them at all, especially since the family I was born into wasn't great. In fact, they weren't even good, or alright. They were horrible.

Mom, as usual, starts the meeting. "Callian," she starts, referring to my brother. "Lilly, welcome home. We've missed you both."

"Missed you too, Mom. What's wrong? Has something happened?" Callian replies as he looks at her. He seems to have picked up on their stress.

Even from upon their three golden thrones lined with rubies and sapphires, they suddenly seem weak. Something they can't prevent is happening. This is about the prophecy, isn't it? All our efforts to change the fates I saw for Callian and Michael all those years ago and we've changed nothing. Dammit. Some peacemaker I've become. Will this be my legacy? The peacemaker who

THE FATE OF ANGELS AND DEMONS

sat back and let two people she loves fall into some pre-destined, world-ending war?

I mean, of course, I'm more concerned with Callian's fate, but Michael isn't just some stranger. His mother was my mom's best friend, and his father was someone she called her brother. He's family in every way that matters. So, what if it's not by blood? I'm not family by blood either. It changes nothing. I should have protected him from this, just like I should have protected Callian. Tears well in my eyes as I ask, "It's the prophecy, isn't it? It's happening."

Mom nods. She seems to get a bit stuck on what to say next, so Dad Jameson speaks up. "We went to see Johanna last night. Once again, she refused our offers of peace. We returned, and late last night, we received word of her passing. As you predicted, her death was a murder carried out by someone close to her. Michael has successfully assumed the throne."

Callian gasps. All his life, he's heard tell of this prophecy and how it would affect him if it came to pass, but now, it's finally real to him. No longer some abstract possibility, but a tangible series of events taking place before our eyes. "No..."

He sounds so broken. I can't let this happen. I have to stop it. "We cannot allow it to unfold!" My words are somewhere between a plea and a demand. "I am the peacemaker; let me make peace. I can do it."

"It's not your ability we distrust, Lil," It's Dad Kai. "I just don't think it's a good idea. You weren't there. The situation is worse than even you can handle."

"Let me do my job." I repeat it with more conviction in my voice this time, feeling the familiar fury that eggs my power on whenever they belittle me in this way. They have to see that I'm willing to go the distance for this.

Mom cuts both her co-kings off before either can utter another word. "We will allow our daughter the chance to rectify this. She is the peacemaker and the fact that it has even gone this far is her mistake, a mess of her own making. She should have put a stop to it long ago."

They both sit back and relent to her. They always do, even when it leaves me taking blame that I don't think belongs to me. In private, they justify her cruelty toward me by reminding me of how scared she is. Callian's life is at risk and she's his mother. According to them, it's normal for her to lash out occasionally when under that sort of pressure. Jameson is technically the one with full authority here in Oceanica, so he could override her, but he and Kai both respect Mom too much to go against her. They even call her their goddess, which leaves me to fend for myself in situations like this. It makes my blood boil, yes, but it also just hurts. Something inside me hears the hidden context behind those words. "*She's his mother.*" She's his mother and not mine, so it makes sense for her to lash out at me because she's under the stress of protecting her biological child, the true heir. It's only natural that her adopted child would take the brunt of that stress, is that it? That's what I'm taking from it. I'm just less important so I should shut up and be grateful that I'm here at all.

I appreciate her siding with me and giving me a chance, although it'd be nice if she could do it without the jabs. I know my dads had good intentions, but sometimes men don't realize how much their good intentions can belittle powerful women. She at least acknowledges this is my responsibility, if not my strength. I've grown. It's beyond time for me to step out of the shadows and actually start doing what the allies put me here to do. Being a placeholder for my mom wasn't so bad when I was still young, but now I can truly carry the weight of the title she gave me. She knows she has to let me do so this time. No matter what she said, she stepped back. It's enough. Trying to convince myself, I repeat the words silently once more. *It's enough. I am enough.*

I take the lead she gave me to carry through. It's time to execute. "I'll need the Chief of Pallentine. He's Michael's grandfather. I'll have a better chance of making Michael listen if he accompanies me."

Mom nods. "I'll get ahold of him. Go, prepare. We should be able to get him here quickly enough."

***

The Chief arrives shortly after dawn the next morning. We ditch the formalities, and I just meet him on the dock. Usually, a visiting royal of any sort would go to the palace and greet my parents, but he's an old family friend and Mom and Dads won't assume it's disrespectful because this mission has a time limit. That time limit being before the threat of war turns into an actual war. Thus, I just meet him at the docks, and he goes straight from one ship to another. Once he's boarded, I greet him. "Hey, Chief. Thank you for joining me. I know this can't be easy for you, but it's the best idea I had."

He hugs me for a moment, then steps back. "It's no issue, Lilliana. I'm glad you asked. This mission is a great opportunity for me to bring a request of my own to you."

I nod. "Of course. What is it? I'll do anything I can to assist you and Pallentine in these troubling times."

He chooses his words with care. "It's, well... a bit more personal than it is political. It's about my grandson. I know my daughter lost her way after what happened to Malachi. However, he has never truly had a chance. He was so young when his father left. His whole life, he's only known the jaded perspective of Johanna. Now, he's grieving over her loss and poisoned by her words. I ask that you exhaust every opportunity to dissuade him from the path she set him on prior to resorting to harming him. Within reason, that is. I understand if it's full-scale war...but we aren't there yet, and I would like your word that you'll at least make the effort."

"No!" I blurt out. "I mean, not no. No, I wouldn't deny him the chance to do better. That's why I wanted you with me. I thought the same thing. He deserves a chance to choose his own path in an informed, unbiased manner. We have to present him with the other side of all this. I won't condone war until we've given peace a valid chance. I admit, we failed to reason with Johanna, but that's her. Truth is, we don't know Michael. We can't hold him responsible for her rule. I want to know who he is as a ruler before anything. Besides, I owe Malachi the respect of not killing his son unless we're sure there's no other way."

The Chief seems content with my answer. "You display the wisdom of a shaman and the courage of a hero, young Lilliana. I hope you don't mind me saying, but you are truly the pride of the alliance."

I freeze up. The compliment makes me so uncomfortable because I never see myself as the pride of anything. I'm just not. He's just being polite, I'm sure. "Me? No. I'm nothing special. Just the great priestess's daughter. The credit is Mom's for raising me so well."

He lets loose a rich laughter. "Oh, I see. Perhaps that is the case, or perhaps you are just blind to your own accomplishments. Either way, I think well of you."

I take a deep breath. "Well, thank you. Even if it is unwarranted, it's appreciated."

With that, I signal the crew to depart with a twirl of my finger in the air above my head. We arrive later in the day than I had hoped. The winds and the seas weren't with us. It's odd, but no men interfere with our arrival. They're there, but they do nothing but stare. They must have orders to let us through to the palace. I take some small measure of hope from that alone. It seems Michael is at least willing to talk, which is certainly more than his mother had been willing to do in the years since Kai's resurrection.

Traveling through Tendu on foot isn't a walk in the park regardless, though. The ground here is so hot that it will melt footwear and burn feet. To compound that, the palace is only accessible via flight or climb. The environment is a natural defense for the island. It's hard for outsiders to thrive here. I'm fine, but I worry about the Chief. He's powerful, but it's not the type of power that would serve him well here. He's also old in age and isn't so accustomed to pain as he would have been in his prime. As any diplomat should, though, he hides his discomfort well. I take it slow so as not to make it more difficult for him.

We make it to the palace hours later. Our palms and soles burned from the hot rock on which we walked and climbed. A maid greets us at the entrance. "Lady Lilly, Chief, King Michael has been expecting you. Please come with me. He awaits you in the tearoom."

We follow her in silence as she escorts us to Michael. We enter the tearoom to see his back to us as he sits, looking out the large glass pane toward blazing poppy flowers that only exist here and in Alacrium. He seems so calm and at peace. For a moment, I wonder if he's not truly the monster I foresaw so long ago. Then he turns around. His unnatural, crimson eyes appear crazed, unlike Malachi's, which only ever appeared warm to me. Even worse is his ungodly smile that seemed to cut through every defense I had prepared to keep my emotions at bay during this meeting. I can't say for sure what came over me, but I lose it the second I hear his voice. Smooth as velvet, it slides right down into my soul, bringing vibrations to my core. "At last, my Seshen has arrived."

"I'm not *your* anything, and what the Hel does Seshen mean? If you're going to insult me, at least do so in the common language so I know what you're saying, ass."

He raises an eyebrow. "Well, that isn't very diplomatic of you, Lady Peacemaker?"

I snap back. "As if you have any interest in diplomacy. You and I both know you welcomed me so you could determine how much of a threat I am, not so you could actually negotiate peace."

"So?" It's infuriating how calm he is.

"So? Are you kidding me? You're an arrogant son-of-a..." My words trail off. "Oh, my gods. I'm sorry. I shouldn't have even thought to say that."

He seems surprised by my apology. Reaching out, he rests his hand on my arm. His dark skin feels so soft and comforting; my reaction to him is confusing. "No need to apologize, Seshen. It's okay."

I nod, but then the Chief interjects. "Is it true, grandson? Have you only allowed us entry to get a measure of Lilly as a threat?"

"It's true." Michael replies, with not a hint of indecision in his stern tone. "In truth, the thought of slaughtering the allies brings me great joy. You are no exception, grandfather. When I picture you piled among countless corpses, maimed beyond recognition, I feel happy." He stands too close for comfort, towering over me as he lowers his head to meet my gaze. "But you, dear Seshen, when I picture you a bloodied corpse, I feel remorse. You must not drive me there. Abandon your supposed moral high ground, join me as my queen, and allow me to nourish the darkness that lurks in the crevasses of your dreadfully pure soul, Seshen. Femininity is so much more palpable in the depths of depravity; you'll be much more potent when surrounded by my jaded aura." He cups my cheek. "Just the thought makes me want to taste you."

I smack his hand away. Still, I can't hide the blush that surely covers my cheeks. Fuck. I want him. I want the bad guy. "Get off of me!"

He laughs. "But I don't want to, little Seshen."

"Stop calling me that. Jeez, what the Hel is wrong with you? Come on, Chief, we're leaving!"

"Uh! Lilliana, what has gotten into you?" I can't blame the Chief for being confused since I'm reacting to Michael's advances instead of negotiating peace.

Michael rolls his eyes. "Don't leave. Stay the night. It's late. Traveling will be dangerous. We can talk over dinner; I have a proposal you'll want to hear. I promise that you and my grandfather will be safe here tonight."

Curiosity or naivety, it's hard to say, but one of the two drives me to agree to hear this proposal of his. "Fine. We'll stay tonight. One false move and I'll kill you, though."

He smirks. "Yeah, yeah. And here you thought I was the violent one. Come on, Ses, let me take you to a guest chamber. I'll give you two adjoined rooms, so you feel safer."

I agree, and he takes us to our rooms. As he opens them, he continues. "Dinner is to be served at seven. Will you come hear me out?"

I try to put some bite in my words, but I'm not sure it sounds as much like I'm displeased by the idea of his company as I was aiming for. "It's certainly better than sitting here hungry all night, so yes."

"Sounds good. I'll see you tonight then, Seshen."

I stop him before he can walk away. "Wait! Tell me what that means."

He chuckles. "Another time." Then he closes the door behind himself. Each footstep he takes further from the room rings in my ears as his dress shoes meet the tile flooring. The sound of him growing further away makes me sad. It's like I'm losing him, even though he has felt gone to us since he was a baby, since Kai's resurrection. I don't understand the things he's making me feel, but

I know that for my sake, I need to explore them, especially since he seems to feel them, too.

***

While I wait for dinner, I head to the baths to collect myself. Here, in Tendu, they use natural hot springs to bathe. I remember, when I was younger, before Malachi left, I learned a bunch about them when we visited. The volcanoes act as a natural water filter and as a heater. It's sort of amazing. Even for rune users, replicating that process would require multiple users from different islands, except in cases of extreme talent, like royals.

As I lower myself into the springs, I note the fact that I'm the only one here. It's nice because I can relax fully. The water is warm and eases the tension that had built up throughout this rather stressful day. I rub my shoulders once I'm fully submerged, helping them to unwind. Then, I just soak for a while, letting my mind wander. Of course, where it wanders is problematic. I can't help but think of Michael, and when he enters my mind, those vibrations that filled my core earlier return. This time, they're more persistent. It's not some vague desire, but a need.

I know it won't fully satiate me, but I decide to do something. I need to relieve some of the desire that floods me at the thought of that deranged man. Leaning back against the rocky edge of the spring, I relax and spread my legs. My hand slips down over my plump thighs, and I gasp as the nerves on the inside of them light my soul ablaze. In my mind, I imagine it as his hand, teasing and preparing me for the pleasure that would undoubtedly obliterate my senses and send me into a numbing bliss, the likes from which I would never return.

Lost in the fantasy of it, I part the lips of my drenched pussy and tease my clit with my fingers in slow, circular motions. I bite down on my free hand, attempting to stifle the desperate plea that leaks from me. The pain further heightens my bliss as I picture it being his flawless, deep brown complexion I'm puncturing right now. The stimulation on my clit in combination with it sends me into a frenzy as I rub harder and harder until I reach my cliff. I dive right off it. Climaxing, I squirt and defile the royal springs of this land of molten lava and ash with the fruits of my labor.

It's not enough. More, I need more. My fingers delve into the depths of my cunt before I have the chance to come down off the high of my first orgasm. As they hit that sweet spot, my mind ponders the feeling of Michael's cock pounding and punishing it. I wonder if it's big; I bet it's fucking huge. This is torture. I need it to be him. "I need him to fuck me!"

The words come out as a cry against my will as another orgasm sweeps through my body, leaving me a trembling, sobbing mess. I hear a dark laughter coming from the hall. Someone has seen me. Mortification rushes me, washing away all the pleasure I experienced moments ago. "Who's there?"

From the shadows, he emerges. Such a stereotypical demon move. "Me, of course, Seshen. Did you think I'd allow anyone else to watch that beautiful performance you just put on?"

Okay, wow. What comes after mortification? Whatever it is, I'm there now. Unable to fathom a response to his presence, I go silent. I'm silent, naked, and looking into the eyes of the man I just finished masturbating to the fantasy of. How could this possibly have gone so wrong?

Michael shakes his head. "Embarrassment is unnecessary, Seshen. You did nothing wrong. I enjoyed seeing you that way. No one need know anything about it. Come now, it's nearly seven. Dinner starts shortly."

With that, he leaves, giving me a moment to collect myself and get dressed. It seems he's not a monster. He didn't judge me. His words made me feel better. It was a kindness. One many men wouldn't have offered; one I won't forget.

***

At dinner, Michael's palace staff serves us roast oxen, rice, and wine. From the head of the table, Michael allows the entertainers to perform a brief dance prior to the dreaded political debate that will follow. I sit to his right as I watch the performance. These women are gorgeous. Their movements are so nimble, and they exude elegance. There's an underlying seduction to them that could lure even the least eager to wonder what curves linger beneath their flowing garments. I admire their ability and hope that they're paid fairly for it, but given the state of Tendu, I doubt that's the case.

The Chief, sitting opposite of me, to Michael's left, doesn't seem to pay any mind to it. He's polite, although not amused, and still gives the performers their kudos when it's over. We both offer them gold coins for their efforts. Michael initially seems displeased by them accepting it, but he lets the matter go when he sees that I'm happy they did.

All the staff vacate the room after it's over, leaving us to eat and talk. The Chief is the first to ask, "So, grandson, you mentioned a proposal you had for us?"

The sly smirk on Michael's face implies that whatever he is about to say will shake us to our core. "I do. It's more for Lilly, to be specific. What do you say, Seshen? Will you hear me out?"

"Sure." I answer, although I'm sure he picks up on the fact that I'm not as enthusiastic about it as he is.

"Okay. Allow me to begin then." He fixes his gaze on me with such intensity that it feels like we're the only two here. In this room... On this island... In this region... On this planet...

He continues. "I want you to agree to a bet with me. If I win, you join me as my queen."

I roll my eyes, though the proposal isn't as repulsive as I try to make it seem, I'll be damned if I'm giving him any inkling of that. "Starting by telling me the stakes rather than the conditions?"

"I have to."

"Fine, then what happens if I win?"

"I let the war, and the idea of revenge, go completely."

I'm pretty sure my jaw hits the floor. He's willing to let it all go. All I have to do is win some stupid bet. It's unfathomable. "What is it we're staking this on?"

His smile is devastating. "The matter is simple, really. I give you unfettered access to me and my kingdom until one of us wins. I'll go a step further and agree not to hurt you until then, even if we meet in battle. Keep in mind, I mean you, individually, not the collective that stands behind you. If you influence me into the light, you win. If I influence you into the dark, I win."

Well, it's certainly an upfront bet. Pretty black and white. I look at the Chief, trying to discern his opinion on this by his expression. He offers a subtle nod to affirm what I already suspected. He wants me to say yes. I promised him I'd exhaust my options before resorting to violence. I'm also confident that I'd win, if I agreed. As a priestess, I'm not so easily swayed from my beliefs. Even though I feel something unexpected for Michael, right and wrong is clear to me. I'm sure his hollow convictions would collapse long before mine did.

I meet Michael's gaze once more. "Deal."

My commitment comes out with a strength that I rarely display. I want him to know that I'm unwavering.

"Perfect. It's a bet then." The simple reply grates my nerves a bit, but then he continues. "Better get some rest, Seshen. I suspect you'll be heading home in the morning to update the other allies."

I nod. The Chief and I leave after that with no more words exchanged. We both know that Mom won't be happy about this. I think she'll accept it, though. If for no other reason, because she knows she owes Malachi that much leniency for his son.

CHAPTER Three

MOTHER FIERCEST

LILLY

Upon arriving home, I give my mission report over to my mother. The Chief comes with me. Nervous, I try to escape before she looks at it, but she asks me to wait while she reviews it. I end up trapped there, waiting for the inevitable rage I knew the report would spark. To be fair, if I were in her position, I'd be furious about it as well. It must come across ill-considered, but to me, it's a sure bet. While I understand her being frustrated because I staked the safety of the entire alliance on a bet, it seems like the more ethical course in my mind.

I question if my mind, having decided that this was the more ethical course, hates me as I watch her face contort while reading the report. In silence, I try to gauge just how angry she is as I watch her read. It isn't but two pages into the ten-page report I realize how unlikely it is for me to be conscious tomorrow.

She doesn't even finish reading it before she summons her power to shred it to bits. The paper scatters so far in various directions that one might think there's a hurricane taking place. Reality, though, is that she used blades of spiritual power and applied a large amount of force to them to create the effect of strong winds. With her level of mastery, it was something she could do subconsciously in a moment of rage, whereas for untrained or new priestesses, such an action would be impossible. Even for a middling priestess, it'd require an obnoxious amount of power and energy. Not for Mom, though. My mother is the fiercest woman I've ever known.

"You agreed to what?" Mom's voice thunders, the vibrations of sound booming throughout the palace. I can't see all the many people in our large home, but I'm confident that they're all frozen in place. "Are you out of your mind, Lilliana?"

She's nothing if not terrifying. Every instinct in my body is begging me to run for the hills, but I just can't this time. She has to listen. This was the only way. I opt for a calm, reasonable approach. "Mom, slow down." I plead with her, hoping I can make her understand. "If you just let me explain."

"I don't need to let you explain." She snaps back. Reason never was to her liking. She simply responds better to power. "This is insane! What the Hel were you thinking?"

Her rage is ferocious. Weak is something I've never been, but something about her anger makes me feel like a helpless child quivering in a corner. I'm not a fan of that feeling because I've been that child before. Back then, I was weak. There was nothing I could do to defend myself from those monsters which haunted my dreams just as easily as they did my waking hours. It's different now, though. I'm not a weak little girl anymore and she will not silence me. I have to make her accept this. Otherwise, killing Michael becomes the duty of the peacemaker, my duty. I can't allow that. The idea of killing him is tantamount to suicide in my mind. It makes me feel like I'd be killing a part of myself I've not even known.

"Oh, I don't know, Mom." The sarcasm in my tone causes an uptake in her power that I can only describe as petrifying. Does that shut me up, though? Nope. I just dig my grave deeper. At this rate, they'll be burying me at the planet's core, instead of the traditional six feet under. "Maybe I was thinking I'd try to help someone who has now lost both of his parents because of a decision *you* made?"

I hate my mouth. Why does it continue to form words at this moment? She's going to lose her tenuous grip on the patience it's taking for her not to strangle me. I realize I must be an idiot as I watch her rage boil over as she summons her spiritual power. She pins me back against the wall, seething as she speaks. "Don't act like I made that decision alone, Lilliana. You were there; you know what happened."

I snap her hold on me with my spiritual power, then use it to push her back against the wall opposite of the one I just free myself from. This is horrible. I'm actually fighting with her. She saved me, adopted me, raised me, and loved me. This is no way to repay her, but it's too late to turn back now. It's too late to repay her for all she did for me back then, but she hurt as much as she helped, and this feels too good to turn back now. "Yes, I do. Congratulations! You asked an eight-year-old for her opinion then used it to justify the ways you made her carry your burdens because you were too weak to take them on yourself. Malachi and Jameson helped make this mess too. We're all at fault. You know who didn't get a say, though, Mom? Michael. Yet, he's the one that has borne the vast majority of the consequences whilst we, you, me, and Dad Jameson, have reaped all the rewards. Rallem lost Pastel. Michael lost his parents. Malachi lost his freedom. What did we lose?"

Her expression becomes sad. She must feel like I'm blaming her for it all, the way Johanna had. I know my words are cutting deep. She suffered so much back then, but it's just not the same as what we put him through. Who knows what sort of Hel he went through after Johanna cut them off from us? The part of me that loves my mom tells me it's not fair to blame her, but something in me can't stop thinking about what he's suffered. It's true that it is her fault. My anger flares even more at the fact that I feel guilty for blaming her for something that is undoubtedly her fault.

Blaming her is honest, and easier than contemplating the forces beyond our reach that have influenced our lives. Why wouldn't I blame her? We met Rettferd and Myrkr on the road before things blew to bits. This master they spoke of was probably the true reason for the suffering we all incurred. I can't deal with that, though, so like Johanna, I blame Mom. "Maybe Johanna was right about you, Mom. Maybe what we did was wrong. I'm sorry, but I think you were selfish."

"We lost my uncle, who yes, needed to die to protect the greater good." Her voice shakes, like she could break at any moment. I hate this. She's answering the question, even though I knew the answer. As she speaks, I'm reminded of all that happened. It feels as if I'm reliving every moment.

My Hel should have been over after those men abandoned me. It wasn't. I had to suffer more. I had to find the family of my dreams just to watch two members of it die. Then, I had to endure a Helish journey to get them back. I had to take lives to complete that journey. It was all bullshit. Apparently not enough of it, though, because I had to lose more people that I loved. Now, I have to face the one man that acknowledges the part of me that is so angry about it all. I have to acknowledge that I contributed to the suffering that made him capable of understanding mine.

Mom continues, each of her words digging deeper into my heart and forcing all these unwanted emotions to the surface. "I grieved for him, though, Lilly."

She breaks my hold on her and falls to her knees. She has the power to fight more, but I don't think she has the will anymore. I really hurt her. Damn. "The man I saw as my brother, who you saw as your uncle."

She's crumbling. My mother is crumbling because of what I said. Devastation floods my veins as I watch her weep. "His wife, my best damn friend. Twice, actually. First by argument, now again by death."

She sobs. "The chance to see Michael, their child, grow into the brilliant king he would have become if Malachi were here."

I run over and hug her before the last sentence comes free.

"We've lost plenty."

"And gained a million times more." I sound so cold, even as I try to comfort her. This is wrong, but I can't stop pushing her. She needs to hear it.

"Fair enough." I can hear the frustration. She's still pissed, but she won't fight anymore.

Finally, the others step in. Dad Kai is the first to do so, resting his hand on Mom's shoulder. "Josie, she has a point."

Dad Jameson looks at her with a softness in his eyes. "You know I'd never go against you, my goddess, but is this really how you want to react to our little girl's first weighty decision as peacemaker?"

His agreement with me doesn't stop him from turning to me and reminding me who I'm speaking to. "And Lilly, if you ever speak to your mother that way again, it won't be her rage you have to worry about. Josie's my wife and I won't have her disrespected by anyone."

Mom looks at the Chief for some kind of confirmation that I consulted with him prior to agreeing to this bet. He nods, knowing what question she wants an answer to. "She did. I think this course will, in time, save my grandson. I saw how he reacted to her. He's softer in her presence."

For a second, I see the vaguest hope light in her eyes before she speaks. Somewhere inside, she thinks there's a chance this will work. "Fine, but if you lose yourself to him, I'm killing you both myself."

I stand strong and proud, although I don't feel either. She needs to see my confidence, even though I want to cry and beg her to forgive me because of this social conditioning I've endured my whole life, the kind that taught me that we're always supposed to give in to her, but I'm not sorry. I was right. It only makes me resent her more that I have to feel bad about being right. "Okay,

Mom. Just leave it to me. You raised me to be strong. I'll handle this."

With that, we all agree. I'm doing this. The Chief heads out soon after. He goes to the docks so he can return to Pallentine. I imagine he has some business to handle back home. The tribe will want updates, but more pressing will be to prepare them for what I'm sure will be a bumpy ride while I work on this. I retire to my room when I see Mom and Dads retreat to the terrace. Most likely to do something I'm not entirely sure I want to know about. I heard her mutter about punishing them for talking back to her. They seemed excited about it, so I've decided not to question what sort of punishment she'll be doling out. It's one of their favorite spots to do that sort of thing, I guess because that's where the three of them got onto the same page for the first time about their relationship many years ago.

Callian, having the same sense that I did about what they were up to, found me on my way to my room. It isn't unusual for him to hangout in my room and chat with me when there's a lot going on. I don't mind it. For there being an eight-year age gap between the two of us, we're still pretty close as siblings. We bonded plenty when we were young, both needing equal respite from the insanity of our parents. We love them and they're great, but being their children comes with some difficulties as well.

I remember when Callian was about thirteen and he first realized how complicated life would be as their child. He had made a friend about six months prior. The boy was the son of a nobleman who had a fair amount of influence, but not as much as he desired. I suppose the father tasked the boy to get close to Callian, hoping that a bond to the heir might gain him more favor from our parents. Long story short, things got messy when Callian found out the boy had never truly been his friend. It was one of the first times I saw his latent power surface.

Of course, he didn't want to go to Mom or either of our dads about it, so he came to me. It was challenging for me not to attack the nobleman, but I knew these were the things Callian would have learn to handle. Not only as a child and heir, but perhaps even more so when he becomes king and is the one people want to curry favor with.

I've always felt badly for him. While I also inherited my position from our parents, I had a choice in the matter. I wanted to become the peacemaker. It's different for him, though. He didn't really ask for a throne. Unlike my position, the sole determining factor in who becomes king is genetics. I've always wondered if he'd have chosen it for himself if someone presented him with another option.

Once we're alone in my room, Callian breaks out in laughter. "Elder sister, you are quite intent on driving our mother to the brink, aren't you? Cutting deals with tyrants. It's unlike you. Tell me, is Michael so alluring to have captured your heart with such ease?"

"He has captured nothing, Callian." I make every attempt to sound smug. "You, however, will capture a fist to your jaw if you repeat that."

"And you will capture our mother's ire if you fail." He quips back, falling into our usual banter. He's right, but damn, it still makes me want to knock his teeth out.

"You speak of Mom's ire as if I couldn't turn it toward you." I look at him with an antagonistic eyebrow raised. "Have you not been bedding a maid?"

"Regularly." He admits with ease, not seeming to think it's a big deal. "Although, letting a tyrant bed you is far worse than me bedding a maid." His poking is annoying and comforting at the same time. "Besides, it's not as if I love her. We're just friends who occasionally offer release to one another. Whoever I wed will be much more suitable for my station. I am the heir to Oceanica, after all."

"How humble..."

He chuckles. "I know you're slow on the uptake in the royal aspect of our lives, but you might start by understanding that royal and humble are antonyms."

"That's not true." I correct him. "I know you were too young to recall, but Malachi was never conceited. He was honest and good. So humble, in fact, that he rarely took credit for successes, even when he was the determining factor in them."

Callian scoffs. "He was also a demon who signed his allegiance over to Myrkr."

I shake my head, my fists balling up as I take a deep breath to calm myself before I say another word. This kid can be so clueless sometimes. I guess that's just part of being a little brother, though. Still, it's not helping anything. The more comments made I see as hateful, the more I have to restrain myself from our actions on that fateful day as the catalyst for Michael's suffering. I don't want to see it, but I'm starting to. It takes everything in me not to tell my family about themselves right now.

They always think they're right, even when their arguments are a mile wide and an inch deep. I doubt my little brother is in the habit of comprehending how little logic they put forth when debating, especially against his older, more experienced, and well-studied sister. "Yeah, Callian, Malachai did. And if he hadn't, you'd have died in the womb." I can't help the resentment that leaks from my voice as I speak. "We had to give Myrkr something to stop the fighting."

He gets quiet. I suppose he sees the sense in what I'm saying, or he just realizes that this debate will lead nowhere. After a few moments, he looks me in my eyes. I want to shove a light spear through one of them for the sheer level of audacity he displays when his expression remains as confident as ever, even as he continues to act as a naïve child. "You got this."

We spend a few minutes chatting and hanging out before a yawn overcomes me, highlighting the exhaustion of my last few days. Realizing I'm tired, Callian wishes me a good evening. With that, he leaves and I'm alone again. The fatigue of the last forty-eight hours catches up to me fast. It's still early in the evening, but I need to rest. I lie down and drift off to sleep not long after.

CHAPTER Four

WAR, SHE GREETS US

JOSIE

Before our fun even got started on the terrace, my bumbling fool of a war advisor stumbled out here in some sort of panic, babbling incoherently about something I can't even attempt to surmise the details of while he's rambling. He truly is a competent man, and one of the most reliable that we have here in Oceanica. His strategic mind, vast network of informants, extensive knowledge of our military, and unwavering loyalty make him invaluable to the kingdom and irreplaceable as a wartime advisor. He just gets worked up so easily that sometimes it overshadows his skill and makes him look like an incompetent idiot. "Calm down, would you? I cannot fix a problem if I can't understand what you're saying."

He tries to calm down, but he's still panting. At least he's slowed down enough for me to understand now. "Tendu and their king have attacked Nollent. The southern half of the island has already fallen, milady."

I can't even imagine the shock that appears on my face. It makes no sense to me. This is reckless aggression that I can't even begin to wrap my head around. It shakes me to my core. I hardly imagined that Michael would turn to one of the runic islands first. Strategically, Loft would make far more sense since they don't have any magic. This is bold. He's not afraid. We've all been framing him as a hurt child lashing out in pain, but we failed to consider the years of training he'd had under Johanna and her generals, which are the same generals who once trained Malachi. His threat may compound even more than we realize, now that I'm thinking about it. What if, like Callian, he can use the power sets of both parents? We're in trouble.

I turn my gaze to Kai and see the devastation on his own. My poor love. All the years he'd spent when he was young fighting to end discrimination in Nollent and unify his fellow citizens, now he finds out that it's being destroyed by a country that was once ruled by some of our best friends. It must be even more heart-shattering for him. He needs to go. He'll never forgive himself if he doesn't do everything he can to stop this. I can understand why. If it were Loft, I'd feel the same. Even though most of my memories there were terrible, I love my origin country, and I'd come running in a heartbeat if I thought it needed me. "Go!" I push him, needing him to snap out of it and go fight. "It's your homeland. Take Lilly with you!"

He gasps as if he had forgotten to breathe, then takes off without saying goodbye to Jameson or me. Before he gets too far, Jameson calls out. "And you better come back to us alive. If you make the goddess cry, I'll come down to the Spirit Realm to kick your ass. Cal will help me, too, I'm sure."

Kai stops, turning back to give a half-hearted smile to us. "You got it. I love you both."

Then he's gone. While he and Lilly get moving, I take charge of things here. I give the war advisor his orders. "Prepare a battleship and men for them. They'll need a means of transporting people away if they can't save the island."

He agrees. "Absolutely, Your Majesty. Ratio of men to space aboard the ship?"

I feel the weight of the reality settle in. The sad truth lies in knowing if the island isn't savable, most the people will have already died. It's riddled with rune users, and they are no strangers to fighting. They'd have fought tooth and nail against an attack. Tendu is much stronger than they are, though, so I know Michael would crush any resistance. "Seventy-five percent capacity should be our men. Save the last quarter for survivors."

I didn't explain my answer, but the advisor's face flushed just the same. It didn't take a genius to figure out that I wasn't expecting many to live. Stunned into silence, a minute passes before he can form his reply. "As you wish, milady."

He turns and runs back inside to carry out his orders. I look at Jameson as the war advisor takes off. "You lock down the council. Make sure they know the war has started and that all of them need to be prepared in case Michael comes for us next. I'll issue a warning to the citizens and have the royal guard place safety measures."

"Of course, goddess. I got you." His wings burst from his back as he takes off, trying to round up the council members quickly. I want to hear their thoughts on things. Most of them are nothing short of experts in their respective fields, so it's always best that we hear them out on how any significant event may impact Oceanica. More than that, though, is the fact that as members of our council, they are also vital targets during times of war. It's safer for them and their families to stay in the palace. I'd hate for one of them to get killed for trying to help us.

I know both of my husbands are powerful men, but I worry about them as I stand by myself on the terrace. There's a lot I have to do, too, though. There's not enough time for me to linger on my concerns for them. I whisper to myself. "Be careful, my loves."

Then, I head off to my study to write up an emergency edict. In it, I include all the pre-agreed upon wartime measures. There's an 8 P.M curfew for all citizens, and a 6 P.M. one for those under the age of eighteen. All points of entry are to be blocked, aside from the few deemed necessary for the movement of logistical and military personnel. In addition, there's also predetermined places for supply stations that ensure our people have access to vital goods that get more expensive during wartime and regular military patrols.

We do what we can to make sure these things affect them as little as possible, but in the end there's only so much we can plan for. So, we keep lines of communication open as well. Frankly, having the nobles communicate on behalf of the people is inefficient. During difficult times, citizens can approach the palace without invitation so long as they have ID. There's a handful of our most trusted people that will hear them directly if the three of us aren't available, but I try my best to ensure that Jameson, Kai, or I hear as many of them as possible with our own ears. It serves to make things more expedient when we do it that way.

After I'm done writing up the order, I have it distributed across the kingdom. Then, I head out to the borders to raise my barriers. The military's help as a support to mine, but mine are harder to get through. We use them as the primary defense. It would be preferable to have Lilly erect them because her living barrier doubles as offense and defense, but we're short on time and she really needs to get to Nollent. Mine are the best attainable option right now. I hope they are enough.

I whisper enchantments, calling on the forces of the Spirit Realm as I raise them. The purple aura of my power spreads and stretches according to my will. I cast layer after layer until I'm exhausted, strengthening them as much as possible. Once they're done, I'm panting. I have no time to lose, though. It's moments like this that I miss Kimble the most. It'd be convenient to have a fox spirit to ride so I could rest on my way to my next task, but I don't. I haven't for a long time now. So, I take off toward the palace. I need to get cleaned up and put together so I can speak to the people. They need to hear me tell them that everything will be okay. They need to know that I will fight for them to my last breath.

Even this tired, it doesn't take me long to get back to the palace. No matter what my condition, my perception of slowness is still quick by comparison to someone of average power. It's one benefit of being one of the most powerful people in the world, I guess. When I arrive back home, I head to my chamber and begin searching the closet for something that says, "I'm regal and maintaining my composure. I'm not nervous, so you shouldn't be."

Of course, that's total bullshit, but sometimes bullshit keeps people from panicking and putting themselves in more danger. I'm not a fan of it; I prefer transparency. Most of the time, it's not such a reach, but there are moments where a façade is necessary. About ninety percent of the people are powerless, unable to protect themselves. If they see the person they trust their protection to as a mess, they'd feel hopeless. There's no purpose in that. It's better to give them hope by showing them I can handle this. I'll give them the truth too, but I won't do so while appearing weak and incompetent.

After I'm prepared, I head out to the terrace. Using my power, I project my voice by willing the energy to carry the vibrations further. "People of Oceanica, Your Queen speaks. Please, stop what you are doing and hear my words." I pause briefly, giving anyone who may have been doing something a moment to redirect their attention. "An attack foreseen by my daughter, Lilly, two decades ago has begun. Do not fret. The insights she gave us have prepared us for the events that will follow. The protocols are active. Plans that will help you protect and provide for your families are on every block. As of right now, there is no immediate threat to those on this island, but there may will be, eventually. We will give our all to protect you should that time come. In the meantime, the direct contact emergency policy is active. Anyone with concerns that need to be reported directly to the royal family can approach the palace. Please follow the procedures set forth. Thank you."

WASTELANDS AND WATCHTOWERS

LILLY

Not long after I fell asleep, Dad Kai comes busting into my room. "Lilly, get up. Tendu is attacking Nollent. We need to move."

Groggy, my brain fails at processing the information. I roll over and groan. "Can't you just tell them to wait until morning?"

He scoffs. "Sure, I'll just tell the dying people to wait until morning because the peacemaker they've entrusted their lives to is sleepy. Get the Hel up, Lilliana."

That one registers. "Dying people? What? On my way."

I pop up out of bed with a far more appropriate sense of urgency, running into my closet and changing into something battle appropriate. From the other side of the closed door, Dad Kai explains the situation to me in full. The more he does, the more I rush. This is insanity. I've always known Tendu held great power; I just never imagined they could take out Nollent in a matter of a few hours.

Of the islands, Oceanica and Tendu are equal in terms of sheer strength, although we outperform them in our economy. Directly after that, though, is Nollent. The gap between us and them must be far larger than I had perceived. How much power do those touched by angels and demons have? It suddenly has me questioning if I could even kill Michael should I try. Or if my little brother also surpassed me. I haven't sparred with Callian since he was twelve, so I don't suppose I'd know if he had.

It isn't long before Dad Kai and I are taking off down the streets at full force to reach the docks. Mom, having thought ahead, had everything ready for our departure by the time we arrived. It's so like her. I swear that woman could still think clearly if the gods themselves attacked us. Chaos just doesn't distract her like it does most people. Even when she thinks she's rattled, she usually still sees things more clearly than the rest of us.

Once we board the battleship Mom prepared, we dole out orders to the men. Our priorities are pretty straightforward here; save lives, engage the enemy as little as possible, and try not to die. With such little warning, we can't launch a full-scale counterattack. The best we can do is attempt to save the citizens and buy enough time for other measures to be implemented.

After we've given our orders to the men, I head toward the stern and use my spiritual power to create more propulsion. My power is much better equipped to do so than Dad Kai's. He's better with raw strength because his runic magic is earth-based. My doing this will ensure we arrive much sooner.

We arrive in Nollent to a nightmare we wish remained in the confines of our sleep. Flames engulf nearly seventy-five percent of the island. Scattered on the street are bodies that will not be identifiable. Charred beyond recognition and blown to bits are the women, children, and men of Nollent. They're dead, and Michael did it. We move through the rubble to a high point, trying to assess the situation the best we can, given the debris and smoke that obstructs our vision and hinders our breathing.

We find our vantage point on top of a mound that almost surely has buried some of the dead in perhaps the least respectful way imaginable. Looking out, we see that almost all the watchtowers across the island have fallen. The only exception is the one that sits in the center. Many of the mountains are gone too. They must have crumbled under the weight of Michael's destructive flames, and those of the men who serve him. Homes and shops have collapsed all around us. We catch the heart wrenching sight of the café where Dad Kai first met Mom. It isn't just destroyed; it's annihilated. Johanna must have told Michael the story because there's nothing there. No ash, no debris, nothing. It's just scorched earth. I wouldn't even had recognized it if not for the pain etched on Dad Kai's face.

He chokes back a sob upon seeing his homeland in this state. He will mourn them, but right now the warrior in him knows we mustn't allow our emotions to take hold until we've saved whomever we can. "You help them," I mutter. "You'll be able to move the rubble easier than I will. Take our men with you to help. I should—"

He cuts me off. "Go find that little bastard. Now, Lilliana."

The anger in his voice is off-putting. It's rare to see him get truly angry. He has more patience than Mom or Dad Jameson, but when he reaches that boiling point, anyone in his way may as well be dead. He's ruthless. In measured strides, he walks away. Glowing runes cover his arms as proof his magic is active. Using it to control the earth-based materials in the rubble, he tosses bulks of it into the ocean so he can reveal any survivors that lie beneath to the men, who will get them to the ship and begin tending to their wounds. With them activated, he's also prepared to fight any enemy who crosses him while he searches.

Meanwhile, I begin my search for Michael. It seems like a near-impossible task between the smoke, flames, and dust. I begin to feel hopeless the longer I search the island, trying to be thorough enough to ensure I don't miss him. If he didn't want to be found, I probably wouldn't find him. In this chaos, no matter how thorough, anyone is likely to miss a ton. This type of environment makes it easy to hide.

He must be watching in the distance because, after I search for a long while, I spot a faint glow toward the lone watchtower standing in the center of the other fallen ones. It has to be him. That glow is unmistakable. It's Helfire, something only demonic royalty can summon. Using my spiritual power, I levitate and propel myself toward the tower. It's quicker, yes, but it also allows me to avoid stepping or stumbling on those who have already died. It's the least I could do to respect them. No one should have their corpses trampled.

I go straight to the top of the tower and land face-to-face with Michael. "Are you out of your damn mind, Michael?"

"What?" He sounds amused and calm, not scared of any consequences his actions might have for him. It makes me want to lose my shit. I want him trembling in terror at the sight of me, but he doesn't even seem to take my presence here seriously. Why is this man so insufferable? "I told you the protection of our bet only applied to you. Besides, you were taking too long to come visit me again. I got bored, so I had to get your attention somehow."

My eyes widen. Less than twenty-four hours that I was away from him, and he did this... out of boredom? Shock courses through me as I realize that he's far deeper in the darkness than I had realized. His convictions are more profound than I ever imagined. This bet won't be easy to win. What have I done by making a deal of any sort with this man?

"Oh, Michael." I can't tell if it's sympathy for the things he went through to become this way or disbelief that he could really do this that makes my voice tremble. "I don't understand. How could you?"

"Because I will do anything," He snaps. "I will burn every kingdom and torch every village in this gods-forsaken realm. I'll kill them all, just to share a moment with you, Seshen. Even if you plaster disgust and hatred of me upon that lovely face of yours, there is nothing I won't do to see it. You are mine, and there is no escaping me."

The intensity of his words, regardless of how depraved they are, sends warmth flooding me in places that should not be relevant during what is supposed to be a war. I'm getting turned on by this beast. His sharp, demonic senses must allow him to pick up on it because he takes a huge breath in, then grabs me by my waist. "Those sweet juices smell delectable, Seshen. Do you want me to fuck you senseless in this watchtower while we're surrounded by such beautiful carnage?"

I gulp, knowing I should say no. Saying anything else would be stupid and ridiculous, nothing but an invitation to move me further away from the person my parents wanted me to be. The more I consider it, though, the less it sounds like a negative. It sounds like freedom. So, "no" isn't what comes out of my mouth. Not even close. "Yes. I want you to fuck me. Fill me with your madness. Evil is where we find our happy ending."

If he had any reservations, I couldn't tell as he stripped me down. Lifting me into his arms, he bites down on my neck with every intention of leaving a mark. I screech in pain, or pleasure, unsure if there's even a difference between the two as I wrap my legs around his waist. My screams blend with the sounds of those coming from the dying as he plunges himself into me with a ruthlessness that makes me question if I'll be joining them in the Spirit Realm. His cock threatens to tear me in half with each brutal thrust he takes. "Fuck, Seshen. Take it. Take this cock like the filthy whore you are. You have no clue how long I've dreamed of ruining this tight little cunt."

He spits straight into my face, and I don't know what's gotten into me as my tongue leaves my mouth, trying to catch his saliva as it drips down from my eyes. The smoke and flames from the ground rise alongside my impending orgasm. He thrusts harder and harder, but doesn't appear to be anywhere near as close as I am.

He is going to destroy me, and I am going to let him. His fucking insanity makes me feel like mine isn't so bad as he barks a maniacal laugh after ripping his cock out of me and leaving me desperate to be stuffed again. The feeling of unadulterated violence he so freely displays speaks to the part of me that hates my mother, the part that wasn't sure if I wanted to save Callian. It lets me know he sees it and understands it even as he fucks me senseless. Robbing my orgasm from me, robbing my orgasm from my, he drops me to the ground. My knees scrape against the brick floors a bit. He doesn't hold back when he slaps me hard enough that I fall to the side, causing my cheek to hit the bricks as well. "Get on your hands and knees like the bitch you are!"

Somehow, I get the impression he meant the word bitch literally. A female dog. Far more degrading than if he intended it as a slur. I won't deny that I like it. Something about it is so erotic. It also highlights something else for me, though. There's this inexplicable contrast between the harshness of his words and action when compared to that look in his eyes that portrays nothing but affection. Using, humiliating, and degrading the perfect little peacemaker by the tyrannical demon lord while innocent people suffer, Michael acknowledges the part of me my mother refuses to see. The part that craves violence and vengeance. It makes me so wet that I need more.

I do as he says, hoping that he'll reward me with more of his sweet cruelty if I'm obedient. He does, of course.

Slamming his cock back inside of me, he wraps both hands around my throat and squeezes so tightly that not even a drop of oxygen gets through as I struggle. His bruising grip remains for his first few thrusts before he releases me, allowing me to gasp for air while he punishes my pussy. He grabs my hair, yanking it back like a rein, pulling me in time with his harshly paced thrusts. I cry out. "I love being such a worthless whore for you!"

His dark, breathless chuckle caresses my soul. "I know you do."

He slaps my ass softly. "Degrade yourself more for me."

"I'm a stupid bitch." I pant, curling my toes a bit.

He rams into my uterus again, then slaps my ass harder. This time, there's a sharp sting of pain that summons a pathetic cry from deep within me. "More."

"And I love to be brutalized by a man who wants to kill my family. You own me. I love to be humiliated by you. You're not just a demon king to me! You're a demonic god!" I just can't shut up. This shouldn't be so hot, but it is. I'm just as filthy as he claims; repulsive.

I can almost picture the smug look on his face as he thrusts again. This time, the slap is much harder. I yelp. "Ah!"

The sound seems to encourage him. "You're so sexy when you're like this, Seshen. What a perfect little cumdump you're becoming."

He leans forward and kisses the side of my head gently enough to convince me he'll take it a little easier. It feels so sweet and affectionate that I could swear he's an entirely different person. I enjoy it just as much as I do the ruthless side of him I'd been experiencing. I'm wrong about one thing, though. Instead, he goes even harder. Relentless. No more stopping or teasing. He rides me brutally until I climax so many times that my body collapses into the brick, scraping against it with each of his thrusts. It feels like forever before he nuts, covering my back and hair in his seed. Yet forever wasn't enough for my needy cunt to be satisfied.

Afterwards, I'm covered in bruises and scrapes. I look around and see that much of the destruction has settled. It occurs to me what I've done, what I've allowed to happen on my watch. Nollent has fallen and I'm the one to blame. I hyperventilate. Realizing what I'm feeling, Michael lies down beside me and pulls me into his arms. "Shh. It's okay. I'm right here, my gorgeous Seshen."

I sob. "How could I? What have I done?"

He whispers, holding me tight. "You've done nothing. My men did it. You simply enjoyed your time with me while it happened."

My voice is shaky as hatred and self-loathing fill my soul. "I... I... I did nothing. While this was happening, I did nothing."

Michael kisses my cheek, his touch sweet and affectionate. His voice isn't authoritative like it typically is. Right now, it's soothing. "Yes, and that's okay. You shouldn't bear the burdensome task of protecting those who have done nothing for you."

I curl up to him, burying my face in his chest so I don't have to see the horror any longer. I change the subject, trying to avoid facing up to what I just did. "Why are you being so nice now? What happened to me being a whore and a bitch?"

I peek up just a little to see his expression as he replies. He smiles, perhaps the most genuine smile I've seen from him to date. His loving touch reassures me he means what he says. "Silly woman, play and reality are very different things. Of course, I love fucking you and being kinky, but that doesn't mean I don't actually love you, too. In reality, outside of bed, I'll always be kind to you. I may be 'evil,' as you call it, but I'm not a monster. I don't think poorly of you, Seshen. If I did, why would I ask you to be my queen? That's what this whole bet is about, for me anyway. I want you to choose to be at my side because you are by far the most important, intelligent, powerful person in the world. At least, in my eyes, you are."

That is the distinction between him and those men who attacked me as a child. Michael was a terrible person, but a good man. My attackers were terrible people and terrible men. Michael made sure our pleasure was mutual and took care of me afterwards. They just did what they wanted and abandoned me. That's why his roughness was blissful and theirs was traumatizing. I get it now. As I'm preparing myself to address it out loud, I catch sight of Dad Kai out of the corner of my eye as he floats by on a rock with an injured citizen in his arms. I gasp and dart to my feet. Throwing on my clothes, I tell Michael. "Try to behave, please. I'll come see you soon, but there's something I have to do now."

With that, I take off, not giving him time to get a word in. As I run toward Dad Kai, I save a few people myself, albeit not as many as I could have had I focused on the mission. When I catch up to him, he asks, "Any luck with finding Michael?"

I shake my head, lying. "No, Nollent has fallen, and we're outnumbered. All we can do is get the handful of people we saved out of here."

He gives a sharp nod and gets moving. That's good. I guess he didn't see us as he passed. Together, we board our ship full of injured civilians. These people are suffering. Many of them lost loved ones. Their homes and businesses are gone. They must feel so defeated. Even now that they're in our care, many of them may still pass from their injuries. Healing magic, though powerful, has limitations. Those that survive will be refugees. I'm sure that Mom and Dads will house many in Oceanica. I may have to approach the other islands in the alliance about caring for the others.

That's the good thing about allies, though. In an emergency, we can count on them to help us shoulder the weight. Some part of me feels as if I've betrayed those friendships today, but I can't bring myself to regret it. After what happened with Michael today, I can't deny my fascination with him and the darkness in which he lives.

The boat ride home is long. Unlike on the trip here, I don't use my power to propel the ship. Rather, I'm too busy using a less potent variation of Dad Jameson's angelic healing technique to keep as many people alive as I can. Before all this, I was exhausted. Now, I'm teetering on the verge of vasovagal syncope—passing out from stress. I'll need medical attention soon if I don't get some rest. Of course, I keep myself together long enough to get back home and ensure these people reach my mother and Dad Jameson. Once I see that they're safe, I stumble up to Dad Kai, who I know won't have to help with the healing. I collapse into the safety of my father's arms, too tired to push through long enough to get to my bedroom. I guess he gets the message because I feel my feet leave the ground as I'm wrapped in a warm embrace. In that fatherly way of his, he presses a kiss to my forehead, and I hear a soft whisper. "I got you, Lil."

I relax, finally allowing the darkness which lingers behind my heavy eyelids to reach out and take me away from this chaos. I drift into a sleep so deep that it borders unconsciousness.

Michael

After leaving a handful of men to maintain control of Nollent, I return home. Hours have passed and I still feel consumed by this jittery craving my Seshen left behind. I need more release. Rather than returning to my chamber, I go find one of the many whores I keep on call. Low on patience, I fuck her against the wall in the hall. Something disturbing happens, though. That fucking priestess' face keeps appearing in my mind. I feel something akin to... well... guilt. I just can't get off on this bitch. No whore could compare to my future queen.

I dismiss her, not just for the moment, but permanently. Taking it a step further, I put the word out and dismiss them all. I'm hooked on Lilly. Addicted. Obsessed. Nothing will satisfy my craving for her. I don't want any of these women, just her. She's a need.

Soon, I'm pacing the halls, itching with insanity, trying to grapple with the grip she has on me. It's a battle I don't want to win and know that I never will. There's no meaning to it aside from a poor attempt to pretend I don't want to be crazed for her. Realization comes like a brick to the brain. I gasp. "Am I in love?"

"No!" I reply to myself, sounding every bit as crazy as I am. "I can't be in love, especially not with Seshen."

I sigh. "Ah, who am I kidding? I'm definitely in love. At least, that's what it feels like. I want to possess her, break her, and consume her. Shit, I want her so close to me I won't be able to tell who's who."

"Dammit, Michael! Stop it. This is insane. She'll never be yours. She's all pink and girly and good. You're a raging fire that will burn her alive. You must stay away from her."

"Or..."

"Or?" I ask myself, still speaking aloud as though I couldn't have this same conversation in my head where it wouldn't make me seem deranged.

"Or you could watch the fire take hold until the little Seshen becomes a field of eternally burning lilies."

I love myself. I have such good ideas sometimes. What if I don't burn her alive? What if I just make her burn brilliantly for all eternity? I mean, she's not weak. The little Seshen can withstand my fire, can't she?

AT THE END OF EVERYTHING

LILLY

When I wake, I'm disoriented. I can't tell how long I've been asleep. At first, I thought it was still the same day, but then it occurred to me it was night when we arrived home and it's day now. I look out my window and from the position of the sun, I know it's about noontime. My mind assumes that it's noon the next day, but I soon realize that's not the case when I notice temporary settlements for the refugees from Nollent have been erected. Either we had way more help than I imagined we would, or I've lost time.

One way or the other, I need to figure out the state of things. The best way for me to do that is to find someone that would be privy to all information, like my mother, either father, brother, or the butler. The butler always knows everything, no matter how secret the information is. I suppose that's the butlery thing to do though; anticipating needs would be difficult if he were unaware of what's happening.

I search the halls of the palace for any of them. For about thirty minutes, I wander the halls, each lined with the Oceanic blue banners hung on white walls with a 24 karat gold inlay running along each edge, into every corner, and around every door. Although, I suppose that the wealthiest nation in the world could afford to do that. It never bothered me that our family spends lavishly because our people have food, housing, and get paid a living wage. We aren't hoarding resources like many royals and nobles. Oceanica just has enough that if every person on this island spent three times what they are now, we'd still have enough to continue providing all the aid we do to other nations for the next three generations without feeling it ourselves. The only times it gets even moderately rough is during times of war, when importing or exporting anything is impossible. That's mostly a matter of safety though, not of economic hardship, and usually fades as soon as the fighting does.

After a while, I grow weary of searching and decide to have a kitchen maid bring me food. I feel as though I'm starving. Just as I turn the corner to head toward the kitchen, I run into Callian. The concerned expression on his face tells me he's surprised to see me up. "Sis? What are you doing? You should be in bed still."

"I'm fine, Cal. Food and an update on what's happened while I was asleep is what I need now."

It only takes my little brother a moment to give in. Unlike Mom and me, he doesn't have quite the same stubborn streak. He nods. "Okay. Go back to bed. I promise I'll bring you a plate of food and update you when I deliver it. Give me about forty-five minutes?"

I smile. He's such an awesome brother. Having inherited Mom's cooking ability, he's well aware that I prefer his cooking to the kitchen staff's. Of course, I'd listen if it meant he'd cook for me himself. "Okay, you win. I'll go back to bed and wait, but at forty-six minutes I'm activating Living Barrier on you."

He chuckles. "Guess it's in my best interest to get there in forty-five then."

Callian takes a few steps before turning to say one more thing. "Glad you're alright, Lil."

I nod. "Always am."

With that, we part. I do as I promised, heading back to my room. On my arrival, I lower my sore body down onto the bed. He was right. I'm really not ready to be up and moving yet. Even just that bit of wandering has me feeling like I want to crash again. I decide to take another brief nap while I wait for Callian. I awaken just moments before I hear his knock at my door. "Come in."

He enters with a tray in hand. The scent of the food makes me salivate. Pancakes, eggs, sausage, and toast. Behind him is a maid with two pitchers, one full of water and the other full of orange juice. They lay the spread out for me, then Callian dismisses the maid so we can speak freely.

Once she's gone, he waits a few moments before beginning. "It's been two days since you went to sleep, Lil. Things aren't good."

"What's happened?" I ask.

"Well, we can't ensure safe transport for the refugees to other allies, so we had to keep them all. Some of the other kingdoms sent aid to help us put up the settlement, but we can't move civilians at all anymore. With Michael's control over Nollent and Tendu, we're essentially cut off from the others. To set sail in any direction, we must go east or west to move around Mallishrine, but that means passing within range of the places he controls. It's just too dangerous. So, aside from fighters, we move no one and nothing. Supply routes are already closed this early in the conflict. Johanna must have passed down her knowledge of the alliance's weak spots and taught Michael how to exploit them."

I can hear how defeated he feels with every word. He must feel so powerless. An heir, but not a king. Powerful, but without the mastery necessary to facedown this kind of enemy. Concerned, but unable to express it behind these palace walls. It almost makes me feel even worse about what happened in Nollent. I had the option to do everything he must want to for our people, but I chose not to. Maybe Michael is right. Maybe I'm better suited to the darkness. I certainly feel evil after what I've done.

"Hey Callian," I look up at him. "I need you to promise me something."

He nods. "What is it, sis?"

"If I fail... if I fall to the darkness, stop me, by any means necessary."

He laughs, but I can hear the anxiety and avoidance in his tone. "I've never seen you fail at anything, Lil. Why would you start now?"

I shake my head. "I'm not saying I will. It's just that I need to hear your promise."

Kai

My wife and I stroll past our daughter's room and hear the rather alarming conversation she's having with our son. Josie looks at me. "Why would she want him to promise her such a thing?"

I shake my head. That beautiful mind of hers loves to run rampant, huh? "Relax, my love. I'm sure Lilly is just scared. It means nothing."

She scoffs, keeping her tone quiet so they don't hear us from inside the room. "That's bullshit and you know it. Malachi's son will be the destruction of our children."

I raise my eyebrow. "Seriously? You came to that conclusion based on a whispered exchange she's sharing with her little brother?"

She juts her chin out. "I know my daughter."

I chuckle. "Clearly."

Taking her hand, I lead her away from Lilly's room and hopefully away from her strange paranoia about Michael turning our daughter into a deranged priestess who betrays everything and everyone she's sworn to protect.

Lilly

Callian pauses for a long moment. His hearing is way better than mine because of his angelic lineage, and I suspect he's using that gift now. He must have caught an interesting conversation. Nosy little prick that he is. After a minute, he groans. "Fine, I promise. Now, eat, would you? The food will get cold if you keep yapping."

I smile. "Yeah, okay. Thanks. We'll talk later?"

He leans down and hugs me gently. "Yeah."

After that, Callian heads out, leaving me alone with my food and my thoughts, the former being the better company, whilst the latter continues to irritate me. Getting Michael off my mind seems to be an insurmountable task, chipping away at my sanity as I try to cope with its enormity. I feel like I'm being split in two. One half of me is the sweet Lilly my family adores and believes in, but this other part of me is one only he can see. They'd never accept it. It's the part that came into existence when evil men forced me to become a woman before my time.

It's the part of me that longs for vengeance against them, and my parents who abandoned me to such a compromising position. There are certain events which create a darkness that is impossible to satiate, events that mar the soul of anyone unlucky enough to encounter them. These things allow me to empathize with Michael in ways the others can't. They prevent me from abandoning him. More importantly, they make me want to be more like him. I find it admirable that someone could embrace their blackened soul even when others reject it.

It sounds easier that way, more relaxed. Michael probably doesn't have to feel like he's being torn in half. What I need is time with him. I need to speak with him again, be with him, and get to know the half of me I've been pretending doesn't exist for two decades. It'd be hypocritical to stop him when I can't deny that he has valid points and we have so much more in common than anyone around me bothers to see.

Thoughts of him continue to haunt my mind for hours, each one that passes fractures me more than the last. It's 3 A.M. before I realize what I must do. Careful not to make too much noise, I open my window. Jumping out of it, I levitate high above the city to keep the guards from spotting me. I move to the docks and carefully slip past Mom's barriers in the only way I know she won't detect the breach. It's done by Realm Walking, which is usually something she does to relax, but I can do it too. By slipping into the divide between our world and the Spirit Realm, I can pass the barriers without ever technically breaching them.

Not having as much experience with this as I do with other skills related to spiritual power, I take more time figuring out how to do it. Understanding the concept and applying it are two vastly different things in this scenario. In fact, it's probable that I fall all the way into the Spirit Realm, which would cause Kimble or Cal, the one Mom named Callian after, to alert Mom. I'll have to be very cautious if I want to escape undetected.

After a few minutes of testing the power commands, I take my shot. First, I harness it to pull myself down, following the power stream like a trail that will guide me into the divide. Once I'm on the right level, I stabilize the frequency of the spiritual power I'm releasing to keep me here. I move forward several feet and then drag myself up on the other side of the barrier. "Yes! I did it!"

I blurt out the words in excitement, realizing I may have just tanked my success by alerting someone. Checking my surroundings, I find myself in luck. There's no sign that anyone heard me. With that, I levitate once more and use my power to guide me toward Tendu.

Soaring over the sea in the matter of thirty brief minutes, I arrive. I recall Michael saying he'd alert his guards to allow me access to him. It's time to find out if that is true. It seems like an awfully large amount of trust to put in an enemy priestess, so I figured it was crap. Yet, as

I land at the edge of the volcanic kingdom and a guard raises his magic to fight me, the commander orders him to stand down. "That's the priestess, Lilliana. She's the peacemaker. We're under orders to let her pass."

The guard who raised his magic leashes it once more. I stand confidently before them, not bothering to make eye contact. It's best I don't show any signs of weakness to this scum. "Take me to Michael."

His discomfort is palpable when he hears me refer to their king as just Michael. I'm sure it registers as either treachery or blasphemy in his mind, perhaps both. Michael is not my king, though. I will not pretend he is. The commander gets past his discomfort and does as I say. He escorts me to the palace. Once I arrive, I'm promptly allowed in by the staff. I ask for the location of Michael's room, and they all continue to cooperate. He must have dropped every procedure there is for me. It's kind of sweet.

I head for his room and knock at the door. "Um," Suddenly, I realize I'm nervous about this. *"Um"* was the only thing to come out of my mouth. This is pathetic.

"Stop being ridiculous and come in, Seshen. I gave you access to my kingdom, my palace, and my cock already. You seriously thought my bedroom was going to be where I draw the line?"

He has a point. I can't admit that, though, so I just scoff as I open the door. "I was trying to be polite, asshole."

He smirks. "Who tries to be polite to a villain then gets surprised when the villain isn't polite in return? It seems you're blaming me for your poor logic."

"Great!" I'm getting frustrated. Why did I come here? "Now, I'm stupid."

He mumbles. "Your words..."

I turn around, prepared to leave. This was a bad idea. I shouldn't have come here. It's hard to say what I was expecting, but it wasn't for him to be a jerk after I came all this way. I just wanted to talk to him. I feel so stupid, but just as I take my first step back toward the door, I feel his hand wrapped around my wrist. His grip is firm and when I turn back to look at him, his expression is almost panicked. "Stay."

The word comes out gruff, almost desperate. Yet, fury rages in those crimson eyes of his. I trail my gaze along his deep brown skin to where he holds my wrist. The way my heart pounds and my stomach fills with an oddly pleasant sense of nausea makes me question my sanity once more. Nausea is not supposed to be pleasant. What is he doing to me? In my flustered state, I make what I believe to be one of the stupidest decisions I ever will. I challenge him. "Why should I?"

His lips curl into a menacing smirk and his nose crinkles ever-so-slightly. "Because I asked you to."

Shock ripples through me. Because he asked? He did, didn't he? He's asking me to stay. That means he wants me here. He must want to talk about what happened between us, too. I give him a firm nod. "Fine, I'll stay."

He uses his grip on my wrist to pull me in, holding me against his chest. "Good. Come, lie down so we can talk."

I look at him as if he's out of his mind. I'm not sure what he's thinking, but I will not be getting into that bed with him. "No, that's fine. I'll stand."

He lifts me by my waist and tosses me back onto the bed without another word. I let out a slight, "*Mmph!*" as I hit the bed. Then I sit up a bit to look at him. "What the Hel?"

He chuckles. "It's fine, Seshen. Jeez, I won't hurt you. You're my guest, though. I won't have you standing in the middle of the room feeling awkward."

I nod, understanding that this conversation will be harder to have if either of us is uncomfortable. Once I do that, he climbs onto the bed and lies beside me. I turn onto my side so we're laying face-to-face. We stare at each other for an allotment of time that I would prefer not to admit to. It's too easy to get absorbed by his presence and forget all the many things that need to be said. Forget that I'm the peacemaker, that I'm Oceanica's queen and kings' daughter, that I'm supposed to save Michael. Forget everything. The only thing that matters any more is us. When I finally find it in me to break the silence, the only words I can fathom are, "I'm yours now."

He wraps an arm around me, pulling me so close that our noses touch. "You've always been mine, Seshen."

I can't help the giggle that escapes me mere moments before his lips lock onto mine. He consumes me in a passionate kiss that sends heat to my core and a whirlwind to my brain. All functions come to an absolute standstill as I feel his tongue invade my mouth, drawing mine into his. He kisses like we're in a war that he hopes never ends. I'm not sure I want it to either. This demon, this king, he's everything to me. I kiss him back, making damn sure that my counterattack is every bit as intense as his initial one. It must work because I could swear that his back arches just as much as mine does. Rough moans escape him and mix with my lighter ones in the air until a symphony of lust and love echoes throughout the halls of his palace.

Amazingly, we refrained from having sex again tonight. We just spent it making out until we both passed out. Next to him, I feel safe and relaxed, so I sleep deeper than I have in years. For once, there is no fear that those men will burst in and attack me again in my sleep because I know that if they did, he'd make them suffer in ways I couldn't when I was a young girl.

The next morning, I wake to a gentle kiss on my forehead. "Are you ready, my queen?"

As I open my eyes, I look up at him and realize what he means. He's asking if I'm ready to be his queen, to admit I've lost the bet and move into the darkness alongside him. I have to say yes. If I don't, I risk losing this connection. Besides, I can't deny that some part of me craves this. It's important that I understand that part of myself. Otherwise, I risk never fully understanding him, who I am, and who we are. That's not what I want. So, I have to do this. "Yes."

He nods, then walks me through everything we'll need to do to publicize it. It's all so official that it sucks the romance out of it. The sadness I feel at the loss of it must show because he notices. "What's wrong, Seshen?"

I shake my head. "Nothing. Not really, anyway. It doesn't matter."

He chuckles, brushing a strand of hair behind my ear. "It matters. Tell me."

I nod. "I just... This all sounds like things I'll do to be with the king of Tendu, as the future queen of Tendu. What about things I'll do as Lilly, for Michael?"

He smiles. "Well, I was going to save this for later, but I want to ask you to go on a date with me. To get to know each other, and for you to get to know Tendu for what it is now."

Excitement rushes me. I can't believe it. An actual date! I guess falling for the bad guy doesn't mean there isn't any romance in the relationship. "Alright. Yes, I'd love to go on a date with you!"

The look of adoration on his face is telling. He must enjoy hearing me get so excited about spending time with him. It makes me wonder if this is as new for him as it is for me. I don't suppose many are so over the moon about hanging out with the tyrannical demon who lords over Tendu. Perhaps he needs this as much as I do. If so, maybe there's still hope for him to be good. Maybe there's still hope for me. What if love heals the sort of darkness that lingers between him and me? That would be something. It would mean that by going into my darkness with him, I could drag us both back out of it. It's a plan, which is something I haven't had until now.

I'll run with it. Either way, it ends with us together, whether it is on his side or on mine. It's a risk, but I think it's worth it. I only hope that Callian holds up his promise if this doesn't go my way. If worse comes to worst, he's the only one I can imagine dragging me back from the brink. I'll have to have faith in him because I see no other way. From here on out, I'm playing the long game.

CHAPTER
Seven

WHEN TRAGEDY STRIKES

JOSIE

I storm the palace, frantic to find her. "Where is my daughter?"

The question booms throughout the palace with authority, ensuring that everyone stops what they are doing and looks for signs of Lilly. Tears flood my eyes as fear sets in. "My daughter, where is she?"

My husbands stand some distance behind me. From what I can sense of their energy, they're terrified too.

We all hate to admit it, but there's no sign of a struggle. Wherever she has gone, she has gone there willingly. Of course, I have no means of confirming my suspicions at the moment, but if I have to guess, she's gone to Michael. I don't know what she's planning or why she's made this choice, but I'm more terrified for her now than I ever have been. It's easy to see that she doesn't know what she's gotten herself into.

I turn my gaze toward my son. "Do you know anything?"

Callian gulps, putting his nervousness on display. "Nothing about her departure, only that I must be the one to bring my sister back. I have my suspicions about what's happening, but I can't be sure. It's likely best I refrain from stating them until I have proof."

I raise my eyebrow. "Are you refusing to convey those suspicions outright, or rather telling me you'd prefer not to?"

I can tell he doesn't want to say it by the way he pauses, looking unsure of himself for a moment. It doesn't take long for his confidence in this decision to beat out his fear of standing against me, though. "I'm refusing, Mother. Not just as Lilly's brother, but as heir to the throne, I believe that for the time being, the best thing for everyone is that I refrain from speaking about this matter. If that displeases you, I'll accept the consequences. Still, you should know that they will not make me tell you."

It's unlike Callian to defy me so openly. He wouldn't do so unless he felt strongly that he was making the right decision. I suppose I have no choice but to have faith in my children. I've raised them to the best of my ability. It's time we see if my best was good enough. As I observe him, he stands tall and confident. He means it. There's no chance that he'll waiver. So, I nod. "Best of luck to you, then, my son."

I glance over at my two doting husbands. "Anything to add, loves?"

Kai groans. "I don't like it at all. She's our baby. We shouldn't be standing around waiting to see if that psychopath kills her or not."

Jameson doesn't hide the fact that he disagrees. "As if that fucking demon could kill her. Have you forgotten that she isn't *just* our daughter? She's the peacemaker, a place she earned by making Josie, herself, forfeit a battle at just eight years old."

Kai snaps back. "I have not forgotten. It is you who seems to forget that Michael isn't some regular demon. He is Malachi and Johanna's son, their heir. Underestimating him would be stupid. Besides, you did not bear witness to the mayhem he caused in Nollent. I did. I saw with my own eyes what he did to my home. It is unacceptable to leave our daughter to the same fate."

The tensions between them escalate higher with each passing moment. The coming of the prophecy is already tearing my family limb from limb, and I feel so helpless to stop it. Lilly is gone. Callian is hiding things.

Jameson and Kai are bickering. I am no longer the unifier I once was. To top it all off, the child of my best friend and my brother is at fault for doing this to us.

This is the fate of angels and demons, huh? First, foreseen by my uncle, Rath, who spent more than one lifetime trying to prevent it. Later, foreseen by the Chief who advised us that Lilly would guide us through it. Most vividly, though, the prophecy Lilly saw with her own power. I think she knew she'd be in the middle, trying to prevent our son of an angelic bloodline from clashing with Michael, of a demonic bloodline. I just don't think she knew that, like me before her, and like Linola before me, she would be the catalyst for all the horror.

Zoning back in on the argument between Kai and Jameson, I try to put a stop to it. "Boys! Separate. The decision is out of our hands. I shouldn't have implied differently by asking. This is my fault."

They both freeze when they hear me take the blame. It's no secret that they're still pissed at each other, but they don't want to make me feel bad, so they shut up. I look at Callian. "We left this matter to Lilly, and we'll uphold that. Further, we will respect your wishes and grant you the freedom to investigate your suspicions prior to telling us about them. Callian, promise me one thing, though? Please."

He nods. "Yes, Mom. What is it?"

I hug him. "If you find that either you or she is in over your heads, come to us. We will help you."

He hugs me back. "I promise, Mom. Thank you."

I keep forgetting they're not children anymore. Listen to me babying them. He's twice my size, and she's twenty-eight years old. It's pathetic that I'm still trying to safeguard them like they're toddlers. My parents never protected me, though. In fact, they almost always made me face the cruelty of this world alone. As a mother, I guess my instinct was to do the opposite. I may have grown overprotective in my attempt to give Lilly and Callian what I never had. I felt they deserved a mother who would protect them come the flames of Helheim or floods of Ragnarök. It never occurred to me that such a thing could keep them from realizing their full potential and chasing their own destiny. I see it now, though, and I will not hold my children back.

It takes all my strength to remove my arms from around Callian, but I do so. Then, my husbands and I take our leave. The two of them remain heated from their argument and I'm not necessarily in the best mood either, so we each take some time to ourselves, not wanting to continue bickering. Not only could it stress Callian out more, but the council and other nobles who roam our palace may take it as a sign of weakness. The last thing we need is to cause a fuss by letting people see all the ways their royal family is falling apart.

Jameson

At my wife's behest, she, Kai, and I all go to our separate corners to cool off after the argument. We each have our own hobbies we distract ourselves with when the dynamic of our three-way marriage becomes turbulent. Josie prefers to either read or go Realm Walking, while Kai goes and uses that runic magic of his to build himself a mountain to climb. After that, he'll sit at the peak of it and stare at the world. I take to much more self-destructive methods of coping.

On this occasion, I'm flying around Oceanica on patrol while mentally berating myself for starting that argument with Kai. I hate arguing with him. Even when I'm right, it hurts. There's no good way to do it. I've never said as much, but I often feel insecure when we argue. Even after all these years of loving each other, some part of me still believes he'd rather I not be in this marriage with him and Josie. It's ridiculous, honestly. My mind seems to understand that the thought is illogical and untrue, but my heart never quite got around to accepting that.

As for Josie, she and I didn't even argue. She keeps stuffing down her emotions to manage everyone else's. She'll end up blowing if one of us doesn't give her an outlet soon. This situation is too difficult for her not to let herself feel the turmoil it's causing her. I suspect Kai has realized the same by now. Later tonight, we'll probably get over ourselves and team up to give her what she needs to relax. It's our pattern. That's actually what keeps our marriage together.

He and I would be explosive without the shared interest we have in keeping her sane. Oddly enough, I think that applies every which way, though. Without Kai, Josie and I would be way too high-strung. Neither of us is as skilled in rolling with the punches as he is. Without me, the two of them would probably get lost in the leftover grief of not getting Cal back. It's my belief that we only work when it's all three of us. I'm sure the other two feel the same, even if my insecurities spend a substantial proportion of their existence trying to erode that surety.

I continue contemplating our marriage with all its euphoric peaks and damning valleys for hours as I fly around, careful to check on any citizens or refugees who look as if they could use help. After several hours, I return to the palace exhausted. While my husband has still not returned, my wife has. She seems tired as well. She and I retreat to our suite and lie down. It isn't long before she falls asleep with her head on my chest. Her presence drives away all the stress and insecurity, leaving only the overwhelming joy that comes with knowing I have the privilege of worshipping this goddess every day for the rest of her life.

As much as I'd like to fall asleep, I want to stay up and admire her even more. I fight the urge to close my eyes tooth and nail just to earn a few more seconds of looking at that peaceful expression etched on her gorgeous face. I love her so much. Still, I can't help but wonder what's taking Kai so long. I'd like to have them both here to dote on. It's a thing for me. I'm the emotional one in this union. I don't care if we argue to the point of wanting to murder each other; when it's time for cuddles, we just have to get over it because I will have my cuddles.

It just pisses me off all over again that he's not back yet. I spend several minutes silently raging over it before wondering if I'd been harsh. Of course he's worried. He had to watch his homeland fall, a fact I'd been so detached from while telling him this enemy shouldn't concern him. Did I hurt him more than I realized? I thought all this time it was just a normal argument between spouses, but it's dawning on me that perhaps this went deeper. I was insensitive to his loss. For fuck's sake, I really am a terrible husband, aren't I? I need to go find him and make this right. He shouldn't have to come to me. I see now that I was the one in the wrong.

I slip out of bed, careful not to wake Josie. Knowing him, my first guess is that he in the training grounds. It's the only space large enough for him to build those mountains he loves to climb and sit on that much. I'm a bit thrown when I get there and don't see him. It takes a moment for me to realize that he'd know this is where I'd look for him. I must have thoroughly pissed him off if he's avoiding me like this. I quickly come up with an alternative list of locations to check and go through several of them before I find my beloved.

When I do, he evades eye contact. No doubt it's because it's harder for him to stay mad if he's looking at me. He speaks first. "Hmph, so you found me."

I can't help but laugh a bit. He's so cute. "Yeah, I found you. You're my husband; I'd find you anywhere, even in a bunch of underground tunnels."

He scoffs. "Some husband..."

I nod. "I'm sorry. That was stupid of me, and so, so cold. I'm an ass."

He glares at me. "That's not good enough. I lost my homeland, Jameson, and you just acted like it was some minor thing."

"It is not a minor thing, I know that." Desperate to help him understand, I try to explain without justifying. My goal is only to let him know I wasn't trying to hurt him. "I wasn't trying to belittle your loss. At that moment, I was just thinking about trying to assuage Josie's worries regarding Lilly. I thought if I was confident in her, Josie might worry less. Kai, I'm so sorry. I shouldn't have done so at your expense."

He nods. "I get that. Frankly, I'm probably not even truly mad at you. I just need some time, okay?"

"Of course. We can talk later." I respect his wishes and turn to leave. Something stops me, though. I realize there's one more thing I must say before leaving, so I pause and look back. "I love you."

He smiles. "I love you, too."

With that, I let him have his space while I return to Josie's side. This time, I'm quick to fall asleep beside her.

Kai

Jameson leaves the tunnels, and I continue to wallow in the turmoil I'm feeling. I'm not one to throw pity parties, but in this case, I feel like taking some time to sit in the distress is necessary to move forward without being burdened by it. My homeland is gone. Nollent was so much more than just an island to me. It was the place where I grew up. I discovered myself there. The memories are clearer to me now than they ever have been.

There was a tiny shop on the south side of the island where I first spotted Cal. He was so cute in his cat-ear hood. It was the first time I realized I was bisexual. I'd felt an attraction to females before that, but he was the first male. I didn't know others on the island saw non-hetero sexualities in such a negative light. It wasn't hard to figure out I was different, though. If there were others like me, they weren't very open about it; I had never seen a man with another man before. So, I hid it, unsure of what would happen if I said something about it. Cal felt something for me, too, though. He introduced himself and we became friends. Of course, we ended up falling in love later.

At seventeen, we both agreed to come out to my parents. My parents acted ashamed and disowned me, but his father's reaction was more aggressive. He became violent and tried to attack Cal. Acting on instinct, I summoned my runic magic and accidentally killed him. Cal helped me cover it up and after that, we met in secret, loved each other in silence, afraid that others would react like our parents did.

I started the rebellion to fix all the injustices that plagued Nollent. It was failing, until I met Josie, that is. Much like with Cal, I knew the moment I saw her, but Malachi wasn't so friendly toward me back then. It wasn't homophobia, just an older brother worried about seeing his sister with a guy. I understood that. His tune changed pretty quickly after getting to know me some. He came to like me and Cal. That's when things got better. We helped Nollent grow through our efforts back then.

Then Cal died, and I did, too, not long after. Then Josie came for us, even though she was only successful in resurrecting me. These past years, I found happiness with her and Jameson. Now, I feel like it was all for naught. Nollent healed just to fall. The man I was fighting for is gone. The family that healed me is tearing at the seams. I feel so lost. This is hard on us all, I know. I just need a little time to deal with the ways it's hard on me, personally.

I walk along the rocky tunnels with my hand grazing on its side. The earth makes me feel so grounded. Whether that is because of the way the runes covering my body react to it or because I grew up in a rocky climate doesn't matter. I love stone. It comforts me. Often, I compare it to the feeling of surety, the unwavering solidity of knowing something will always be there if you call on it. Nothing compares to knowing a thing is reliable. I had thought many things in my life were, but aside from my loves, living and dead alike, nothing aside from stone has proven to be so.

Wandering aimlessly through these tunnels has the desired effect. It soothes my soul and helps me to cope with the chaos that has erupted around me in the wake of Johanna's death. Before I know it, several hours have passed. I head back to the surface. Upon reaching it, the sunlight causes me to feel disoriented. I squint to help myself see with more clarity until my eyes adjust. I must have been down there longer than I thought if the day had already come. I know I should get back to the palace soon. Josie and Jameson will be worried if they wake, and I've not returned.

It takes some time for me to get home. When I do, Josie and Jameson are still asleep. I want to climb into bed beside them, but I'm in dire need of a bath and food. I have the staff prepare my bath and order them to make food as well. Knowing my spouses and son should wake soon, I ask them to prepare enough for us all so we can sit and eat together. I think that sense of family is what we all need right now.

I wash and soak for about forty-five minutes in the bath. The warm water helps to ease my body. Without Jameson's magic, though, it cools bit by bit, and I decide to get out. After I dry and dress, I walk along the halls to the dining hall. Joy cracks in my expression when I see them all sitting at the table, awaiting my arrival. I take my seat to the left of Josie, who is at the head of the table. Callian sits beside me, and Jameson sits opposite.

Callian

As my parents and I eat, we make the effort not to let the conversation lean in a political direction. None of us can afford to think about that right now. At this moment, we just need to be there for each other. After taking our space and time to ourselves, it's important that we come back together like this. My parents always taught us it's okay to need a break, but when that's done, it's vital to let the people you love know you're still with them.

It's a healthy practice that allows individuals to have boundaries while also making sure the unit stays bonded. I've learned to respect it over the years. I'm glad they took the time to teach us that. Otherwise, what example would I have to follow? While I agree with Lilly that sometimes having such icons as parents is daunting, we've never exactly agreed on this matter. She doesn't seem to think it's good for us, but I do.

The thought makes my heart ache a bit. I miss my sister. Even though I see the importance of it, not thinking about her is a struggle for me. I don't let the passive thought pull me too much away from the goal, though. I still enjoy having breakfast with my family, knowing in my heart that I will get Lilly back, even if it's the last thing I do.

After we finish eating, I get to work on my actual plan to confirm what I've been thinking all this time. I'll admit it's not the most surefire plan I've ever come up with, but it's my only hope. If I'm right, I should be able to speak with my sister directly. If I'm not, well... Let's hope I am because I don't know what happens after that. I just know that it won't be good.

I search my room for the journal she wrote the instructions in when she taught me how to do this. It's small and made of brown leather. I haven't touched it in years, but I'm sure it's in here somewhere. I scan every shelf and dig through every drawer, but there's no sign of it. It feels like it's not here until I remember another spot that it could be. I go into my oversized closet which is filled to the brim with all my princely jewels and formal clothing I acquired when I came of age. In the back, righthand corner of it all, is a hidden door Lilly and I created to hide away things we didn't want a maid to find and tell our parents about.

I open it to find the journal, along with a few other mementos. I pull them all out and promptly get sidetracked with reminiscing over them. My favorite is the dusty antique vase. We stole it from mother and used it to hold our secret candy stash. She spent a month looking for it, but neither of us rolled on the other. Comradery among siblings is strange in that way. We'll nearly torture each other to death, but we stand together when it's something that absolutely doesn't matter, as long as it's against someone we agree needs to be taken down a notch.

I chuckle a bit as I recall all the time we spent together. We were such menaces. Now it's time I get my lifelong accomplice back. I open the journal and find the page with the instructions among the many other rituals and spells we weren't supposed to be doing. "Ah, here it is, establishing a telepathic link."

The spell is far more complex than I remember. Leave it to Lilly to have mastered something like this at ten years old. Nerd. I've never been as adept at learning stuff like this as she is. It takes a few hours to get everything ready. I have to gather herbs, crystals, and candles. I hate making altars. You'd think a damn angel could bypass all this nonsense, but no. Apparently, we actually have to follow the rules like normal people. So, here I am turning my bedroom into a priestess's dream to contact my sister, who clearly doesn't want to be contacted. It's annoying, but whatever. No one else is going to do it.

Finally, I have it all set. I sit and chant, trying to establish the link. Unfortunately, this spell is one that only works if the other person accepts the connection. Forcing a telepathic link on someone is a much different spell. The good thing is that how Lilly responds will tell me what I need to know about her plan. If she rejects the link, confirming her fall is true, then my only hope is for my survival. She could use the rejection to hurt me.

I guide the magic, trying to find her, the physical distance between us making it even more difficult. I've never done this before. It's tiring me out. I manage, though. The magic does its work, essentially knocking on her mind like a door, asking her to let me in. I can feel when she becomes aware, but she tries to push the link out. Not wanting to fight her or give her the opportunity to hurt me, I let her. This ends the spell. This is bad. She's not just playing at being on his side so she can sway him to ours. If she were, she should have accepted it and communicated since he wouldn't know. That's not the case, though. She's really gone to him. This information tells me what my next steps are. Things are going to get rough.

CHAPTER
Eight

THE QUEEN-TO-BE, LONG LIVE SHE

LILLY

Oh, this is so ridiculous. I cannot believe I've found myself in this predicament. Surrounded by eager maids fussing over which stuffy clothes they plan to shove me into so I can appear beside Michael publicly was not in my plans. This is miserable. I wanted to be with him, not to be paraded around as the future queen of Tendu. I mean, I knew it would come one day. Since he's king, it's a given. Though, I'd hoped he'd fulfill the date promise before doing this. It's whatever, though. I'll do it because he asked me to. Oddly enough, I seem to care about him deeper than I'd thought.

The maids make up their minds at last. I end up in a suffocating gown that looks better suited to a princess than it does to a priestess or peacemaker. Its floor length with a train that seems as if it never ends. The color of it is nice. It's about the same red as Michael's eyes. I love that red. Its silken material feels nice, but I'm not a huge fan of the design. Sewn into it is a cascading series of jewels that makes its weight less comfortable. I feel burdened, like I can't move to defend myself properly if the need arises.

Although I'm not the biggest fan of this garment, my feelings about wearing it become positive when Michael walks in. His face goes from stern and serious to elated in mere moments. He rakes that intense gaze of his over me time and time again as his eyes become a little brighter each time. "You're gorgeous," he states as if it's fact rather than his opinion. "The most beautiful creature to walk this world, without a doubt."

I giggle. "Why, thank you, Michael. That's sweet of you to say."

The maids surrounding us seem to fade into the background as we stare at each other. We must look like fools right now, but I don't care. It seems pointless to hide that we're obsessed with each other. We may not have been together long yet, but Niflheim, if I won't say we're in love. Hel, yes, we are. After all, how could I not be in love with someone like him? For all his hatred and loathing for this world and everyone in it, he found it in his blackened heart to make an exception for me. Coming from him, such a thing must count as only the highest form of praise.

Michael offers me his arm, ready to escort me to do whatever it is he wanted me to do before our date tomorrow. He leads me through his palace at a casual pace. As we walk, he stops a few times to point at random relics and arts to tell me the history of them. I noticed that the collection had grown substantially since I visited when I was young. It makes some sense that he and Johanna had expanded it over the years.

It's nice to see what pieces he chose, though. You can tell a lot about someone by their taste in art and such. His tastes are very distinct. They aren't pieces one would normally want to collect. None made by famed artists and not a single classic piece. Rather, each seems to be made by small, independent artists. It gives me the impression that he cares much more about his people than I thought.

He's clearly using his wealth to support independent art, possibly trying to stimulate the economy as well. The art itself is interesting. It's dark. Anger and loneliness echo throughout every piece. There's no sign of love or warmth, which is further highlighted by the fact the relics are all gruesome. Its bone shards and teeth, a few skulls, and vile after vile of blood from every species. Human. Demon. Angel. Even one of god's blood.

Who knows which god it came from, or how he got it? I don't ask these questions as he shows me all these things because I don't think I want the answers. Also, because I'm enjoying this. Somehow, I'm fascinated by these brutal, sad pieces. That other half of me, the one I don't know all that well, comes to life some around this sort of beautiful cruelty.

Together, he and I relish in it a bit on our way to wherever he's taking me where I'm supposed to look all queenly. After a while, as we're nearing the destination, he changes. Once again, he becomes cold, serious, and frightening in that way that should scare me, but... it doesn't. For some unknown reason, it only makes me want him more. There's something about that darkness of his that gives the impression that what happened between us in that watchtower was surface level. His darkness is like a void. I could go deeper and deeper, spend eons exploring it, and there would still be no end to it. That sort of striking evil must be what most people picture when they picture a demon. I'd only known demons like Uncle Malachi previously, who, regardless of his bloodline, had nothing in common with the stereotype of being demonic.

We arrive in front of a massive oak wood door just before Michael looks at me. "Smile." He commands. "And try not to embarrass me. This all goes much easier if they like you. I'd rather not have to fight them over the decision to be with you, especially since it's not one I'm willing to budge on."

Offering him a nod, I reply. "I'll do my best."

Of course, I don't tell him about my doubts that my best will be any good. He seems satisfied with my answer as he queues the guards posted on either side of the door to open it. In one synchronized push, they open both sides for us to pass through. Michael pulls me closer, making damn sure everyone inside what appears to be his war room knows that I am with him and should have their utmost respect.

I stand tall, making sure I elongate my posture and appear confident as I stride in at his side. His generals and advisors surround the long table within, each of them glaring at me with some mix of apprehension and loathing. Michael pulls out the seat at the head of the table, but he doesn't sit in it. Instead, he looks at me. "Sit, my love."

He wants me to sit at the head of the table. It's a gesture that can't be mistaken. He's not demanding equal respect from those in this room to what they give him. He's making it clear that he sees me as more important and expects them to do the same. I see why Mom loves my dads so much now. It's an amazing feeling. To have a king, a leader, an idol uplift you until you are above even a king. It is like being a goddess. Queen is more than just some title when you are this loved by your king. It's an honor. A position of unequivocal power. Who dare stand against the woman the king, himself, bows to? I dare say no one would be that foolish. If any were, I don't think they'd live to tell the tale. For all my power, Michael would kill them before I ever lifted a finger to defend myself. I know that in my core. He's made sure of it.

He addresses those around us in a collected tone after I'm seated. "This is Lilliana, former peacemaker of the allied kingdoms and daughter of Queen Josella Spade, as well as her co-kings, Jameson and Kai. She is no longer to be counted among them, though, nor held accountable for the sins they committed that drove me to war against them. From this day forward, she is to be known only as Lilliana, the future queen of Tendu, and my fiancée."

Eyes, all glued to me, fill with horror the likes of which I've never seen. They do not want me here, but they won't openly oppose Michael. One by one, they walk over and kneel before me, each placing a reluctant kiss on my hand. Despite the show of reverence, I know better than to think I won't face opposition from them at every turn. They'll all try to drive me away whenever they think Michael isn't looking. They won't succeed, though. I'm not going anywhere. I'll just have to earn their trust and respect.

After we finish up with them, we go public. From the King's Podium, a traditional point at the pinnacle of the palace of Tendu from which the king can speak and reach the entire island with ease, he introduces me to his people. Hearing the announcement seems to give many some sense of renewed faith. They must think that a wedding to the peacemaker is a step toward peace, or at least a sign that someone in the palace is looking out for their interests. As much as it shames me to say it, they may come to be disappointed. I didn't come here to look out for them, or anyone else for that matter. My only goal is to be at Michael's side. Frankly, I have no intention of interfering with his plans. A fact my brother learned when he tried to penetrate my mind.

I know what he was thinking. He thought I came to Tendu to grow close to Michael so I could sway him. That's not the truth of it. I just wanted to be close to him. To me, it no longer matters which of us sways the other. I will be whatever this man needs me to be, and I know he'll do the same because he loves me, he sees me, he showed me a way out of the Hel I spent years suffering. We may not be good people. I used to think I was, but maybe I'm not. Not anymore, at least. It just doesn't matter, though. We're excellent partners. Good lovers. Good to each other. That's what I value. I won't give it up, no matter the chaos that ensues because of our love. I will let this world burn if only to let him know he need never feel alone again.

When we're done addressing his people, he brings me in on his plans for the war. I try to hide it, but I rejoice in secret. He trusts me. I stand beside him as he shows me the strategies, listening. "As you can see, our next target is in Loft. Not the entire kingdom, just Queen Josella's duchy there, the one she inherited from her parents. It's the first step in undermining her stronghold on the allies. Attacking her in Oceanica is a much larger task, so we thought attacking her in some far-off duchy she rarely visits would be a good start. We can weaken her from the outside before we ever have a direct confrontation with Oceanica."

His plan isn't bad, but there's one gaping hole in it. I think he's drastically underestimating how willing the allies are to defend each other. If he wants to bring down my mother, he'll need to do better. The part of me that loves her and is grateful to her for adopting me screams at me to leave it be, so he'll fail, but that darker half of me is much louder than it ever has been before. It drowns out whatever guilt I feel about betraying her and makes me want to help him. "They won't let it happen. Oceanica will send aid to the duchy, as will the rest of Loft. Your biggest worry is Pallentine, though. They're close and can get there fast. It'd be unwise to underestimate them."

He smirks. "Me? Underestimate the tribe that produced my fearsome mother? I think not, Seshen. I have a general that can hinder their arrival. He's like my father and me, in the sense that his magic borrows from more than just fire runes. As a descendant of royal demon blood, I have my Helfire, just like my father did. Noble demons, though, have a variety of slightly weaker, but equally useful special powers. This general has venomous smog. He can use it to block them off. They won't be able to sail through it without dying."

I shake my head. "Many of them can harness wind. They'll blow it away. Let me help. I may have a solution, but we'll have to see if my power is compatible with the general's to know if it will work."

He nods. "Sure. We can put it in the books for the day after tomorrow. I'd hate to cancel that date you were so eager for."

With a single arm placed around my waist faster than I could keep up, he pulls me close, eliciting a sharp gasp from me. Our bodies touching turns me into a quivering fool. Why does he affect me so? His hard, muscular body against mine weakens me. I hadn't realized how drab the official business of the day felt. Only when his fire ignites every nerve in my body does the weariness slip away, replaced by the fire he gifts me with every touch.

I melt into his sturdy frame, relaxing into his arms. When I do, I notice this pit in my stomach driven by a question I believe would be unwise to ask. When have I ever been able to hold my tongue, though? I look up at him, resting my chin on his chest as he caresses the pudgy little love-handles just above my hips. "Is this what our love will be? Stolen moments at the end of busy days?"

His eyes widen a bit. I'm shocked to see that he hadn't realized the impression this day gave. He kisses my forehead, then looks into my eyes. "No, beloved Seshen. Never that. That was what today was like, and there will be more like it occasionally. Most days, though, I will spend bringing joy to this precious face of yours." He moves one hand to my cheek. "This is my promise to you: For every star in the sky, I will spend ten seconds looking into your violet eyes. If that time accumulated doesn't pass before I die, at least I'll know I spent most of my life at your side."

A tear forms in my eye from the sheer earnestness packed into his rich voice as he speaks. I never knew words could taste so sweet. Coming from him, each one makes me weak, yet somehow I feel so damn strong. The sound engages every part of me. It sparks an electricity in me, shooting from my labia, right through every limb and ligament in my lustful body. I have to search for the willpower to answer him. "Oh, Michael..."

My words fade. I have nothing to match the loving words he gave me. I want to tell him how I feel, but my brain is failing me even though my soul wants to pour it back into him tenfold. He must see the emotions flailing around in my eyes because he kisses my forehead. "I know, Seshen. I know."

He lifts me off the ground to carry me in his arms back to our room. After laying me on the bed, he hovers above me. He's gentle as he lifts the skirt of my dress. "Just relax and let me give you the reassurance you need."

Before I can reply, he tugs my undergarments away. The feel of his rough hands running over my thighs as he breathes me in. "You smell so sweet."

He indulges himself with no regard for my tenuous grip on sanity, spreading my lips wide. I gasp as he swipes his tongue over me, tasting my wetness. He makes this sound that I could have sworn came from the depths of Hel. That growl sending vibrations through my core is all I need to know that he's loving this every bit as much as I am. His next moves are anything but slow and gentle. He shoves his face in me, sucking and licking on my clit so intensely that I shoot straight past gentle moans into screaming for the pleasure he gives. For several blissfully excruciating minutes, he locks onto my clit, and I don't think even the strongest person alive could tear him off.

Then, without warning, he moves down, plunging his tongue into my hole. His demonic heritage shows when his tongue elongates, becoming just as enormous as any cock. He teases my g-spot with it, devouring me until I'm a submissive puddle. Fuck. I'm such a whore for him. I love it. My hips buck, riding his tongue as he uses it to get me off. His eyes lock on mine and that glowing Helfire red does nothing to prevent me from coming undone all over his face. Goddesses, I want to see that gorgeous, ebony skin soaked in my juices. The pleasure has me squirming, but he won't let me get away. He reaches up and locks his arms around my thighs to hold me in place.

I plead, "Oh, Michael, fuck... I'm... I'm going to!"

It was too late; I squirt all over him. He's all too eager to let me ride out the orgasm on his tongue. When the last wave subsides, I assume we're finished and try to get up, but he grabs my waist and flips me forcefully, putting me face down on my stomach. He doesn't even give me a moment to collect myself before he spreads my ass cheeks and swirls his tongue around the hole.

I can't believe the shockwave it sends throughout my body. I sound so desperate as I speak. "Wha—What are you..."

He gives me a sharp slap to the ass, causing me to yelp. "Shut up and let me eat this thick fucking ass, Seshen."

I go silent. There's not a sound between us for a few seconds as he holds my ass splayed. "Such a good fucking slut."

He delves back in with such reckless abandon, circling the rim furiously until I'm sobbing. Then, he thrusts his tongue inside with it still in that demonic, lengthened form, pinning me so I have to take it all. I'm amazed at the way my hole relaxes and widens to accept it. I didn't think it'd be so willing. This all feels too good, though. I'm sure I'd take just about anything he gave with pleasure. Soon enough, I'm writhing for him again. As he tongue fucks my asshole, I'm consumed by the excruciating ecstasy of it. The way his saliva drips down from my ass over my pussy is euphoric. I don't think it could get any better, until... Oh, fuck. What is he doing?

MINE

MICHAEL

I slow my pace as I eat her ass, wanting to drag out this moment for as long as possible. A sweet, trembling moan comes from her as I inch my tongue out of her ass until only the tip is inside. I wait, watching her become desperate as she struggles against my grip on her to get it back inside of her. There's a sick sense of amusement I get from watching her struggle like this. Lucky for her, I can't resist her long enough to make her wait too long. After I get a taste of her desperation, I plunge my tongue all the way back in with a single thrust.

She hollers. I didn't think it was possible for my cock to get any harder, but it does. I'm tempted to stroke it while I eat this ass, but right now, this isn't about my pleasure. It's all for my Seshen. I need her to see how much it pleases me just to please her. I need her to know in her mind, heart, soul, and delectable organs just how much she means to me. Easing my tongue back out again, I continue to torture her with the sole goal of ingraining that in her so deep that she'll remember it in her next nine lives. I continue plunging in and easing out for a while, ensuring she's got the message before ravaging her like the disgusting whore she is.

It's nothing short of paradise when she squirts for me again. And again. And again. Hel, I made her squirt so many times she was barely conscious by the time I stopped. I make sure she drinks plenty of water before I let her fall asleep, though. She won't be much fun for me tomorrow if she's half-dead from dehydration. I want our date to go well. I've never cared so much about a woman before. This is the first time I'm even taking one on a date. For some inexplicable reason, I feel all giddy and excited about it. It's gross, but whatever. Apparently, this romance mush makes her happy, and that makes me happy, so I'll do it.

She sleeps like a rock beside me. Niflheim, this woman could wake the entire palace with the way she's snoring. Something so grotesque would annoy me coming from anyone besides her, but when she does it, it's adorable. My heart flutters a bit. It's never done that before. I love this madwoman, don't I? She's taken over my life. All the things I thought I knew about myself crumble in her presence. She's redefined me.

After a while, I tune my thoughts of her out and fall asleep with her bunched up in my arms. Nothing has ever felt so perfect before. Somehow, even with her snoring, I sleep better next to her than I ever have. I get up just after dawn. Lilly is still asleep, but that's not a problem for me because it gives me time to prepare. Careful not to wake her, I slip out of the bed and head down to the kitchen. I'm having the maids make a special breakfast for us as part of the date I planned.

I'm relieved upon seeing that they haven't screwed it up. My maids are competent, but I have high expectations for this day, and I needed to be sure. When I'm done there, I head to my dressing room. Knowing my Seshen, she'll want to discard the burden of politics for our date. I had my seamstresses make me basic tunics and breeches. I've never put on anything so bland before, but we can hardly remain inconspicuous if I'm dressed like a king. This is the only way to ensure our date remains intimate. Courting is a lot of work. I'm insane; no man in his right mind would do this. Then, I think about how she smiled at me on the balcony after meeting the generals. It'll be worth it to see that smile of hers.

It's mid-morning before my precious Seshen sees fit to wake. I've already been up for hours checking on every detail of this day. After she's bathed and clothed, the maids escort her to the dining hall where I await her. Her eyes widen when she enters to see the breakfast feast I planned. At first, it looks like horror that caused her reaction, perhaps because of the amount that will inevitably go to waste, but then it turns to excitement when she spots...

She's infuriating. All this food and she heads straight for the pancakes. No meat, no fruit, nothing that might actually give her body nutrients, just pancakes. She's lucky I feel like I can't feasibly survive without her, otherwise taking care of her would feel like an insurmountable obstacle that wasn't worth trying to conquer.

After she piles about ten of them onto a plate, I take it from her, lifting it over her head as she tries to reach for it. She pouts as I circle the table to put some more diverse food choices onto the plate. "I don't need you telling me what to eat, you know?"

I roll my eyes, conflicted between fawning over how adorable she is and the need to give her a stern redirect. "Contrary to what you may believe, Seshen, it's obvious that you do."

She huffs. "Contrary to what you may believe, Michael, I've kept myself alive for twenty-eight years and don't need you, or anyone, telling me how to do it."

This woman, doesn't she realize that after last night she'll feel like crap all day if she doesn't eat a proper meal? I'd rather not have her pass out on our first date.

It wouldn't bode well for our relationship. I give her a warning glare. "Lilliana..."

Her eyes widen, and she almost looks hurt? Did I hurt her feelings somehow? No. There's no way. It must be something else. Yet, she goes silent. She takes the plate with the stuff I added to it and sits down to eat. What just happened? I thought the conversation was fun and teasing, but she just shut down on me. Perhaps the look I gave was too much for her? Maybe she thought I was more serious than I was? I didn't take her for the type to be intimidated into submission, though. Not by me, or by anyone. This is strange. I tilt my head, trying to figure it out. That was unsuccessful, so I ask her. "Did I do something wrong? There was a dramatic shift in your demeanor just then."

She shakes her head at me. "No, it's nothing. Just forget it."

"If it caused that reaction, it isn't nothing to me." My voice is firm yet caring as I speak. "Don't you see, Lilly? You are my life now. When something causes you to dim yourself, I will destroy it. I'd protect you from anything, myself included."

She snaps. "Stop calling me that! Stop calling me Lilly, Lilliana, or whatever. You've always called me Seshen. Why the sudden change? I don't even know what it means, but I see it as a term of endearment."

Her words shock me a bit at first. I didn't think the nickname meant that much to her. I can't help but smile some, knowing that it matters to her. "Seshen is a word in my native tongue. It refers to a specific type of lily called a blue lotus. It has many healing effects, but also some more abstract ones. The ancients used it in rituals related to sex because it causes euphoria. I call you Seshen because you, my beloved, your presence and your being, bring me healing and euphoria, just like the flower."

Lilly

Damn, this man has me reeling. He's just told me I'm so intoxicating to him he nicknamed me after an ancient flower with psychedelic effects. "I don't know what to say, Michael."

He shrugs. "Say you'll never leave."

I shake my head. "Wouldn't dream of it. I love you."

He smiles. "I love you too, little Seshen. Now finish eating, we have a date to go on."

I do as he asks, finishing my food. We depart not long after heading out into the village to see the market. For as much havoc that has torn through the economy here since Tendu broke off from the alliance, the areas immediately surrounding the palace were still stable and wealthy. A tactical move, I would guess. Surround yourself with those who love you, so those that don't can't easily reach for your neck. Most of these small villages around the palace are full of the merchants the palace trades with. Of course, the people who fill their pockets and feed their family on coin they receive from the royal household love Michael.

This village is stunning, though. The surrounding volcanoes make for some of the most vibrant flora one can find. It helps that the people here are also fire rune users. Even the weakest among them have this unnatural ability to withstand the heat of lava. I'm not sure if it's caused by their magic or some freaky evolutionary mishap, but they can swim and bathe in it like normal people do water. Many here even believe that swimming and bathing in lava makes their skin clearer and more beautiful. I guess I wouldn't know if it were true or not because if I touched lava, it would certainly result in my being burned. My power as a priestess protects me from many things, not from lava, though.

That's the issue with people like us. We'll never know if one type of being is stronger than the next because each power has such unique properties that they aren't comparable to each other. For example, just as my power can't protect me from lava, his power can't protect him from an attack across a realm divide. We're unique, but neither is definitively better than the other.

When we arrive at the market, he shows me to a small local bookstore with a café inside of it. I'm overjoyed by his excellent choice in dating locations. He rests his hand on my shoulder as I enter the store. "Look around, get anything you want. On me, of course. I'm just going to run to the bathroom."

Wandering off toward the back of the store, he leaves me unsupervised with permission to get whatever I want. On him. He'll come to regret that pretty fast. I head down the one aisle with a sign hanging above it labeled "Romance" and start picking up book after book. While I'm busy piling up more books than I can carry, some guy comes up behind me, tugging at the sash I used to tie my miko.

I whip around, turning to look at him. "Hey! What're you doing?"

He cuts me off. "You're the king's new plaything. I'm going to defile you, so he loses interest."

All my books tumble to the floor as he tries to cover my mouth with his hand. I'm afraid to retaliate and damage the store's property. My mind shoots straight to not wanting to cause any trouble for Michael. Attempting to fight him off without using my spiritual power proves useless. He's much stronger than I am in terms of physical strength. I let out a yelp as he moves to open the miko. Before he can, he jerks back, flying off of me. I'm confused at first, but then I get myself together enough to focus in on Michael standing behind him, holding him by the collar of his tunic. The barbarian quakes in fear, knowing Michael won't let this go without retribution. As far as Michael's concerned, an attack on me is an attack on him.

I follow as he drags the man from the store. He searches the street to find guards posted nearby. When he spots two of them patrolling, he calls out. "Men!"

They recognize their king and their attention snaps to him in an instant. Michael continues, issuing his order. "Take this man to the dungeon. Offer him nothing.

Lilliana and I will be there later to show this douche what happens when he touches what is mine."

Both guards reply in unison, "Aye, sir."

With that, they drag the man off. Michael's attention shifts back to me. "Are you okay?"

I nod. "Yes, I'm unharmed."

He lets out a deep, primal growl. "Answer the question I asked you, Seshen."

I inhale a sharp breath. "I'm rattled. It was frightening, and I didn't know what to do."

"Defend yourself." The tenor of his voice tells me it's a command. "At all costs. If there are repercussions, I will deal with them. Nothing is worth you compromising your safety."

Not knowing what else to say, I just look at him. The intensity of the situation brought back memories I hoped would never return. He must see the fear and trauma clouding my eyes because his expression softens when his gaze meets mine. "May I touch you?"

I look down as I nod. He wraps an arm around my shoulder. "Do you want to go back to the palace, or do you still want to go book shopping?"

Lifting my hand, I extend my index finger toward the bookstore. "I still want the books."

He grins. "I thought so. Come on. Let's get them."

He keeps his arm around me, its soothing presence calming me as we go back inside. Michael wasn't lying. He bought me every book I wanted. A grand total of three hundred gold coins, two silver ones, and five copper ones. We had to borrow a wooden cart from a local to transport them back to the palace. They didn't seem to mind, though. Michael sent a servant with a few coins to bring it back to them. I liked him showing gratitude for the loan.

Upon our arrival, he helps me to organize them on a special shelf he's dedicated to me in his library. "A gift," he explains, "So you know that this is your home just as much as it is mine."

I can't help the blush that I feel rushing my cheeks. He's so sweet, going out of his way to help me get comfortable here. This feeling of comfort is so new to me. I've never felt so free to be myself before, like I don't need permission to exist in my most natural form. There's no part of me he'd reject or make me feel bad about. We spend a few more minutes stacking my books neatly onto my new shelf. As I look around, I notice that most of his collection is on battle tactics, history, politics, and other relevant subjects. He must think it's goofy of me to read all these romances. I hope he doesn't think I'm frivolous. Yes, I enjoy romances. That's not the only genre I read, though. I've read many of the titles in his collection. The simple fact of the matter is that romance is more entertaining. It's my belief that reading for entertainment is both educational and healthy. The benefits of reading aren't exclusive to certain genres. Every book has something worthwhile to offer.

After a while, we finish up. I don't want our date to be over, but the sun is coming down. I look up at Michael as we lay on the floor of the massive library, cuddled into a ball. He looks back down at me. His eyes are so full of awe that it makes my heart melt. The love in his expression is unlike anything I've ever seen. Seeing it makes me want to love him even more than I already do. It's a scary thought since I'm not sure my heart could take it if I did.

When we finally stumble into enough willpower to force ourselves out of each other's arms, he helps me up. A mischievous smile comes across his face as he says, "With me, Seshen. I have one more surprise for you."

I follow him so willingly that I wonder if he could lead me into Hel and still have me follow without a fuss. He leads me down to the dungeons. Bound to a pillar of stone in its cold, dark depths is the man from earlier. The guard on watch whispers something in Michael's ear as we enter. From the way my love's face contorts, it's not anything good. He snarls as we approach the prisoner. "Who paid you to attack her?"

The man's face was emotionless. He feels no fear. "I'll never break."

Michael laughs a laughter so dark that it would traumatize even the most beastly of beings. "Oh, I beg to differ."

His power heightens, becoming more palpable as his body morphs. He's taking on his demonic form. The full transformation doesn't take long. When it's done, I stare at it in awe. It's a grotesque, repulsive sort of beautiful. Heavy hair, almost like fur, sprouts from his rippling muscles as his shirt tears off from the sheer enormity of the form. With the body of a beastly lion and horns of a ghastly bull. Of course, there's that serpentine tongue as well. I must remember its power too well because I become aroused at the mere sight of it. Fuck, what is wrong with me? The look of him would repulse most people, but I'm horny.

He speaks to me in a distorted, demonic voice. "Join me, my love. Help me break him."

I've never tortured a man before, but that part of me—the part that made me come here, the part that's turned on right now, the part that grows every time I see Michael—that Lilly is even more excited at the prospect of torturing this man together. I call up some spiritual power, shaping it into two glowing, purple jambiya-shaped blades. One for each hand. "Let's do it."

The emotionless expression on the prisoner's face eradicates as he observes our derangement. His fear is delicious. I lick my lips at the sight of it. Then I take the first move, using the blade to cut his pants away. "You were going to defile me, were you? Let's see how you like someone *defiling* your genitals without consent."

I cut his cock, careful not to hit either branch of his penile artery. Wouldn't want to kill him too quickly, now would I? Michael laughs hysterically as the man hisses. "This bitch is crazy."

"You're damn right she is. Hot, isn't it?" Michael replies to him.

I laugh in return. "Aw! Thanks, babe. That's so sweet of you."

The man's horror, terror, and pain fill the dungeon. Michael follows up on my torment by setting fire to the soles of the bastard's feet. He makes damn sure it's hot enough to drive him insane while keeping it from spreading as he commands. "Now, answer my question. Who paid you to fucking attack my bride?"

Sobbing or seething, I can't tell anymore as the man once again refuses to supply us with a name. Infuriated by his stubbornness, I jab one blade into the side of his hip, just high enough to miss his superior gluteal artery. This time there's no debating it. The sob that tears from his throat is clear as day. Still, he doesn't break. I can tell we're getting close, though.

After several more minutes of what I'm sure is excruciating pain, he relents, coughing up a name. As I suspected, the culprit was a general. One of those who appeared most perturbed when Michael introduced me to them yesterday. With that answer, I assume it has come time to kill this prisoner, but Michael, thinking with clarity, insists that death is a privilege he'll have earned only after we can confirm that the name he gave was true. He had a point. The man may have just named a random person so he could protect his true master while also escaping the agony of the torture.

We leave him in the dungeons, tied up, and order the guard to make sure he doesn't bleed out, as well as to give him only enough food and water to sustain his life.

With that, our date has come to its end. The idea doesn't bother me so much as it did earlier, though. I'm more than confident that there will be many more. All the days of our life, Michael and I will be together. We're well beyond the point of no return. He and I are forever. Our love will be eternal, like the flames of his ancestral home.

After such a long day, we rest well cuddled up in bed, although some part of me had enjoyed the library floor a bit more. Tomorrow, we have to work on my plan to help with the attack on Loft, and devise another to confirm the words of my attacker. Tonight, though, it's just him and me. All our worries seem so far off when we're close like this. I spent so many years being the light everyone needed me to be that I forgot how wonderful the darkness is.

Right and wrong blend together when love is the question at hand, the distinction between them becoming just as unclear as the boundary between my person and his has. The emotion isn't exclusive to good. That's the beauty of it, in my not-so-humble opinion. It's a morally grey emotion that doesn't discriminate, nor does it adhere to societal definitions of good and evil. It takes everyone on the same emotional rollercoaster. No one is immune to loves highs or exempt from her lows. Love is the same great equalizer that death is. As I fall asleep in the arms of a demon who taught me that, I know it to be true.

CHAPTER Ten

TREASON, TORTURE, LOVE

MICHAEL

Another night with Lilly in my arms comes and goes, yet it still feels heavenly having her close. That fact is of growing concern to me. As a demon, I'm a being of darkness. For as blissful as her presence makes me feel, it also comes off ominously. A demon should never feel like something is heavenly. That's a sign. For the life of me, I can't seem to put my finger on the problem, though. Every time I turn around, more of that evil I saw lurking in the depths of her soul has become a little more prominent. She can't be a threat to me. I trust her. Those she's connected to from her past life, though, are still dangerous. Maybe it's not so much my Seshen as it is the lengths they'll go to bring her back to their side of the line.

With that in mind, my determination to see them ruined multiplies one-hundred-fold as Lilly and I make our way to meet with General Pythias, the one I'd mentioned to her previously that uses the venomous smog. He's one of my most loyal generals, so he'll remember his place if I leave her there to work with him on our plan to attack Loft while I go deal with another general. One that is in trouble if there is even an inkling of truth to him being behind that failed attack on her. I wait a few minutes to make sure she's as comfortable as I thought she'd be dealing with Pythias. He may be loyal, but asshat is his most friendly setting, and I need to know that she won't let him treat her like a doormat.

Once I see her in command of their exchange, I know it won't be an issue and sneak off without telling her. Knowing my Seshen, she'd want to be involved in this. As her fiancé, though, it is my preference to keep her away from people who may or may not have planned an attack against her. She can hold her own, but it's a matter of principal. My queen shouldn't have to deal with my subjects, *her* subjects, rising against her. They should be ready to die for her. Every one of them. That's my expectation as king of Tendu.

It's easy enough for me to find the general in question because I have all their schedules. Right now, he's in the meditation room on his break. He often spends his breaks here. His name is Nyft, a first rank general. He's always been on the shady side, but I haven't had issues with him before this. I want to give him a chance to prove his innocence, but without tipping off that I'm onto him, just in case he's not innocent. I'm going to give him an order, one that will make him see a window of opportunity to dispose of Lilly without alerting him to my suspicions. "General," I call out in my usual monotone voice. "Do you have a minute?"

"Of course, Your Majesty." His reply is immediate. He gets off the ground and stands, as he's supposed to in the presence of a royal.

I nod. "I need you to handle my bride's security. Some ruffian tried to attack her yesterday in the village. I've handled the man and believe he was acting alone, but it'd be safer if I had someone looking out for her, especially with the impending war. I know her loved ones wouldn't try to kill her, but I'm sure there are rogue factions within the alliance that don't hold the same level of loyalty to her that her family does."

"Yes, sire. It's an honor to be trusted with such an important task." There's no shock in his reply, nor is there any empathy. It's not enough to condemn him, but his lack of concern is enough to earn him more suspicion than I'd placed on him using only the attacker's word. If he is guilty, he must also feel confident that the son-of-a-bitch wouldn't have cracked during interrogation. I don't like it. Either way, hearing me broach the subject should have triggered some type of reaction. I'm cruel, but this sort of behavior is just antisocial. Have I had a psychopath under my command all this time and not realized?

I school my features, not letting him see an ounce of my growing suspicions. "Very well. I leave it to you, then, General Nyft."

We go our separate ways. After I'm sure he's no longer watching, I set the trap, having my best friend and most loyal advisor, Hilo, tail him and report his every move. I don't give Hilo much of an explanation, not wanting to skew his perspective. This way, whatever he reports comes from him noticing an issue rather than searching for one.

Once he's off to follow the orders, I return to check in on Lilly. She and Pythias have made impressive progress with merging their powers. We may launch this attack using our original timeline if they keep this up. I settle into a corner, observing them in silence so as not to distract either of them. They get along well enough. Perhaps he's the man I should truly charge with her security detail. Giving her a security team is bound to go over with less resistance from her if she likes the person in charge of it. Besides, he's competent and his loyalty is unquestionable. It's a solid choice to keep her safe when I'm not physically present to defend her myself.

THE FATE OF ANGELS AND DEMONS

For about another hour, I watch them without being noticed. In the end, I've reached a decision. After I sort things out with Nyft, I'll have Pythias take over her detail. In the meantime, I'll let them continue working on this together. Having that in mind, I clear my throat, alerting them to my presence as if I'd just entered the room. They both turn to look at me. Pythias bows, but Lilly's eyes just light up with excitement. "We can do it! We can merge our powers. You'll be able to move forward with the attack without worry."

I smile. "That's very good, Seshen. Thank you for working so hard to help me with this."

I wrap my arm around her waist and give her a kiss on the forehead. All too easily, she melts into my arms. I'd take her here and now, but then I'd have to kill Pythias and waste all her hard work because he'd have seen her naked. More than that, there are other things in need of our attention. Like the obnoxious roar coming from her stomach, for starters. My little Seshen must be starving to make such a sound. I should treat her to something special tonight, and I know just the thing.

I take her down to the kitchen and dismiss the servants. She giggles. "What are you doing? How are we going to get food if none of the servants are here?"

I look into those eyes of hers. They damn near steal my breath away. "I'm going to cook for you, Seshen. And you are going to sit there and talk to me while I do."

She arches an eyebrow. "You can cook?"

I chuckle. "Yes." I pause briefly. "One thing. I can cook one thing."

Her laughter fills the air. "Okay. Well, what would you like me to talk about while you do?"

"Anything," I reply, "Anything at all. Tell me something about you I don't already know."

Lilly

I watch idly as Michael scans the kitchen to gather ingredients and whatever cookware he needs to make the food. He wants me to tell him something about myself he doesn't already know, but nothing comes to my mind as I search it for something he'd want to know. The question mark lingering between us seems to choke the life from me as I stumble over myself trying to come up with something to say. It makes me feel vulnerable. Because of that, when I get around to saying something, it's something sensitive. "I'm not what other people make of me. From the exterior, I seem so strong and confident. Intimidating, even, according to many. That's not me, though. Not internally, at least. I often feel more insecure than I let on. If you only knew the absurd amounts of time I've spent pestering myself about my every flaw."

"Specifically?" He asks.

"What do you mean, specifically?"

He smirks. "I'd like you to point these flaws out to me. I seem to have missed them, as I was admiring the woman I see as perfection."

"Fine." I groan. "It's hard to explain. I think the word *see* is an important part of what you said there. I see myself as attractive too. Confidence about my appearance isn't an issue here. The type of insecurity I'm talking about goes deeper than that."

"Do you not see yourself as smart or strong enough?"

I shake my head. "Still deeper, believe it or not. It's the question of if a culmination of traits is all I amount to. Yes, I'm attractive, strong, and smart. Most people like looking at me and even talking to me. Yet, most people don't like me, if that makes sense."

He raises an eyebrow, looking back at me some as he stirs some ground beef in a saucepan. "No, I'm going to need you to break that one down more for me."

"It's like... Have you ever been hanging out with someone and they laugh, talk, and joke with you? They complement you; tell you how attractive you are. They engage, open up, tell you they like who you are. Even when you warn them that these things they like about you might not be as likable after a while, they assure you that's not going to happen. No matter what you've experienced with other people, they aren't like that. They insist they'll like you just as much in a year as they do now. You want to believe them, so you do. After all, they would know how they feel, right? No. They don't. That person doesn't even make it a full year before they're gone."

He pauses what he's doing and turns to look at me, seeming to realize that this is more important than he thought at first glimpse. "No, I haven't. That sounds... painful. I'm here to listen more if you want to tell me about it."

That's nice to hear. Some part of me wants to open up to him. After all, I'll never be able to trust him if I don't do it. It'd be hard to know he won't run unless I take the risk and give him the chance to show me he won't. "I appreciate that. As hard as it is to talk about, I think I should. It's important for you to understand."

The attention he places on me is intense. It would be enough to scare the Hel out of a normal person, but to me, it just feels like someone is finally ready to listen the way I need them to, the way no one ever has. It feels like a risk opening up like this, even to someone I have so much faith in. The problem is, if he lets me down... That is, if he abandons me, it'll hurt more than it ever has before. When it comes down to it, I always knew in my heart that those people would bail one day. I've gotten used to it. With Michael, though, it's not like that. No matter how hard I try to stop myself from expecting anything, I do. I expect him to stay, even after he realizes how damaged I am. He could do even worse damage if he doesn't.

I take a deep breath, calming myself as I prepare to speak. "It feels like I'm the woman men adore when we're behind closed doors, but don't want to be seen with. It feels like I'm a famed piece of art, renowned by all, who someone spent their whole life saving to visit in-person, all to experience something that fails them.

THE FATE OF ANGELS AND DEMONS

They push all that excitement and eagerness onto me, time and time again, then get surprised when I'm exactly who I told them I am."

I feel the sadness inside me ignite, turning to rage as I speak on. For once, someone is going to listen to my words. "It feels like being told I'm crazy after I told someone I'm crazy, only to go crazier because they make me feel crazy for it. It's loving who I am, yet hating the fact no one else can love me unless I mild myself to become more palatable, as if it's my fault they're too weak to handle the full weight of my brilliance. Hating myself for loving myself even after being taught repeatedly just how unlovable I am is the bane of my fucking existence. I don't understand how countless people love being with me; but cannot bring themselves to love me. You would think I could find just one. I cannot. One person who sees me for who I am and commits to loving me has become entirely too much to ask. I understand that none of this is your fault, and it's not your job to fix a mess you didn't make. Anyone would understand if you heard this and erased all traces of my existence from your life. I have to ask you not to, though. For you are the one person whose loss I don't believe myself capable of enduring."

"Shit." That singular word from him leaves my mind reeling. I can't tell if he's repulsed, stunned, or if it's about the smell in the air.

"Shit!" He screams again, rushing to douse the fire that started as the food burned. The moment had become so intense that neither of us realized it. Lucky for us, his magic is just as capable of snuffing out fire as it is setting it. It only takes an instant for him to stop it. That didn't save the food, though. He must have listened intently to have allowed that to happen.

I know how big of a transition it is to move right back into the topic after a fire, but I need him to say something. I freeze, though, unable to force the words to ask him to reply from my throat. All I can do is stare at him. He takes a few deep breaths before he notices the worry I'm sure is showing in my expression. Huffing a laugh, he wraps me up in his arms. "You're psychotic if you think their stupidity extends to me. I'll never let you go."

I relax into him, a half-hearted laugh escaping me. He's not running. His instinct when hearing how damaged I am is to pull me closer. For a man known to be so destructive, he's doing nothing but healing all the tiny cuts others inflicted on my soul. So many that I didn't think any corner of it was unscarred. One move from him, though, and all the many years of bleeding it out in the slowest, most agonizing way imaginable got wiped away.

We stay like that for a long time. Michael is sure to offer me all the reassurances I need. It feels so good to be loved in this way. He makes it more of an action. Love is something he does; not some word he uses to describe an abstract emotion. It's amazing, in its own way. Love has never been more than a concept to me. Now, meeting him, it's become so tangible that I can't see it as that distant idea that's an anomaly in reality.

After that day, we spend several more developing the collaboration plan between Pythias and me. Michael comes in and out during the practice sessions. I can't say what he's been working on behind my back because he won't tell me. For all my stubbornness, he's twice as much so. I don't mind as much as I pretend to, though. In the end, I know he'd never hurt me, so I have no reason to be concerned aside from my insatiable curiosity.

It's not until the day before our attack on Loft that his activities come to light. Hilo comes over and whispers something into his ear. Michael's expression contorts into one of rage upon hearing it. "Seshen, the captive wasn't lying. Come with me to get this bastard."

My eyes widen. All week he's been working to protect me, and I hadn't even realized it. I'd forgotten about the matter altogether and moved on. Goddesses, I'm so in love with this man. What a thing to do.

We head down to Nyft's private chambers. Michael burns the door open. Taken aback by our sudden entry, Nyft leaps back. It doesn't take long for him to realize we know the truth. I can see it as the puzzle pieces fall into place. He knows his life is over, but also that his death will be far more excruciating if he lets us detain him. Leaping forward, he reaches for my neck with a nasty sounding, animalistic hiss. Michael moves to kill him, even realizing what's happening, but I get my barrier up before he can, trapping Nyft and blocking Michael's magic at the same time.

Michael offers an amused smirk. "You're pretty good. Nice move, Seshen."

He's right. If I'd have failed, Michael still would have saved me by killing him, and I knew that. In the moment, it was a decision made to turn Nyft's immediate death into the backup plan. I risked nothing and gained the privilege of watching this asshole die the slow, painful death he deserves. There's a feeling of pride that swells up inside of me when Michael praises me for thinking so fast.

With Nyft detained in my barrier cage, we move him to the dungeons. We grant his hitman death without further suffering, as we promised to do if his information proved factual. As for Nyft, he'll suffer a long time before being granted execution. I look forward to his torturing becoming a sort of foreplay between Michael and me. We'll enjoy it. After all, all couples need a mutual hobby to encourage them to spend time together. We're getting rid of a terrible man and taking care of our relationship. I see nothing wrong with that. It's hot to think about. Already I feel drops of arousal between my thighs as I contemplate the excitement I'll experience when I make this man bleed for me. I want nothing more than to see Michael's cock straining against his clothing as he sees me act on the urges I've repressed for so long. It'll be amazing, but first, there is other business he and I must attend to. The night passes slowly as I continue to think about the excitement of our future ventures. Tomorrow, our attack on Loft will take place. We should save play time for after that success when it'll be even sweeter for us to enjoy.

***

With two battleships prepared, we depart from the docks of Tendu long before the sun reaches the horizon, moving through the cover of the night to avoid being detected as we sail southeast to Loft to bring my mother's duchy to its knees. Some part of me feels conflicted about doing this because she was such a wonderful mother. Even now, I consider myself lucky that she adopted me. I just wish that she would have allowed me the space to explore the parts of myself she didn't want to see. My moral lines have more flexibility than hers. I think that's a good thing. That's something I contemplate as we sail.

I make my way below deck where I can get some space from the others. As soon as I'm alone, the thoughts roll in like a storm, laying seize to my mind and tearing my composure apart. My mother is a brilliant woman with so many accomplishments. She built herself on challenging societies' expectations yet tried to stuff them down my throat. She clings to the very things she fought so hard to end. I grapple with it, trying to reconcile the person who made her who she is to the world with the person who spent years trying to suffocate me. It's like seeing someone say, "do as I say, not as

I do" in a moment where they don't have your best interests at heart.

My thoughts run wild as I try to sort out the emotions encroaching on the few parts of my mind that still cling to the light. I don't fight them. I don't want to because I am too damn tired to care. Why? Why does she hate me enough to do that to me? Does she resent the burden I placed on her by being a child in need when she was little more than a child herself?

I try to muffle the sobs that seep from me as the panic sets in, but it's of no use. My breaths become heavy and frantic as an invisible weight tantamount to a sack of bricks settles on me.

I don't understand why she thinks I should conform to her rules when she doesn't even try to conform to anyone else's. Do I not have the right? Because she did something that saved me from an abhorrent fate, I now owe her complete obedience for the rest of my existence? I got lifted out of my trauma, so I don't get to explore its long-term effects on me? Instead I'm forced to ignore the fact that it happened. Is that the message I'm supposed to get from her behavior? I expected the conflict I face to be much more taxing than it's proving to be. While I still have parts of me that don't want to do this to her, the parts that don't give a shit anymore are so much louder and make so much more sense than she ever has. In the end, the part of me that wants to be the one to ruin her for doing this to me is too rampant at the prospect to cause any true hesitance.

The panic gets replaced with something much more sinister as I allow myself to think the many thoughts I've held back for so long. Hatred and rage flood my being as an eerie calm settles my breathing. *Fuck my mother.*

That's my final thought before I turn it all off, detaching myself from the situation. I disassociate until the next time I'm needed, staring blankly at the wooden planks above me. I only snap out of it when I hear yelling on the upper deck. Orders. It's time.

With two separate tasks, Michael and I move to different ships. His ship will go straight for the attack. Mine will go for the waters between Pallentine and Loft to set up the blockade to prevent them from helping. On the ship with me is General Pythias, with whom I've become close over the past week developing this plan together. I'd call him a friend at this point. Out of the generals that answer to Michael, he's the one I trust most. Unlike Nyft, the others don't plot against me, but they don't want me here either. Pythias has made it beyond his initial apprehension and seems glad that I'm with them now. Hopefully, as the others get to know me, they'll be able to do the same.

Once in position, Pythias releases massive clouds of venomous smog. As it forms into a wall before the ship, dividing Loft and Pallentine, I release small bursts of spiritual power into it. It appears like pink glitter surrounded by the black smoke. As harmless as it may appear, those little pieces of glitter will cause an explosion of spiritual power if they touch a person or ship. Our prediction is that Pythias and I can maintain this wall for about an hour before they can gather the power needed to use air manipulation to push our own magic back at us. Since we're holding it in place instead of leaving it to be blown away, they'll have to first wear us out before they can blow it in our faces. It should buy Michael and the others enough time to destroy a duchy full of people who have no runes and no magic.

CHAPTER Eleven

HELSCAPE BE THE HOME OF MY MOTHER

MICHAEL

A flare from the men on the ship with Lilly and Pythias lets me know they have the wall up, preventing the Pallentinians from coming to assist Loft. I give the order for my attack on Queen Josella's duchy in Loft to begin, reiterating that they are only to attack inside of the duchy. If we take out the entire kingdom like we did in Nollent, my message won't come through as vividly as I'd like it to. I want it known that this is an attack on her, not the entire alliance. I'll come for the others later. Right now, my priority is Josella. She's the biggest threat to my plans, so I have to shake her up and loosen her grip on power.

Tearing through the duchy, my warriors light buildings aflame. Carnage ensues as citizens rush from their homes, many with children in their arms. We slaughter them all with equal brutality. It's not long before the bloodshed floods the streets. We take extra care to demolish the estate. Just like in Nollent, we want spots with sentimental value to Josella to be as if they never existed. I want the thought of what we will steal from her next to be all she can ponder when she lies in bed at night beside her co-kings. She needs to suffer, just like I suffered when she stole everything from me.

I relish in the smell of burning flesh and the sound of fear that rings throughout this place. The demonic energy within me surges, craving more. No amount of it will ever sate me. Shredding this duchy is thrilling, and all the more so knowing that Seshen is helping me do it. Glowing runes covering the bodies of those under my command shine through the smoke and ash of the destruction, allowing me to watch my dreams become reality. It's such a beautiful sight to bear witness to. Most people find this sort of cruelty repulsive, but for me, it's art worthy of the highest praise. I'll be rewarding those with me for creating such a masterpiece.

The chaos rages on for nearly an hour before I spot another signal from Lilly and Pythias. They must tire from holding back Pallentine. Unlike us, they're up against other rune users, so I imagine that it's harder to sustain for a long period. I need to get my people and leave before the wall comes down. No matter how much I'm enjoying this, I won't risk someone laying hands on my Seshen over it. Besides, the mission is a success. This duchy is destroyed.

"Men!" I call out, making sure they can hear me over the booming sounds of war. "Back to the ship! We're done here!"

One by one, they all pull back. I stay where I am until each of them has boarded. Then I turn to head back to the ship myself. A few steps in, I see a young boy, one not so unlike myself. There's a fire and rage in his eyes that I recognize. I could save him from those injuries if I took him to Seshen, but I know that look. If he lives, he'll come for me as I came for Josella one day. Yet, I can't bring myself to do it. His chest heaves in pain, but the look never leaves his eyes. He's strong, not to be un-underestimated. I stare down at him. "Are you suffering? Do you want me to end it?"

In a small, shaky voice he replies as he forces himself to rise to his feet regardless of the immense pain I'm sure he's in. "Yeah, I'm suffering, but not nearly enough to let myself die by the likes of you."

I tilt my head, intrigued by his willpower. This child would attempt to fight me, powerless in this condition? Normally, I'd call that stupid, but not with this kid. He knows he'll lose. It's hatred fueling him, not a lack of understanding regarding his predicament. I like him. I smirk. "Settle down, kid. You're not dying today."

I lift him up and throw him over my shoulder. I'll bring him to Lilly.

Lilly

Once I see the signal letting me know Michael and the attack force are clear, I queue Pythias to help me set up our escape. We take a few moments to ensure the wall of smog and spiritual energy will hold long enough for our ship to get away. I doubt Pallentine will give chase, but it's better to make sure they have to wait if they decide to. Though their priority is probably getting to Loft and helping quell the chaos. I'm sure Michael left more than a little behind.

After we secure the wall, I give the command to get us away from there. The crewmen turn the ship, and, at full speed, we sail to catch up to Michael's ship. If they catch up, it's safer to have our forces grouped so we can take our stand together.

Pythias and I use our combined power to further propel our ship. By the time we catch up to Michael, it seems Pallentine has broken through our wall, under the Chief's command no doubt. As I expected, he steers his people toward Loft, more eager to help them than stop our escape. Kind hearts are so predictable.

After we clear any potential dangers and make it back to Tendu's waters, Michael signals for me to come over to his ship. I levitate over right away. He stands before the dying body of a young boy. "Can you save him?"

I nod. "Maybe. Let me look."

It occurs to me to ask why he wants this one boy saved, but I see no purpose in asking that because he'd probably not survive long enough for us to have the discussion. Given his condition, I need to save him first and ask questions later.

Moments later, I've assessed the boy's injuries and determined the best course of treatment. We call it angel stitching, but anyone with light energy, such as an angel or priest, could do it if they had someone to teach them. I've only use it a few times. Dad Jameson is much better at it, which makes sense because it's a technique he created when Mom's life was in danger. So far as I can tell, though, Dad Jameson has only taught Mom, Callian, and me. His mistake, I guess. If he had taught others, Oceanica would have a much greater chance against us. Since he hasn't, I don't expect many to benefit from it aside from this child, because I certainly won't be saving a soul on their side.

I take my time stitching the child up, starting with the most severe wounds. Michael commands the crew to keep the ship as still as possible while I work. When I'm done, I look up at him. "I think he'll live. Still no promises, though. He needs fresh water in his system and plenty of rest. Avoid adding anymore stress than he's already experienced."

Michael nods, still not offering any additional information about why this child is worth saving in his mind. I'm tempted to ask, but he seems preoccupied with his own thoughts. It feels like a question for when he's in a better state of mind. Instead of prying, I encourage him to sit down. When he does, I sit at his side, resting my head on his shoulder. He remains silent. His only response is to tilt his head, resting it atop mine.

We return to Tendu, safely, then plan a party to celebrate our victory in Loft. Our men should enjoy themselves before the war is in full swing. One will come when my mother finds out what we just did. Her love for me is no matter; she's a leader. She'd kill anyone she thought was too deep in the darkness to be saved. All those years ago, she even took the life of the only biological family member she'd ever felt a connection to. She believed Rath's soul to be tainted, no longer a suitable peacemaker. Mom was mistaken to believe mine was ever pure enough for that vital role.

Callian

At about nine in the morning, the Chief once again arrives at our home, asking my parents and me for an audience. There was a sense of urgency in his request that prompted us to gather quickly. We opted to meet in the war room for security, but also because the nature of his plea gave the impression that we'd need to plan a response to whatever event has occurred. Mom is the first to ask. "Chief, tell us why you've come?"

Discouraged, he looks down. It pains him to share this news. "It's Lilly. The situation is worse than we thought."

A growl comes from Dad Kai's throat. "What happened?"

He's pissed, and he doesn't even know yet. I'm not looking forward to seeing his reaction when he does. It seems the Chief isn't either. He hesitates before answering. "Tendu..." He stops and shakes his head. "Michael launched an attack on Loft this morning, before dawn. More specifically, on the Spade Duchy lands. We spotted the chaos from across the water and rushed to help. On our way, we met Lilly. She was on a second ship with the general known as Pythias. In conjunction, they worked to prevent us from aiding Loft. Their actions forced us to wait. By the time we could get through, she, Michael, and those helping them had fled. Upon our arrival in Loft, we found no survivors left inside the duchy."

Mom's eyes widen. I can't imagine what she must be feeling. Her childhood home, the neighbors and families she grew up with, all gone. "No," she whispers.

The Chief nods, reaffirming his statement. Sensing Mom's fury, Dad Jameson wraps an arm around her waist to keep her from running off and killing... well, possibly all of Tendu, given the look on her face.

I can't help but think about the promise Lilly asked me to make. She must have known she was vulnerable to giving into Michael before she even left. I have to keep my word to her. Finally, I get myself together. "We're losing ground and fast, Mom. Nollent has fallen entirely, and Loft is defenseless without what few rune users lived in the Duchy. The alliance is crumbling."

"I can see that, Callian," she says tightly.

Before I can reply, the war advisor busts into the room panicking. I can't imagine what could be wrong now. Things can't get much worse.

"Tendu took advantage of the Chief's absence. Pallentine is theirs!" He blurts out.

Or they can, in fact, get much worse. This is insane. In mere days, most of the island alliance has fallen, only Oceanica remains. This is unfolding too damn fast. We're in real trouble here.

Mom groans. "Fuck."

Lilly

Okay, so it wasn't exactly a normal party. We celebrated our victory by claiming yet another. What can I say? The warriors are all fired up now. We're on a winning streak and there's no point in slowing down. Michael and I didn't even go back home after that. We went to Mallishrine, my original home. The one where my biological parents tortured me, abused me, and abandoned me to be taken advantage of by cruel men.

Having heard of our recent feats, Mallishrine knows better than to fight us. Instead, they welcome us onto their island. The head priest meets us at the docks, bowing his head as we off board the ship. "King Michael, Lady Lilliana, welcome to Mallishrine."

Michael glares. His suspicion is obvious. "What is this about?"

The priest explains himself. "We have heard of your recent accomplishments and are in awe of your pursuit of justice, sire."

From the look on my lover's face, he thinks the priest is a coward. He waits, letting him finish, though. So, the priest continues. "In reverence, we prepared an offering. One that we hope will prove our loyalty to your cause."

"What is your offering?" Michael inquires.

"The priest and priestess responsible for the suffering of Lady Lilliana."

My parents? They're offering my parents and an opportunity to take my revenge on them. Michael looks at me, trying to judge my feelings on the matter. I wish I knew how to answer his silent question. I don't know how to feel, though. Getting that sense, he decides. "We will accept your offering, so long as your loyalty remains true. You are now in alliance with us and us alone. That way, when she's ready, Lilly can decide their fates."

I'm grateful for his initiative. Not having to decide now is best. It's nice to have a guy that would rearrange his own plans to give me time to make my own. This isn't such a poor offer, anyway. It leaves Mom and Dads standing alone in Oceanica. Rallem isn't strong enough to help them, and I doubt Alacrium will bother.

After considering it, I speak up. "Take me to them."

The priest acknowledges my command and leads me to the cell my parents are being held in. Upon looking at them, I have my answer. Even now, they both have dead eyes. Soulless. I walk over, never taking my eyes off theirs. With not a single word, I take a blade of spiritual energy and, in one swoop, slice off both their heads. As their bodies go limp, I take solace in knowing I've finally taken from them just as much as they stole from me.

Michael, standing behind me, runs a hand down my back. The simple action reassures me it was okay for me to want them dead. It's reasonable. After what they did to me, they owed me their lives. Anyone capable of doing such horrific things to a child of their own blood doesn't deserve to live.

He gives me a few moments to look at their bodies in silence. It's necessary. They were giants in my mind; obstacles I could never overcome. Yet, here they lay, defeated. In the end, it's I who won, I who stands. Unable to deny the relief I feel, I cry. True peace would have always escaped me so long as they walked this plane. Many would say that's dramatic, but I say they have never known what it is to scan every face in every crowd for the ones who hurt you. The feeling of knowing the people responsible for your trauma are alive and well, capable of hurting you again is horrible. Sometimes, I think the world overlooks the depth of that sort of pain and fear.

Michael scoops me into his arms, bridal style, then turns to the priest. "You don't mind us staying a night?"

The priest shakes his head. "I'll have a room prepared right away."

His kindness is out of fear. We aren't stupid enough to forget that. His usefulness, however, allows us to overlook it. So long as he doesn't betray us, there's no point in betraying him. I'm sure Michael agrees.

We get settled into the room the priest prepares for us. The space is small, all quarters in Mallishrine are. They are of the belief that comfort weakens priests and priestesses. That's not true, as one can see by the strength of my mother and myself. I don't have the energy to care at the moment, though. Given my exhaustion after the events of the day, I don't feel like traveling back to Tendu. Michael and I will be fine here overnight. We curl up on the bed together and try to get some rest. Even in uncomfortable surroundings, his presence is enough to set me at ease.

Callian

Queen Alexandria,

Many years ago, you offered my mother, Queen Josella, your aid to call upon if it should ever become necessary. I'm writing this letter with the hope you would offer her heir the same. By now, I'm sure you've heard rumor of the events unfolding on the islands. We are in need.

To clarify what exactly it is I'm asking of you, there are several things. First, our enemy surrounds us on three sides. I've growing concerns about that. No matter what Oceanica's strength, we haven't enough to fight four kingdoms overflowing with rune users alone. We need backup. We need someone we can count on. Rallem simply doesn't cut it. We need the full weight of Alacrium's support. From our economy to our military, we need it all.

I know what a big ask that is, but if you'll recall, we are in this situation because your father insisted on taking Malachi. Not that I'm placing blame here, I know there's so much more to the story. I'm just saying that Alacrium helped us into this hole and should help us out of it, too.

That leads me to my second big ask: is there any chance Myrkr might let us borrow Malachi? I think a visit would go a long way toward resolving this while also minimizing bloodshed. Just see what you can do for me. From the stories I've heard, your father isn't completely without reason. Surely you can persuade him to give Malachi some leeway, given the extreme nature of the situation.

Please, reach out to me and let me know what can be done.

Respectfully,

Prince Callian of Oceanica.

After writing the letter, I give it to a messenger, instructing him to take it to Alacrium via the most direct route. I ensure he can leave from the northeast part of the island to avoid being spotted by anyone now under Michael's control. I can't be sure that Alexandria will lift a finger to help us out of this. How could I? I've never met the woman, but I know our odds are much better with her than they are without her.

The messenger takes his leave, and I return to planning. Mom has placed a lot of trust in me by believing that I can get my sister back. I think she and my dads are stepping back some so I can build my reputation as a leader since I'm to rule Oceanica one day. What better way to grow into my role than by proving I can manage a war against Lilly and Michael?

I spend my time working out several strategies. The first, and most ideal, is if we have sufficient aid from Alacrium. The second, which is not ideal, but not horrific either, is the plan we'll use if Alacrium gives us something, but not enough. Finally, there's a worst-case scenario that'll almost certainly fail. It's an adequate and realistic approach as a last-ditch effort, though.

By the time I finish developing each of them, the whole day has escaped me. I decide to take a break between that task and my next by going for a late-night walk. A realm walk, to be more specific. I guess I take after my mother in that way; though, I'm like Dad Jameson in most others. Taking a deep breath, I lower myself into the void between realms. Nothingness surrounds me, its arms envelop me like a long-lost lover. I embrace the contradictory presence, indulging myself in the nothingness that feels like everything. With a single stride, I propel myself forward to explore the divide.

It's both the darkest and the lightest place in existence. Pitch black and pure white at the same time. As such, there is every color, and no color. This divide is beyond the comprehension of almost any living being. Most would go insane within its boundless confines. It isn't healthy to spend so much time in a place beyond time. I'm an exception, not the rule. Higher-level priests and priestesses can maintain a presence here easily, like Mom. Of course, I'm more than just a high-level priest. I'm also a part angel. So, I could survive in any realm or divide.

My mind goes numb as I walk, the silence consuming me as the instinctual need to join the nothingness, blend into it, become it, brings me peace. Soon enough, weightlessness follows, and I no longer need to give myself the periodic propulsion I did when I was starting out. Lost is what I become in the void.

I've often heard the term "lost" used in a negative light. Over time, I've found I disagree with that perspective. To someone who has had their identity handed to them on a silver platter and stuffed down their throat by golden forks, being lost is a luxury full of possibilities rather than certainties. If you ask me, being lost is the opposite of being trapped. I think my sister would agree. Otherwise, she'd be home instead of in Tendu at the side of a man she, herself, foresaw fighting me to the death. Back then, I doubt she could have fathomed such a fight would take place *over her*. Now, though, I think we all know the reason either Michael or I will die is our love for her. In the end, she'll have to choose between his life and mine.

When I return to the Living Realm, I'm met with the realization that I'm too tired to get anything more done tonight. At least, not if I want the work to be useful in the events that will unfold soon enough, which I do. Given that, I lie down to get some rest. Sleep doesn't come with as much ease as my body would prefer, but my mind insisted on exhausting every drop of energy it could squeeze from my weary vestige.

When I find it's at last willing to rest, I let the sleep overcome me without resistance. Even in that rest, though, peace of mind escapes me. I spend the night tortured by dreams of the many potential outcomes. All of which made one thing clear: I cannot afford to lose.

CHAPTER

Twelve

PLEAS AND BARGAINS

ALEXANDRIA

Julius, my butler, and the man I trust most in this world, stands before me as I read the letter from Oceanica. After I finish, I look at him, pout, and slouch down into my throne. "I guess I should probably do something about this?"

He tries to school his grin. The effort was a failure; I saw it. "I think so, milady. It would not be good for Alacrium if the alliance between the island kingdoms failed."

I huff. "Yes, I know that. You recommending something for me to do would be infinitely more helpful than you telling me that."

No sane person would want Oceanica as an enemy. I think Malachi's heir is crazy for even going down this road. Long ago, I witnessed for myself how powerful Josella and Jameson are, and from the rumors, the other king is no weaker. Odds are that their offspring is even more terrifying. I'd give Callian my right arm if it'd convince him I'm not his enemy. It's not even that I think Alacrium would lose to Oceanica. It'd be more accurate to say that it's mutually assured destruction. To be frank, that's no more appealing than losing would be.

He shrugs. "There is one option. You won't like it, though."

My eyes roll back into my head. "My father. Of course it's my father."

I rise from the throne and force my body to move, dreading the amount of begging I'll have to do. Julius follows me without being asked. We've worked side-by-side for so long that by now, he's well aware that I dislike doing anything without him at my side. All my other advisors, my half-sister included, have ambitions of their own. Julius's only ambition is to strengthen me and my rule. Thus, my trust in his council is substantial. A queen must always have at least one person who wishes for nothing more than to serve her. Many would find that not doing so is a mistake most female monarchs don't survive. After all, how many mistakes get avoided by having that one person whose council never holds ulterior motives?

He and I make our way up to the palace's tower. It's the easiest spot to access the alternate realm my in which my father and Malachi reside. Most people call it Hel; it's not what they imagine, though. I call it home. Alacrium is our home in the Living Realm, but Hel is our true home. It's the difference between a villa and a primary estate to us. While we can't realm jump like someone with a derivative of light power, we can still travel across realms with the same level of ease. Our methods are unorthodox, but just as effective. We just overwhelm the divide with enough magic to create a fissure, which we pass through, and then close from the other side. Since we possess ample magic, it doesn't take much of a toll on us.

Julius holds his hand out, searching for the thin spot between Hel and the Living Realm, where we've been breaking through for eons. It's the easiest spot to use. Once he finds it, he pushes out a compact burst of magic with enough force to create a fissure. Then he steps back, allowing me to pass through it first. Julius follows not even a moment later, then waves his hand, mending the fissure. We arrive at the tower of Hel's palace, where my father lives. I take a deep breath, inhaling the warm, still air of my home and exhaling the stress of my rule. Looking out over the edge of the tower, I observe Hel. It's just as I recall.

THE FATE OF ANGELS AND DEMONS

From this point, I can see the bustling city below where demons buzz around in their natural form without fear of rejection—or straight up malice—from humans. Some walk, others fly, lesser demons crawl. Most of us keep them as pets. They're fluffy and have a sweet demeanor. They also struggle to survive without us because their magic drains faster than their bodies can replenish it. When bonded to a high demon, though, they can sustain themselves by feeding off our magic energy. We once viewed them as pests because of it, but my mother put a stop to that. Her fierceness, though notable, was often overshadowed by her kind heart.

I continue looking over this land, reminiscing on all the memories I have of my time here as a girl. I gasp when I spot a food cart that sells galinma, a common festival food here in Hel. If I'm not mistaken, that's the exact one I begged and pleaded with my father to visit almost every day. It's the best galinma in all the land. Sidetracked, I allow my wings to sprout. One of the many reasons I prefer dresses with an open back is that I can let them loose whenever I want. I swoop down toward the cart with Julius following only a heartbeat behind.

"My Queen!" He calls out. "We're here on kingdom business."

I giggle. "And Your Queen has decided on a detour from that business. You wouldn't want me managing our kingdom on an empty stomach, now would you?"

His laughter is so free. It's always like this with us. In Alacrium, we're queen and butler. In Hel, though, we can't help but revert to being just two inseparable best friends. I love it. Stuffy, proper Julius never quite appealed to me the same way as the wild man who used to steal bottles of millennia-aged wine to drink with me while we wrestled around in Lake Hedonic. We land in front of the cart and the person manning it recognizes me. "Princess Alexandria! What a surprise. It's been some time since you visited last. I see Sir Julius is still at your side, as always."

I'm taken aback when he addresses me as a princess. It's easy to forget that I'm not actually a queen here. I rule Alacrium, the capital of demonkind in the mortal realm. My father prefers to keep his title as king in Hel. Some part of me knows he will never forfeit it, at least not while he lives. After I relax, I hug the shopkeeper and order my galinma. Julius gets one, too. We walk back to the palace so as not to spill the creamy, sweet liquid in the center of the cakey outside, or drop the crunchy chocolate topping.

We don't rush back to the palace to meet my father. Together, Julius and I frolic our way through Hel, leisurely making our way toward it. When we arrive, my father is standing before us as we enter. The audible breath that escapes him causes me to tense a little. "You just show up and wander off without even saying hello to me?"

I relax and smile a little. "Come now, dad, you know Mr. Miles gets first dibs on me."

My father chuckles. "Oh, of course. How could your father ever compete with the guy who makes your galinma?"

Julius returns his lighthearted laughter. "My apologies, King Myrkr, I should have reigned her in."

My father shrugs. "You're welcome to try. I'm not sure my beloved daughter is going to take well to being reined in by any man, though."

Julius smiles. "You make a fair point. I'll pass. Prefer to keep my head."

I giggle. The two of them are too much. They speak as if I'm the most unruly woman ever. I'm up there, but I'm far from the worst. "Anyway, father. We come to ask your permission for a... sensitive matter."

His face goes blank for a second. "I see. Come with me then."

He guides us back to his private meeting room as not to be overheard. Given the heightened abilities of demons, extra precautions are necessary if one wishes for confidentiality. This room, for example, is surrounded by charms and wards. My father, having been an angel once, can use some weaker forms of light magic when pressed. Sound-blocking is among those weak forms. Luckily, the spells hold up well and he hasn't had to replace them since becoming the first demon. The lingering light magic in his blood would fade quickly if used regularly.

Of course, what he considers being a menial amount of light magic still lingering inside of him may not be as little as he thinks it is. His benchmark for comparison is the full power of him as an angel. I'd be willing to bet that his "little" is about the same as an average angel's. Plus, since he descended, he has the oldest Helfire known to demonkind and extensive mastery of all demonic abilities.

"Well, out with it." Dad says, taking his seat.

"It's the islands. Things are bad. Malachi's wife has died. The poison she felt from losing him, however, has not. That resentment has twisted her son. He's now at war with the entire alliance. To make matters worse, Lilliana is siding with him. She seems to have caught feelings for Michael and descended in order to be with him."

His eyes widen at the severity of the situation. "Queen Josella reached out to you for help?"

I shake my head. "No, her son did. His name is Callian."

"And you want my blessing to send the help he requested?"

I sigh. "No, Dad. I'm the Queen of Alacrium; I've made that decision myself. They will have military and financial support from me. My purpose in coming to you is because there is another thing we can send. One only you can permit."

"Malachi." His tone is contemplative.

"Yes, dad. They need Malachi."

He sits back. It doesn't take much to see he's not fond of the idea. Still, there's hope in the fact he didn't just say no and send us back to the Living Realm empty-handed. "How time sensitive is this? Do I have time to mull it over?"

I nod. "Yes, I think you do."

"Fine. I'll do that. In the meantime, traps shut. I do not want him hearing about this prior to me deciding. Otherwise, we risk him going without permission and that would be a breech in contract."

The unspoken context is that the binding ritual they took part in would kill Malachi the moment he acted against his word. As much as I hate it, my father has a point here. Telling Malachi would be unwise. My cousin and I may not be close, but I don't want him dead. It seems wrong, but there's no point in him knowing unless he can go without killing himself. So, I agree with the terms. "I won't, but Dad?"

He looks at me. "What is it, sweetheart?"

"Try not to take too long."

He nods, then stands to give me a hug. We embrace for a few long moments before separating. At which point, I turn to Julius. "With me. We should go home and prepare our offer of aid while my father thinks this over."

Julius follows me back to the transport point. Once we step through the fissure that returns us to the Living Realm, his façade of the obedient butler locks back into place. I try to ignore the frustration I feel because of it. It's so annoying. I never asked him to do this. It was he who decided that, in Alacrium, he needs to be formal and subservient to me. It takes so much for me to let it go, but the simple truth is he thinks he's less than me because I'm a queen. It makes me want to set his hair on fire.

Still, I've no time to concern myself with our drama. Why would I when I could focus on the drama of a kingdom several thousand miles away from me?

Callian

"Mom, you gave me permission to handle this myself, so stop butting in and let me do it!"

She scoffs as I follow her through the halls. "I gave you permission to look into suspicions regarding your sister, Callian, not to command the largest military force on the planet."

I roll my eyes. "How do you think one stops a war, Mom? That's what saving Lilly means. I have to stop this war. Stop treating me like a child. Look at me."

She continues walking, refusing to make eye contact. I love my mother to the moon and back, but if she's not the most obstinate, infuriating person I've ever met. "Mother! Look at me."

Still, she persists on her path. Fed up, I leap in front of her, blocking her path forward. At last, she makes eye contact with me. "I'm not a kid anymore, Mom. Don't you see, I'm a man. One that you and my dads have trained well. I can do this."

Wistfully she says, "I know you aren't my little boy anymore. You're right. I need to let you take command. It's better you get authentic experience leading an army while your fathers and I are still here to fall back on. Go, you have my blessing."

I smile, lifting her up into a hug and spinning her. "I won't let you down, Momma."

Her laughter reverberates through the air. "Callian, put me down!"

"Fine, Mom. Well, I'll get to work. Update you at dinner?"

She nods, and I run off with a smile on my face. It's nice to know that even in the heat of all this chaos, we can still maintain some level of normalcy within our family.

Josie

My children are not children anymore. That is the thought that stays with me as I watch Callian go. My little girl, Lilly, is all grown up. Falling in love, finding her own path, and making her own decisions. Decisions that I'm now powerless to stop. That's not the worst part, though. Any mother of an adult daughter will tell you the same: The hardest part of seeing her carving out space for herself in the world is when you realize she's talking to you less because she feels like you're the thing preventing her from living as her truest self. I seem to have fallen into the same trap as generations prior, clinging to outdated beliefs, even when they jeopardize my relationship with my daughter.

With Callian, though, it's different. Worse, in a way. He's not even pushing against me. He's just making a name for himself, the same way Jameson carved out his legacy at that age. I should be proud. I'm not, though. Terrified is the description I'd use for what I'm feeling about him. I've seen what it is for a young royal to step out from the protection their parents' shadow provides to them and make their legacy their own. It establishes them as a ruler all their own and lets the people know that the line of succession is strong by assuaging the fear that they'll be exchanging experienced rulers for a boy king. It's a dangerous step, even if it is necessary. One wrong move and he may never recover from it. Death comes far easier than power. Confidence evaporates much easier than it builds. The difference between a prince and a king is nothing more than a beating heart. Between a student and a ruler, though, it's a leap much larger than any realm jump I've ever seen.

I miss the time when they were young. I miss being able to shield them from the harshness of this world. My babies... There's nothing more I can do for them now aside from trusting that I raised them well and that they'll find their way. It's a powerless feeling, but one I will have learn to live with.

I go to my bedchamber where my two husbands wait. Falling face first onto the bed, I groan in what is, perhaps, the most unseemly way a queen could. However, I feel the need to be dramatic at the moment, and we have a relationship rule that allows for such episodes in private, ensuring we each have a safe space to vent. Kai chuckles. "Aww, what's wrong, my love?"

Jameson smirks. "Is our goddess having a rough day?"

I mutter. "Freakin' babies aren't babies. Stupid aging."

"Well, dear, I imagine you knew they were going to grow into adults. You have a pretty thorough understanding of the human life cycle." Kai's sarcastic reply causes a smile to form. I have to keep my head buried in the pillows, so he doesn't see it. Otherwise, I'd have to stop being grumpy.

Jameson, also amused by my tantrum, puts an arm around me. "Oh, my goddess. I hope my wife, the priestess, war hero, queen, and protector of realms survives the maturing process of our children."

I huff. "Jerks."

The room gets quiet, but in a good way. The two of them snuggle up on either side of me. Now that they got their need to pick on me out of their systems, they're moving on to comforting me. I embrace that, knowing it's what I need right now. While I appreciate them making me laugh some, it's still nice to just be in their arms receiving reassurance.

Callian

A few days pass and now that I have Mom's permission to command our forces, the pieces are falling into place. This morning, I received a letter from Alexandria, Queen of Alacrium. The offer of aid is extensive. I'll meet with her butler, Julius, in three days to coordinate our efforts with their aid. Until then, I'll keep doing what I'm doing.

Behind the formal offer of aid, I find a note. It simply reads, "*I'm trying. Right now, it's a maybe.*"

She's talking about Malachi. She's trying to get Myrkr to let him come. It's not a guarantee, but it's hope, which has been in short supply lately. If Malachi returns, it'll change everything. Michael would certainly be more amenable to peace if the father he lost came back. Lilly would have to feel something. I've heard her speak of Malachi so many times over the years. I never met him, but I know how much she loved him. His name is so honored in my country and by my parents that I believe him to be a great equalizer. There's no doubt that his presence would be a development everyone would have to yield to.

I spend the next few days preparing for my trip to meet Julius. Not that I think preparations are necessary; it's not likely to be a trap or attack. I trust their word. It's just if a crowned prince of Oceanica shows up to something like this without guards and some grotesque display of power and wealth, it looks bad. I'd hate to impugn the reputation I'm trying to build before I get the chance to establish it.

With that in mind, I select a few military members I'm already acquainted with to attend alongside, sure to choose ones that can keep up with my speed so as not to derail my arrival timeline. Next, I select suitable clothing for a meeting with a foreign dignitary. Of course, I consult the stylist my mother uses. I don't want to seem like

I'm trying too hard by overdressing, but I'd also like to be dressed appropriately for someone of my status.

With the stylist's help, I chose a blue himation that resembles the color of my eyes. It's called angelic blue because it only occurs naturally in angelic bloodlines. It took centuries of color experimentation to even get dyes close to it. Luckily, about five hundred years ago, someone—in the court of whatever ancestor ruled at the time—figured it out. So, it became the royal family's official color. Its design is intricate as well. A flowy pattern of waves that feels humble and distinguished at the same time. With the himation, I select a chiton and some sandals.

Once I've selected my clothing, I move forward with reviewing the actual proposal and identifying how best to coordinate what Alacrium is offering. My priority is identifying a route where they can safely transport supplies and fighters to us. We need a new one that Lilly wouldn't already know about. As things stand, she's already cut us off from the other islands. We need to prevent her from cutting us off from Alacrium as well. By examining our current supply maps, I should be able to find a route that avoids anything she'd have Michael monitoring.

It takes a few hours, but I find something that works for our purposes. It's simple, but it's not something she'd be expecting. With that, I move on to other ideas for the coordination effort. I come up with some good ones to present to Julius. I assume that if Queen Alexandria is sending him, she's given him authority to agree to anything he thinks is viable on her behalf. Here, a butler is nothing more than a butler, but to her, Julius's position seems to be a position of government just as much as it is one of servitude. In fact, I know that he's her most trusted because she didn't even mention consulting any other advisor. Maybe they're lovers? It's hard to say.

A MATCH MADE IN JUBILEE

CALLIAN

The few hours of travel by flight don't take a toll on me. I find it so strange to hear that when my parents took this journey before my birth they considered it arduous. It makes some sense because they had to walk since their guide was mortal. I'm not fully human, so I don't know what it is to have a body incapable of flight. I learned how to fly before I learned how to walk. To me, it's the most natural form of movement.

My father can't say the same. He started flying much later in life than I did. That may be why he insisted on teaching me so early on, not wanting to deprive me of the experience of my angelic heritage becoming an integrated part of my upbringing.

I appreciate him doing that. I've never felt as though I had to choose one half of myself over the other, which I know many mixed-lineage people do. Since we are so few, I do sometimes feel like being mixed lineage makes me a reject from both sides, but at least I can say I'm my full self. None of my parents can protect me from what others think. They did, however, give me the gift of knowing others' rejection doesn't have to split me in two, and that's enough for me.

I arrive in Jubilee, a small town belonging to no kingdom, located an equal distance between Oceanica and Alacrium. It's surreal; I feel like I'm walking in the footsteps of the history my parents made. This town is one they passed through as they journeyed across the continent to resurrect Dad Kai. It was where Mom bonded with her Uncle Rath for the first time, only to later find that he used the same stop to organize his betrayal. Being in Jubilee is bittersweet. I welcome the opportunity to make history like they did all those years ago, but I also hate knowing how much they suffered as they did it. It sparks a mild fear that I may also have to suffer to make my mark. I call it mild because I don't think it has to be that way, although history doesn't seem to agree with me.

THE FATE OF ANGELS AND DEMONS

Heading to coordinate with Julius at the exact inn where Rath coordinated with Nubella to betray my parents when they travelled across the continent to bring Dad Kai back, I have the lingering hope that what we accomplish today will lessen history's pain. When I arrive, he's already seated at a table on the inn's lower level. I look around, trying to decipher the situation and how freely we can speak.

Julius shakes his head. "It's alright. I bought out the whole inn for the day. No one else is here."

I nod and take a seat. "Very well."

I don't know how to begin this conversation. It's awkward. I've never had to lead in negotiations for anything like this before. Julius shifts in his chair and I get the impression he's picking up on my lack of experience.

"Relax, Prince Callian. I am a friend here to offer assistance. My queen wants to help your kingdom. I have no plans to use this deal to harm you. We just need to know the best way to get the aid we offered to you. That's all this is. Depoliticize it in your mind. Talk to me like you would a friend. If you asked me for something, and I agreed to send it, you'd tell me where and how to send it, right?"

His point is valid. They are trying to help us. That makes sense. I should stop focusing on being perceived as a king and focus more on doing what I came here to do. I take a deep breath to calm myself before I speak. "I think the best transport route is also the most direct. Traditionally, all transports to Oceanica have routed through Loft and the network of the islands. However, the most direct route between Alacrium, a mountain kingdom on the mainland, and Oceanica, the island on which our kingdom exists, is through the northeast of Oceanica. It's the only route that avoids passing any other kingdom."

Julius nods, thinking for a moment. "And I suppose it's also safer because it'd be difficult for Tendu to get anywhere near that route without either of our kingdoms noticing. You may be onto something, Prince Callian."

I can't help the soft huff of relief that escapes me when I realize he doesn't think I'm a total moron. "Yes. Further, since my kingdom's specialty is water, it boosts efficiency because we can help transport ships from the mainland to our island faster."

"Saving both us and our men one Hel of a lot of extra travel time." He adds, confirming that we're on the same page.

I did it. I found the best route. Excitement courses through me at my first independent success as a leader. This is important, and I did it on my own. That matters to me. It gives me hope I can be a wise leader who makes intelligent decisions even under immense pressure. That's the sort of king my people deserve. There's a sense of honor in knowing I might fill those shoes with dignity, integrity, and effectiveness once my parents are gone. I continue on this path, hoping to see that Julius finds more of my ideas worthwhile. "Great! Then, we'll use that route. Now, as for command of the warriors you're sending, I think it's best they answer to someone they trust. Someone who has fought alongside them before? I understand that it'd be difficult for experienced soldiers to answer to some random prince with minimal experience, so I won't ask that. Instead, I ask that whoever you put in charge of those men be willing to act as my partner in commanding the army."

Julius smiles. "Wise choice. We had a similar idea. I can't tell you who my queen will choose to send, but I assure you they'll have adequate trust from the men and be open-minded enough to work with you. Whoever it is, I'll also let them know I've spoken with you and believe you to be competent. It'll go smoother if they know one of our own has already assessed you."

I'm glad to see we agree on that too. As we talk, we continue to find common ground. By the end of our three-hour discussion, we've hammered out all the details and I feel more confident than ever before. Julius and I part ways on a pleasant note. I'd even say a friendship may bud between him and I. He seems like a trustworthy man and one I wouldn't mind having in my circle. I hope one day that will be the case.

Triumphant, I return home to Oceanica and I can't wait to tell Mom how well I've done so far. Now that I've done this, I'll arrange a time to meet with our military. I want to bond and train with them to get them accustomed to the idea of following my lead. It's important to our war plans against Tendu that they trust me.

Mostly because I'm going to need them to take a risk. The one element we're most short on is the one we'll have to fight for. Time. Our years of planning for this prophecy to unfold all went down the drain when my sister caught feelings for a lunatic. While we once had formidable plans with years to prepare, we now have the scraps I've been able to throw together. If we have any shot at winning, we need the troops to sustain a siege while I get the pieces in place. Otherwise, we'll deplete what resources we have before the aid from the Alacrians ever reaches us.

Lilly

Having given Mallishrine the order to stand by and wait for us to make a move, Michael and I returned home to Tendu. We've accomplished a lot and now, we really intend to rest awhile before taking on Oceanica. It doesn't quite matter what they do. We've won. Every other island has fallen. They are simply waiting to do the same. No one can oppose us united. Soon, my parents will be dead, as will my brother. When that's done, the war will be over. Once it is, I can just focus on being happy with Michael.

There's so much I look forward to in that future. Planning our wedding, a ton of sex, perhaps even a few little ones running about the palace, causing mayhem. It'll be a good life. He'll have his revenge, and I'll have him. I don't even care about my family's fate. That's not who I am anymore. This is freeing, and it feels amazing. Finally, I'm free to relish in the parts of me others wanted to overlook. I can force them to really see me now. All of me, darkness included. That's worth everything. Michael has my eternal gratitude for giving me that freedom. I don't think I'd have ever reached this point without him.

I'm sure back home they're in a fury, thinking he manipulated or blackmailed me. It's not true, though. He didn't have to do any of that. He just saw me. That's all someone has to do when half of who you are has been invisible your whole life. I love him for that. No matter what anyone says or thinks, I chose this. I will not choose people who made me feel like half a person over someone who encouraged me to be whole. Such a thing would be foolish. I will always appreciate what they did for me, a random orphan girl who needed help, but I will never forget what they didn't do, either.

I choose Michael and will continue to choose him for the rest of my life. *In madness we thrive, in evil we lie, until the end of time, it's he and I.*

I recite the chant in my mind a few times, crafting it into a binding promise using my spiritual power. From across the room, Michael senses the magic tie me to him. "You just bound yourself to me?"

I smile. "Yes. I want to be bound to you. I cannot wait for our marriage to bind us."

He runs his hand over my metallic purple hair. "Thank you. Please allow me to reciprocate."

I giggle. "Oh, please do."

He kneels on the ground before me, spreading my legs wide as I sit back in the chair. Pushing my unmentionables to the side, he grazes his tongue over my pussy, making it instantly soaked. Pulling back just enough to speak, he makes a binding from his end as well. "May my throne be her temple; may my life be her toy. Let her exploit me, for it gives me joy."

Fuck. I can feel the binding taking hold, his worship heightening my arousal as it ignites the power he's giving me over him. I hiss. "If you don't put your fucking dick inside me right now, I'll strangle the life from you, Michael."

He smirks. "As you wish, Seshen."

Rising up enough to get a better grip on me, he wraps his hands around my thighs and pulls my hips to the edge of the chair. The way he rams his cock inside of me is ruthless. It elicits a wild moan that, when he hears it, makes those red eyes of his come to life. I dig my heels into his back, trying to keep him this deep. He's patient as my body adjusts to him, offering a few slow strokes, dragging his cock out until only the tip remains and then driving it back in until it meets my cervix. Fucking Hel, it feels so good.

Michael picks up the pace as my body welcomes him inside it. I feel myself clenching around him as he gives me more and more. His hands cup my breasts as he leans forward to nibble the left one. The brush of his teeth and artful teasing of his tongue cause my nipple to stiffen to a peak. The ecstasy overcomes me and I'm quivering beneath the weight of his body. "Fuck, keep going."

As if I had to tell him. With each stroke, he hits my sweet spot. The stimulation drives me wild. Apparently, it does the same to him because lustful groans vibrate against the supple skin of my breasts, sending vibrations all the way through me to my core. We get lost in the steady rhythm of his thrusting, my hips rising to meet him every time. I feel myself getting close and he doesn't hesitate to send me flying over that edge. The warmth of his seed pouring into me as he finishes with me is the most erotic damn thing I've ever felt.

Still, this man is far from through with me. Over the course of the night, every time we finish, he makes a point of getting me aroused again, and each time the sight of my arousal makes his dick hard. By the end, we've both cum so many times we're barely conscious. It wouldn't be exaggerating to say I'm seeing stars. With him still buried inside me, we cuddle, resting our tired bodies as we slip into a sleep that consumes.

The next morning, I awake to the feel of his cock twitching inside me. His eyes are open already. I can't help the laughter that overcomes me. "You woke up and still didn't pull out?"

He huffs, trying to appear composed. "I didn't want to wake you. You looked so peaceful, but well... This stupid thing has a mind of its own, Seshen. It's not my fault."

Is he blushing right now? Oh, my goddess. I don't think I've ever seen anything quite this adorable. I've flustered the fearsome tyrant king of Tendu, the great Michael, by pointing out that he hasn't the strength to remove himself from me even after we went endless rounds last night.

Callian

After updating my mother on my progress, I visit a military barracks. This barrack houses a revered unit. If they choose to follow me, the rest of our military will fall in line. I step inside to see them all standing at attention, awaiting me.

"Prince Callian, welcome." Their commander says.

"Thank you, Commander Luca," I reply. "I've come today to walk you through my plan for the impending war. Please listen carefully, because at the end I will ask you to pledge your support to it."

His eyes narrow. I can tell he doesn't love the idea of following me into battle, but that doesn't mean convincing him is impossible. I continue speaking. "My plan is as follows. Over the past days and weeks, I've coordinated with the kingdom of Alacrium, acquiring substantial aid from them. It will come as supplies, financial support, and fighters via a new trade route we are carving out to protect it from my sister's betrayal. As such, it will take time, but Oceanica is strong enough to withstand until that point. Our primary goal until the pieces are in place will be to withstand all attacks against us as we would any other siege, focusing on preserving life until the ideal opportunity to counterattack arises. To do this, we will need to work hard. Since Lilly's living barrier is our island's current shield, she could turn it against us. We will need to abolish it. Then, with a combination of barrier type spells from me and my parents, we will reestablish a barrier that should be difficult for the enemy to neutralize."

The commander and soldiers seem to focus on what I say. None of the men make the mistake of giving a reaction to the plan. Rather, they remain expressionless and silent, waiting for their commander's thoughts before expressing their own. There's no doubt that no matter what they think, they will follow his orders above mine. I can't blame them for that. He has led and fought beside them for years. As far as they are concerned, I'm an entitled kid who thinks my title gives me command of them. I haven't earned their trust as my parents and their commander have. They have no reason to follow me. I don't want to ask my parents to order them to because that would undermine my leadership. I want to earn it.

After a few long moments of silence, the commander hisses. "Your first order to us would be to take the road of cowards? Who do you think you are to come in here and order some of the best soldiers in the world to do such a thing?"

I stand strong, getting the feeling he's testing me. "I am their prince and future king."

He scoffs. "You are an insolent boy and a bastard."

Shock ripples through me. Why would he think I'm a bastard? That makes no sense. "Like Hel I am. You may dislike me, Commander, but raising questions about my legitimacy is quite another matter. In fact, through an unkind lens, one could see it as treasonous."

He chuckles. "You're mistaken if you think I care about accusations of treason coming from a bastard."

He must be confident in these accusations to make them so directly. I can see the shift. His men went from neutral to being in disgust. There is no winning this now. My best strategy is to retreat and discuss the matter with my parents. I need to know if there's anything they're keeping from me. I cannot lead with a blindfold and ignorance to my own circumstances.

Maintaining my composure, I turn and leave the barracks. Before I even make it back to the palace, they've spread rumor of the commander's claim all over the kingdom. Of course, they could accomplish such a thing. With their training, connections, and expertise, destabilization is an effortless task. I think I misjudged the situation. This isn't a challenge to test my abilities; it's a political hit job. So far, the commander is winning. We can't afford to be in a civil war right now. Why would he raise these accusations now, when Oceanica must appear stable? What could he gain from doing this? I understand so little about what just happened.

Peasants and nobles alike glare at me with disgust as I make my way inside the palace. Dad Jameson meets me in the entry hall with a sympathetic expression on his face. "Son, I think we need to talk now."

THE FATE OF ANGELS AND DEMONS

I must look at him like he's out of his mind. "You think? Care to explain why I'm being accused of being a bastard?"

The way his face twists tells me that he's irritated that this subject even came up. "You are not a bastard. Your conception was indeed before my marriage to your mother, but your birth took place after."

I raise an eyebrow, finding his words suspicious. He continues. "Son, why would you have angelic power if you weren't my son?"

Okay. That's a valid point. Not a very high possibility of Mom having slept with more than one angel, or person of angelic descent. "Point taken. Okay, then, I'm your son. Your legitimate heir. That's good. Then, these are all vicious rumors, and I need only put them to rest."

He nods. "Good. Get to work, then. We'll be here if you need us."

I do exactly that. I need to check that commander in order to overcome this. The plan I devise is on the reckless side, but it's also brilliant. These are military men. They respect power and brotherhood. So, that's exactly what I'll display. Doing so should bring them to heel.

I can't deny that the very accusation still eats at me, even knowing what Dad said. There are those more traditional factions, though, who believe that conception outside of wedlock still makes a bastard. Personally, I think it's all nonsense. Lilly wasn't even born to my parents, yet I've never thought of her as an illegitimate princess. The only reason she's not inheritor was because her skills were better suited to being the peacemaker. Of course, she abandoned that role now, but I don't think anyone would have questioned it if she were the heir instead of me. Yet, they question me because my parents are so deep in love that they couldn't keep their hands off each other. It sounds stupid. No. It doesn't just sound stupid, it *is* stupid. Yet, I'm the heir and I have to deal with the fact that some people are stupid. They're my people just like the smart ones are, I guess.

A MATTER OF HONOR

JAMESON

My wife and husband lie on either side of me in bed as we discuss the rumors our son is up against. We have always known it may come up at some point. Some people are so uptight about things like this. Of course, we discussed it back then and already have a consensus about how we'll handle it from our side. Not to say we doubt our son, but it isn't something he should have to deal with, so we can at least provide some help while still allowing him to show his ability to handle things on his own.

My wife is furious. "How dare he? I have half a mind to appear before the general myself and see if he has the gall to say such a thing to my face. We should see if he has the nerve to say it to someone he knows will beat his ass."

Kai looks over at her. "Josella, stop it. You know why we can't do that."

She scowls. "Yes, yes. Adult, blah, blah, blah. Callian must become his own person, blah, blah, blah. Don't want issues with an influential commander, blah, blah, blah. Well, I don't care. Callian doesn't get to be his own person. He's my son; I made him. It's my right to defend him."

It's so difficult not to find her adorable when she gets all worked up like this. "My beloved goddess, listen to you. Don't go getting yourself all stressed. I'll make sure our son is okay. You should conserve your energy for matters worthy of your attention. Besides, we'll need all that fire of yours in the war to come."

For just a moment, she freezes. Her cheeks flush red and she looks flustered. That's the look I live for. Every time I see it; I'm reminded of why I worship at her altar. I love this woman so much. Not to mention the man on the other side of me. It's so sexy when I see him look at her with the same adoration and love that I do. He doesn't even realize it. At least I don't think he does. The thing I love most about this throuple of ours is the equality of it. None of us love either of the others more or less. We're all obsessed with each other to the extent we can't function in any other way.

It means so much to me for us to have that with each other. I've always wanted our children to find the same, whether it be with one person or any other number, of any gender whatsoever. I think it's important that one finds one's partner or partners all-consuming. Of course, I wish Lilly could have felt that way about someone who wasn't trying to kill her little brother and wage war against her country, but I don't blame her for leaving if that's what she found. In truth, I'd betray anyone or anything for these two, so I can see why she feels that way.

As I promised Josie, I move to support my son by putting some basic measures in place. While I don't want to do too much outright so he can address this himself and earn the respect of our military, I want to do enough so that he won't end up facing any major consequences if he fails. It's normal for him to make mistakes since he's still getting used to being active in ruling, so my job as his father is to ensure those mistakes don't cost him anything he can't afford to pay. Of course, there will still be repercussions should he mess up, just not any life-altering consequences like losing the crown.

The first measure is to prepare counter information to be spread in case things got bad. Things like witnesses who can attest to the events of that time. A few strong, credible people come to mind, but they are the same world leaders who rule the kingdoms that have fallen to Tendu. Thus, I opt to seek some witnesses closer to home. The advisory council of my father's rule is the best place to start. They're all loyal men and women, so it's likely they'd be willing to speak in public about what they saw during that time to help us, especially since we aren't asking them to lie. My account to Callian is true. Even more, Josie only found out she was already pregnant just before our wedding.

I freeze, silently repeating that thought to myself. This isn't public knowledge. She only found out shortly before our wedding. That commander wasn't around back then. We appointed him just a few years ago. How does he know? "Tch- Dammit. There's a fucking traitor in my palace."

Stepping back from the situation for a moment, I reassess everything that's happened since Lilly went to see Michael the first time, trying to identify anyone who has done anything suspicious. If there's one traitor, who knows how many others there are? I can only hope I'm the first to piece it together. One act of treachery will surely embolden others who plan to do the same. Whoever did this must have the position necessary to know, which means they're close to me and my family. We're in danger. Threats are coming our way from both inside and outside Oceanica; no one but blood has my trust from this moment onward.

Stalking through the palace, I find my husband, my wife, and my son, telling each of them to pack their things. "Get ready. We need to leave the palace. We're going to stay in the castle for the time being instead. It's safer."

The defensive accommodations are much stronger there. It'll shield us in case of a siege and hopefully disrupt any plans the traitor could have, too. I hand select the guards to come with us, choosing only those who have proved loyal, but have never been in our inner circle or my fathers. People who know nothing they can use against us.

Callian

After my father moves us to the castle, he takes some time to talk things over with Mom and Dad Kai so he can locate the traitor. Meanwhile, I resume my mission as if nothing has changed. In part, this is because it might alert the traitor if I stand down. They must know me well enough to recognize it's against my instinct to do so. The rest, though, is just because I want to do this. If I'd have given up, my parents would have accepted that decision, not wanting me to scare or feel like my life was in danger. I persisted, though, once again proving that I'm more ready for this responsibility than they realize.

The guards selected by Dad Jameson escort me to the barracks. After my arrival, I dismiss them to return to the castle. I find the commander and his unit on the barracks training grounds and approach, giving no regard to the nervousness swelling in my stomach as I move toward him. "Commander, I'm here to end this."

He holds his hand up, letting his unit know that training is on hold as he addresses me. "How do you plan to do that, *prince*?"

I can hear the mocking in his tone. It causes me to grit my teeth, biting back my anger. "That's right, I am a prince. By birth. Make no mistake, Commander, I am the only legitimate heir this kingdom has, and I will protect it by defending that claim."

My words seem to get to him. I know it from the way his shoulders tense. He may not like me, but this reaction lets me know Oceanica does matter to him. That brief flicker of fear, not for himself, but for the kingdom he swore his life to serving, tells me a lot about the type of man I'm dealing with. He worries about its future and knows it's dangerous to attack my claim. Then why is he doing this? Someone is blackmailing him, that's my guess. I'll have to back him into a corner in that case. I don't know what's being used to blackmail him, so it's too risky to make it his choice. The best way to do this is for the blackmailer, wherever they are watching from, to see that he had no choice but to stand down. "I challenge you," I say. "I challenge you to a holmgang. Make the square."

He cuts his eyes at me, likely realizing that I'm making such a bold move to help him. There's a sense of warning in that stony gaze, though. He won't hold back. Whoever is blackmailing him must be too familiar with his power. I nod and repeat my words. "Make the square, commander."

He nods. "You heard the prince, men. Make it."

They form into the traditional square around us. Holmgangs are an old practice, most don't use them in this modern age. They still have so much respect, though. Any warrior would honor the outcome of one. "Incapacitating is a win?"

He asks me to confirm. I nod. "Yes. Fighting to the death would be contrary to my goals of gaining your support."

His second-in-command steps forward, looking at us both before calling out. "Fight!"

We circle each other, face-to-face, each waiting to see what the other does. He makes the first move, using his powerful runic magic to unleash a tsunami, hurling it toward me. I respond by activating my own runes, not wanting to lean into my angelic power and risk causing him serious harm. With my own runes, I sway the magic of his, seizing control of the tsunami and redirecting it toward him. It hits, knocking him off balance. I don't miss the opportunity to follow-up with water blades honed to such sharpness that anyone watching would think my intent was to kill him.

He narrowly evades the ones aimed at lethal points, understanding that I have to at least appear to be trying. Despite his speed, several others slice through his body, hitting tendons in his arms and legs. I don't think he was expecting me to be as skilled as I am. There's a shock on his face that implies he's impressed with my ability. Even though he is trying, and I'm holding back substantially, I have the clear advantage. Forcing his body to fight through the pain so as not to appear like he gave up with too much ease, he launches another attack. This one comes down from the sky with a fierceness that forces me to use my angelic power to block it. The water falls from the sky like rain, but with the same sharpness of the blades I threw at him. I have no choice but to raise my power to repel them.

Little did I know that was his goal. I can't defend myself from this lethal rain and from another incoming attack at the same time. He comes fast from my right and takes a massive blade to my side. I hurl over in pain, instantly releasing some more angelic power, accelerating the healing of the wound. He looks at me in awe when he realizes I can heal myself and fight at the same time. It's not a common ability, but certainly one that the royal son of an angel and a great priestess can attain.

The rain stops coming, and I can counter now. My body is lethargic, and I struggle, but I manage something. By altering the temperature of the water, I summon and flooding the ground around his feet with it, I essentially trap him in boiling hot quicksand. I hate to do it to him, but it's the fastest way to end this, so I can heal us both. Screams of agony hurl from him into the environment as his legs burn. He can't escape. I've won. "Yield!" he screams, "I yield!"

Right away, I withdraw my magic, darting over to heal him. I do a quick inventory of his injuries, noting the most severe. The water blades tore his ACL. The boiling sand got into the injury. I should focus on that first. It has the potential to become infected and make him go septic. Turning my gaze toward the commander's second, I order him. "Hold him down."

He follows the order, urging a few others to help as well. Two pin his wrists, one his shoulders, and two more help by holding his legs where I need them. First, I summon more hot water to rinse and sterilize the wound, ensuring all the sand comes out. The commander writhes as I work. I'm sure it hurts like Hel, but I have to do this or so much worse could happen. His second reassures him, talking calmly to distract him from the pain. "Sir, it's alright. He's trying to help you. Relax. Once he's done, we'll take you out for wine and dinner. Mostly wine."

The commander's laugh is weak and gruff, but he settles some, allowing me to work easier. Now, I call on cool water. Not cold, just slightly below the temperature of tap water. It'll help the burns. After a few minutes, I use angelic stitching to heal the muscles and stop the bleeding. With the most serious wound closed, I'm able to patch up the others fast. His men appear relieved when they see that the worst has passed. They aren't just loyal to him; these men care about him. I admire that. I hope one day soon I'll be able to inspire the same from those I lead.

Michael

"Seshen?" I peek my head into our bedroom. I haven't seen her in hours. It's worrisome. Where could she have gotten to? I wander the palace halls searching for her, but there's no sign of her anywhere. Then a giggle rings through the air like a symphony. That's her alright. Nothing else could make my heart skip beats with such ease. It acts like a damn schoolboy whenever she's nearby. I guess that makes sense in some ways, though. She is the first woman I've had these feelings toward. No doubt this is what first love feels like. Except... In my case, she's my first, my last, and every number in between.

I head out to the courtyard where I heard that laughter to find her and Pythias. They seem to have found some sort of creature. It looks like some strange mixture of a cat, dog, and fox. Possibly a ferret, too? Either way, they both appear to be enthralled by the mammals' antics, as it plays with a wad of paper that I can only assume is their attempt at creating a makeshift ball. She laughs again when it loses control of the paper ball and sends it flying into Pythias' head. He snarls, but in a lighthearted manner, feigning annoyance with the creature even as awe lights his eyes. Something deep within me grows with discontent as I watch them. I don't like how close they seem. It may have been a mistake to allow him to spend so much time with my Seshen. I'm wondering if Pythias might take her from me. I approach them, smiling to hide the urge to kill him.

When she sees me, she smiles back, her expression joyous. "Michael! Look what we found."

I ask, "what exactly is it?"

She shrugs. "Aside from adorable? I have no clue. Can I keep it?"

She doesn't even know what it is, and she wants to keep it in my palace. I bend down to touch the thing, trying to judge it. When I extend my hand, the little shit bites my finger. I jerk away. "It's not tamed, Seshen. It's aggressive."

She giggles. "It's all of five pounds, my love."

I growl. "You do not know it will remain that way."

"You do not know that it won't."

I rub my forehead, realizing that there's nothing I can say to deter her. "Keep it, I suppose. Just try to ensure it doesn't shred every linen in the palace."

She hugs me, so excited about this thing. I'm not sure she realizes I could never deny her something she wished for. That would require a type of strength I do not possess, the kind that would enable me to resist her. I wrap my arms around her, holding her firmly against my body. "Thanks, Michael. I promise, he won't be any trouble."

The freaky little monster was, in fact, trouble. As soon as we brought it inside, it took to clawing at the banners. Pythias's amusement leaks into his face as he watches me fail at ignoring the thing. I growl at him, then ask Lilly, "What will you call your new beast, Seshen?"

She contemplates her answer for about a minute, then briefly checks to see its sex. "His name will be Ace."

I nod. "Ace? I like it, Seshen. It suits him."

That seems to make her even happier. I may not like the beast, but I'm glad its presence affects her so. I'll have to bond with it. That seems like something she'll like. There must be some way to make the thing like me. I look at it again. She's not wrong, after all. It's kind of cute. I've never had a pet before. It might just take some getting used to, but I think I can grow to like it.

It must notice me looking at it because it shifts its little eyes my way, then wanders over. I lower my hand again, apprehensive, but open. It sniffs me a few times, then butts its head into me. I smile. "Hey, Ace. You want to be my friend now, huh?"

The thing seems so content as I pet it. Okay, I see why it makes her so happy now. Adorable was an apt description of this beast. I look at her as I pet Ace. The soft expression covering that otherworldly face of hers shifts my center of gravity. In this moment, I realize for the first time that I would do anything, sacrifice anything, endure anything for this woman. She is all there is in this world for me. Beyond her, nothing exists. Or perhaps everything does, and I just don't care. It's hard to imagine giving a damn about anything else when I have the option to focus all my energies on loving her.

Pythias steps between her and I. "I'm getting the sense you two need some time alone. I'll go sweep the premises for security and give you both a few minutes."

I nod and he wanders off. Despite my earlier flare of jealousy, I'm glad I assigned him to Lilly's security. Contrary to what it may have sounded like, I consider him a friend. Albeit a very dead friend, if she ever smiles at him like that again. After he's out of sight, I rise to my feet, lifting Ace into my arms as I glance at her. "You should be more careful with Pythias. The two of you appear too friendly, from a distance."

She scoffs. "Michael, stop. Pythias is great, but I love you."

She loves me. I repeat the statement in my mind. The smug tone it repeats in causes me to laugh a bit. Lilly must have heard it, because she chuckles. I don't bother hiding the blush that I feel heating my cheeks as I say, "I love you, too, Seshen."

Ace climbs from my arms to hers just before we retreat to the library. Settling on to a big, comfortable chair, I lean back, spreading my legs on the fótstól so she can fit herself between them and lie back on me. She does, then loosens her hold on Ace so he can be in her lap. I reach onto the table beside us and grab both our current reads. Mine is about the philosophy of the Five Rings; hers is about two people falling in love, both are valid. I'm no snob. I believe there's just as much to learn from fiction writing as there is from philosophy and academic writing. There may even be more to learn from books like what she's reading because it explores emotions, something one can hardly use logic to comprehend.

We sit together, cuddled up with our books and our beast for quite a while. In time, she falls asleep on me. I don't budge. It's cute seeing her like this, and I love having her close. Of course, that doesn't stop it from becoming uncomfortable. After three hours, my legs are numb. I need to piss, and I'm starving, too, but I still can't bring myself to wake her. Not when she looks so peaceful. Thus, I remain where she holds me.

Alas, the flower blossoms from her rest, which was feeling eternal. With sleepy eyes, she tilts her head back to meet mine. I meet her gaze with affection in my heart. "Good evening, Seshen. Did you rest well?"

"Evening?" She asks, still groggy from her nap. "I slept all day?"

I nod. "You did, dearest one. May I perhaps escape you to handle some of my bodily functions?"

Her answer is a groan. "No, you're too comfy."

I laugh. "But I need to pee."

"Hmph, get over it."

Stubborn woman, she's lucky she's so cute because I'd strangle her if I wasn't laughing so hard. "Seshen! I need to pee, please."

She huffs, then looks at me with such seriousness on her face. "Fine, but only if you give me kisses first."

One Hel of a negotiator, this one. I shower her face with kisses until she's squirming and cracking up. "Okay, okay. That's enough." She slinks down to the floor, out of my lap. "You can use the bathroom now."

I stand. "Oh, but I was just getting started."

As I walk away, she throws the pillow from the chair at me. It bounces off my ass to the ground as I continue my retreat. After relieving myself, I return to find her teaching Ace tricks. I ask, "What do you think he eats?"

She shrugs. "No clue. I think he's carnivorous from the shape of his claws and teeth. Maybe we could just put some meats in front of him and see what he takes to."

"Not a bad idea. I'll have the kitchen work on it."

DISRUPTING THE SYSTEM

CALLIAN

A few days pass as the commander recovers. During that time, we figure out who was blackmailing him. The investigation was tedious since the person in question had the skills necessary to cover her trail. She'd been in a position of power and that always helps someone hide their misdeeds. We caught a lucky break when we check Luca's trunk in the barracks for evidence. As we searched it, one of his people mentioned that his behavior toward the royal family shift around the time I came home. That let us know that whoever blackmailed him did so because my return triggered their resentment toward us. With that, we began looking into people that were negatively impacted by my existence or my parents' decisions around that time. That led us to a handful of suspects, and we successfully apprehended the one responsible.

Her name was Elaine. She was on the advisory council around the time of my conception and has a foul taste in her mouth about being relieved of that duty when my parents brought in their own council for their rule rather than keeping my grandfather's. She used the commander's daughter as leverage for her blackmail. We rescued the girl, though, so she's safe now. We're fortunate to find that she's the only traitor because it means we can return home to the palace. I appreciate the defensive power of castles, but they're nowhere near as comfortable.

Now that it's settled, and the commander is healthy again, he offers me his unwavering support. His first day back at the barracks; he bends the knee to me and tells his men the complete story, including how I saved him and forgave his treachery because of the circumstances. Now, I look merciful and understanding. They rally around me, willing to do anything for me now that they know I'm on their side. With this unit behind me, the rest of the military falls in line with no need for persuasion. The rumors and questions regarding my legitimacy cease as well.

The full backing of the military allows me to gather them to issue my orders. There's an excitement within me that sparks now that I know I can issue orders. I'd say that it will be fun, but given the circumstances, that doesn't seem appropriate. Instead, I'll say that it will be a valuable experience for me, as a future ruler, to gain an understanding of the joys and pitfalls of leading an army. That sounds more prince-like, right?

I step onto the podium and look out at all the troops gathered before me. With the commander at my side, I feel little doubt as I begin my speech. "Hello, and thank you for joining me here today. I consider it an honor to speak to you. For those of you who may not have seen my portrait before, I am Prince Callian, son of Queen Josella Spade, as well as King Jameson and King Kai, heir to the throne of this great kingdom known as Oceanica.

"Yet I cannot take pride in the events that have led me here because they are signs of war. This foe, old as it is, once again comes with the threat of tearing our beloved kingdom apart. Each time it rears its ugly head; we suffer the destruction it brings. While we've known it to have many faces, this time it hurts more than ever. I say that because this time it is not the face of an enemy it bears. Instead, our foe comes wearing the mask of our friends in Tendu who have lost their way.

"These friends—poisoned against us through years of compiled grievances that require a level of diplomacy so beyond the reach of mankind that even those of us with angelic and demonic blood coursing through our veins cannot grasp it—are misguided. They have attacked our alliance, slandered our esteemed names, and shredded our peace of mind. Now, we must face them in battle. However, we will *not* face them with the same malice with which they face us.

"We will face them with the kindness we have always born them, for we know that our friends and loved ones still exist within them. In this war, the goal is not to destroy our enemy, but to let them know they cannot destroy us, and perhaps, with luck, we can return them to being the people we, in our hearts, know them to be. The task I place before you is not for the faint of heart. There will be bloodshed and heartache. Many will die, but not nearly as many as would die if you all did not gather here to lend me your strength.

"Allow me to ask you now, knowing what I've just told you; are you with me?"

The crowd erupts into an uproar of cheers that sends one decisive message: *We will fight.*

I repeat it, feeding off their energy. "I said, *Are. You. With Me?*"

The battle cry becomes even louder, a roar that tells all of Oceanica that these men and I will fight for them until our last breaths. After it settles, I continue speaking. "Awesome. You're all awesome. Thank you so much for your support. Please report to the station with signage labeled in correspondence with your unit numbers.

There, you will receive your orders from the officers in charge of your units. May the gods be with you all."

The crowd of warriors disperses to the stations set up all around them as I make my way down from the podium. The adrenaline catches up to me as soon as I'm out of sight. Anxious breaths catch my lungs as the enormous weight of the responsibility I have on my shoulders takes hold. There are far too many lives in my hands now. I see now that I've thought far too little about the lives I am risking and far too much about my ambitions. These men who are all willing to risk their lives for this cause deserve someone who sees them as heroes, not as tools for political gamesmanship. I don't deserve them, so I must strive to become someone who does because it would only compound my unworthiness if I were to abandon them now. In the meantime, I'll rely on the council of those who have the experience to guide me.

Overlooking the fact that he got blackmailed into treachery, I believe the commander of the special unit may be my best bet as a primary advisor. He sees potential within me and believes my plan has merit. I need only allow him to help me execute it. Yes, Commander Luca is the best choice.

A few minutes pass as I get some water and stabilize my breathing patterns to a reasonable level. Then I go find Commander Luca. He's with his unit at their station. As I approach, they all move to attention. I wave my hand. "As you were, I'm just here to chat."

They all resume their prior activities as I approach the commander. He asks, "How can I help you, my prince?"

I sit in the free chair, designated for his second, who is making the rounds to give each squad within their unit the orders best suited to them. "I want your unit to be the one I stay with."

He thinks for a few moments. "That makes sense, actually. We're the follow-up team for when Lilliana's barrier falls. It puts you in a prime position to help erect a new one."

I nod. "Yes, and I'll post my mother on the western point to erect hers. Dad Jameson to the south makes sense. That leaves the north for Dad Kai and me to the east, where I'll be designing a special barrier that will allow the Alacrians to send aid there. More than that, though, Commander Luca..."

I hesitate, but he reassures me. "It's okay, Prince Callian. I know how nerve-racking it is your first time commanding such a large force. I've been there, and I didn't have the burden of being a prince on top of it. Tell me how I can help."

That encourages me. "I need council, and I want you to be the one to give it."

He shakes his head, laughing a bit. "That's what had you so nervous?"

He takes a slow, deep breath to calm himself, then continues. "Don't be ridiculous. Everyone needs wise council. Your parents are perhaps the finest leaders in the world, and they take council. I, myself, have my second to council me. Asking for it means you're already wiser than you think. Of course, I will be your council through this war, and even beyond it, if you require that of me."

His words make me smile. I find I'm quickly coming to idolize him. He's a sort of hero in my mind, someone to aspire to, as odd as that may sound. Not only is he a magnificent leader, but a gentleman. Intellect, combined with brute strength and a kind heart, makes it difficult for me to see him as anything less than a hero. I think it's healthy for me to have someone, aside from my parents, who exemplifies the things I want to see within myself. I think everyone should have that. Seeing it in your own family feels like pressure; seeing it in some random person feels like inspiration.

With that settled, each unit enters the preparation phase, gathering materials, strength, and getting civilians clear of any areas that may become dangerous while we implement our plan. It takes quite some time to accomplish, allowing me the time I need to go retrieve my parents and walk them through their part in this. Commander Luca sits at my side as I explain the details of my plan to them. They seem rather impressed with how I've created a strategy, gathered the support I need to implement it, and even showed the wisdom to keep wise council at my side. "You're shaping up to be one Hel of a king." Dad Kai says.

Dad Jameson follows up. "That's true, Callian. I remember when we were your age. The transition from a prince who believes he's entitled, to a king who is a king before he ever gets crowned is challenging, but you've shown yourself capable of handling those trials."

I feel pride welling up within me as I realize I've earned their trust. By the time I look at Mom, I'm nervous. She gets overprotective and I'm afraid that this still won't be enough to show her I'm ready for this responsibility. Much to my surprise, she just smiles at me. "They're right. You've earned this. I'm sorry for treating you like a kid all this time. I'm proud of you. You've done well."

That does me in. The pride and acknowledgement spark tears of joy as I at last feel the relief of no longer being scared that I'm not good enough. As the tears stream down my cheeks, Commander Luca appears uncomfortable. "Uh, my prince..."

Mom giggles at his reaction. "Now, now. It's alright, Callian. This is good."

"I know," I reply, "but Mom, for so long now, I've felt inadequate. It means more to me than any of you could know that you've all found me worthy."

She glances at Dad Jameson. "He's definitely your son."

He chuckles. "I couldn't tell."

I raise an eyebrow. "What are you guys talking about?"

Dad Jameson replies. "Nothing of note, just a memory."

"Tell me." I command.

"Once upon a time, I, too, felt inadequate." He explains.

I ask, "And how did you get past it?"

Mom's facial expression goes haywire, and I can't tell if she's flustered or on the verge of laughing hysterically. Dad Kai answers, "Your mother told him he was her property, and that she did not own worthless things."

I regret asking the second he says it, feeling as though I just stumbled into information about their private lives I didn't need. It's obvious, now that I think about it, given how openly he's always worshipped her, but I did not need confirmation. Some idiotic part of me drives me to ask another question I don't want an answer to. "You, too?"

Dad Kai nods. "In this life and the next, Josella is our goddess."

It's sweet if you ignore the explicit implications. I hope to love someone that much one day. The three of them still make me want to gag sometimes, though.

After we finish talking, we all head out to reach our assigned checkpoints along the barrier. With Commander Luca at my side and his unit at my back, we stand behind the first unit on the eastern border of Oceanica, where they launch relentless attacks at my sister's barrier. It's nearly thirty minutes of consistent attacks before we can see any visible cracks in it. Regardless of the fatigue they suffer, the unit doesn't stop, not even for a moment. The same is true of every checkpoint, if things are going as planned. They can't stop, otherwise, it would give Lilly time to realize and repair what progress they have made.

For five hours, they endure until the barrier comes crumbling down, causing mass amounts of spiritual energy to leak into the atmosphere. The second unit moves in, creating an overhead shield that protects the first unit while they retreat. As soon as they're clear, we move in. Commander Luca and his unit provide me support while I get the eastern barrier up, careful to watch my intentions so it will allow the Alacrians through. In the end, we're successful. I know the other checkpoints were too because the barrier connects, forming a sphere around our island kingdom.

With phase one of the plan being a success, a few days later, phase two begins when the first shipment from Alacrium arrives. It's nothing major, just a test to see how well our new system works. They send a handful of men with some gold and medicinal supplies. Even something this simple is a tremendous help. The gold will keep our economy from collapsing now that our trade with the other islands is nil, and the supplies will help because angel stitching is so rare. It'd be impossible for the few of us who use it to treat everyone in full-scale war. We'll need to supply the traditional healers so they can tend to a majority of the wounded. We have plenty of them, but if things get as bad as they seem like they might, we'll need more supplies than we can muster without this shipment.

After we unload the shipment, I say to the men who brought it, "Rest here tonight. I'll have rooms made up for you at the palace so you can recover before returning home."

Most of them turn an awkward gaze on the man I assume is leading them, awaiting his permission to accept. He steps forward. "Thank you for your kind offer, Prince Callian. We consider it an honor to accept your hospitality. Then, tomorrow morning, we will head home to tell our queen this mission has been successful."

I give him a nod. "Perfect. Follow me."

I lead them toward the palace as those men from my side unload and direct the supplies to where we need them under the oversight of Commander Luca. These Alacrians have come far to bring us these things; they needn't assist us with that.

The next morning, after they've rested, they set off back toward Alacrium. A few days more, larger shipments arrive, as do more each day after that. After they get us all the supplies and gold, the warriors will come and stay. Right now, Queen Alexandria needs them since she's constantly sending men on transport missions, but after that, they'll get stationed here, under my command until the war passes.

Michael

Seshen and I wander along the coast of the mainland, starting at Loft and making our way north. We need to see Oceanica from every angle to determine where best to attack. Unlike the other islands, this one will not fall with such ease. Besides, our grip on Pallentine is tenuous at best. With the Chief's return, they've already attempted four rebellions. Each one failed, but it's proving rather difficult to break their will as we have on the other islands we've seized. One wrong move and they could join Oceanica in opposition to us. This warrants additional caution.

On the bright side, walking along this shore with my Seshen is serene. I enjoy spending time with her this way. I can't wait to finish this, so we have more time to enjoy our love. There's so much I wish to show her and so many things I want to do with her. Some of them are mundane, sure. Normal things people in relationships do together, like travel or try new things. Others are darker, but that's just who I am. Things like teaching her methods of torturing people she's yet to consider. Watching her in the dungeon made me realize how hot it can be to see her relish in bloodlust.

It's hard to put my finger on what about her makes me feel the things I do. I've never given a damn about a woman before. Most, I treated similar to how I did that noble girl, but I can't even imagine doing that to my Seshen. In fact, I sort of like the idea of her doing that to me. I want her so depraved she makes me look innocent by comparison. She wants it too. We've broached the topic in private, and it turns her on. She's asked me to help make her into the dark queen that I will allow to brutalize me. I'm more than glad to oblige her.

As we continue strolling up the coastline, I decide to ask her something to get her talking. "You knew my father well, right?"

"Yes, I did." She answers. Her discomfort with the topic isn't so hidden as she seems to think. "What about him?"

I shake my head. "Nothing. No one has ever talked about him before. Mom never brought him up besides to explain why we hated your mother. I know nothing of who he was. I thought you might tell me about him."

She nods. "That's understandable. I can try, but I assure you my words won't do him justice."

A half-hearted chuckle escapes me. "You sound ridiculous, Seshen. Whatever kind of person he was, and however great he was, anyone whose name passes those luscious lips of yours receives more honor than they deserve."

She blushes. Unable to form a response to that, she just moves past it. "Malachi is the best person I've ever met. His loyalty to Mom was unlike anything I've ever seen. He never failed to show up for the ones he loved. His rule was just and levelheaded. The people of Tendu adored him. He and your mom were cute together, too. They met shortly before my mom found me. Johanna loved him from the start, from my understanding. He took longer to come around to it. Not necessarily because he didn't reciprocate. It seems to me it was more about him not being sure of himself. He got past it, though, and married her. I've never seen him so proud as I did the day you were born, you know?"

Her words give me pause. I had expected her perspective to be different, but I never thought it would be this sweet. She loved him a lot and seems to understand how he felt about me. If I made him so proud, why did he leave? Why did he choose to sacrifice himself? I don't understand it. "Really? If that's so, why did he abandon us?"

She sighs. "I'm not sure that's how he saw it."

The frustration caused by that statement makes me lose my temper. "I'm not sure there's any other way to see it, Seshen."

She tenses up when I snap at her. An immediate sense of regret floods my heart. "I'm sorry. I shouldn't have snapped at you. It's not your fault. It was your mother's choices that led him there and his that sealed the deal. None of it falls on you."

She shakes her head. "That's not true. I mean, the part about me not being at fault isn't. I was there, Michael. My role was just as substantial. My mother gave me the power to call it off, and I decided not to, even though I knew the risks. There were so many moments that I could have changed the course of things, and I didn't."

"You were a child. They were not." I reply matter-of-factly.

"I was a child with the power to stop it." Her tone shifts from irritated to soft. "I was a child with the power to stand up for him."

"Your talents do not change the fact that you were a child. It was his responsibility to think of me, not yours. It was your mother's responsibility to handle her grief like a normal adult, not yours. A child does not have the level of development necessary to have authority over decisions that involve such complexities."

She scoffs. "Normal children, maybe, but me, yes, I did. By that age, I had taken life already. I had faced trauma of my own. Do you believe that someone with trauma like mine couldn't have fathomed the ways something like that would have affected you? I assure you I could. Besides, how can you blame Callian and not me? That makes no sense because he hadn't even been born yet."

"I do not blame Callian. I never have. However, I resent him. He has all that he does because of what I lost. It's only fair that his loss restores my peace after all these years."

"You're right," she answers. "It makes sense when you put it that way. If only one of the two of you can thrive, I choose you every time. I love my little brother, but my love for you is far deeper. You must promise me one thing, though?"

"Anything at all."

"You must let me be the one to take his life. Emotions get messy, often in ways we cannot predict. I know myself. If I do it, if my heart goes haywire, I will loathe myself. If you do it, there's a risk of my resenting you for it."

I'm hesitant to agree to it, but when I stop walking and look into her eyes, I realize refusing to promise her this would cause a fight I'm unlikely to win. "Fine, I promise, Seshen, but I must be with you when you do it. For all your power as a priestess, Callian isn't to be underestimated. You'll need backup."

She seems okay with that. We walk a while more before stumbling across something suspicious. There's a group of men approaching the shore ahead of us with carts full of supplies. Lilly realizes what's happening. "They got the Alacrians to send aid."

I nod. "We have to cut off the supply line. It's too dangerous to leave them with an ally that powerful."

Lilly agrees. "Go ahead."

I call up my magic, summoning Helfire from the core of the planet, so it consumes the Alacrians and their shipment. Their screams ring through the air as they perish. Soon, silence comes, confirming they have died. I let the fire burn well beyond it to ensure they won't be able to use this little trade route they carved out again. After, I send for a few of my own soldiers to post them here on surveillance.

BETWEEN A FIRE AND A HOT PLACE

CALLIAN

"Gods dammit!" I burst into Commander Luca's barrack. "What the Hel happened?"

Commander Luca shoots to his feet as he answers. "They must have found the alternative route, sire. When the shipment became late, we sent some people out to check on the Alacrians bringing it and we found nothing but scorched earth and bone. They were incinerated. Further, it seems King Michael has posted a watch on that area. My men narrowly escaped without being detected."

Rage pulsates through my veins. "Well, we certainly can't depend on any more aid from the Alacrians then. Take an inventory of what we've already received and revise our plans in accordance. I'll look over the revisions when you're done. In the meantime, I'll try to contact the Chief to see if he's made any headway in freeing his people. For now, though, proceed as if we have no allies."

"Aye, sire." Commander Luca replies. I can see his mental recalculations beginning already. No doubt he's reliable. If I'm not mistaken, we've received enough that we still have significantly better odds than if we hadn't attempted this strategy at all. At least, I hope that's the case. If not, then I just wasted precious time on a failing strategy and gave Tendu that much more time to prepare for no reason.

While Commander Luca works on that, I go home and report to my parents. They don't seem too worried about it. I suspect they prepared backup strategies to employ in case I fail. Of course they would; why would they ever give me unequivocal trust? I'm untested and, apparently, unreliable as well. I hate this.

To cool myself off, I go for a walk, wandering around the entire border, observing the barriers, and thinking about my next steps. Regardless of what an utter mess I've made, I'm not ready to give up just yet. Once I hear from Commander Luca, I'll have more information about whether this is as bad as I fear. If I'm lucky, I'll at least have got us enough to improve our chances. If not, then this is nothing more than a massive screw up.

A few hours pass before Commander Luca tracks me down at the western border. "My Prince, I have the assessment you requested."

I look at him, hoping for context. "It's good. With the time you bought us, we received fifty-two percent of the aid promised. Aside from the extra warriors, it's everything. This puts us at a likelihood of success of about sixty percent. That number is rough, though, given the unpredictability of the foe. I think sixty is good, though. Prior to the aid, my assessment was closer to forty percent, so at least you flipped the odds in our favor, even if it's by a small margin.

The relief that takes hold of me is unlike anything I've felt before. I did it. These new numbers mean this wasn't a mistake at all. Any scrap of advantage I could muster makes it worth it. If nothing else, now the men fighting for Oceanica know I will not risk their lives without first making sure I've done my part. I heave, feeling the weight of failure lifting off my chest now that I know it was all worth it. Commander Luca is patient, giving me a moment to recover before he continues. "We should go through the assessment together and create a new strategy that will put forth our current strengths and cover our weaknesses."

I stand back upright. "Yes, we should. Let's go back to the barracks, where we can speak freely."

Together, we walk back to his barracks and, with the help of some of his men who have expertise in various areas, strategize. It takes a long while for us to find a method that works all the way around, but by the time we finish, we created and approach that we think will force Tendu to fight on our terms and exploit our advantage. Our island is surrounded by water just like any other and most of our military uses some type of water runes. While some from Tendu have overcome the 'water puts out fire' thing by making their flames hot enough to evaporate water faster than we can douse them, that's only the upper echelon of their ranks. Most of them have flames that just go out. This means our military can face them head on as long as we match the stronger people one-on-one. We come up with a semi-complete list of people and pair them off with ours. We start with Michael, of course. Either Dad Jameson or I are the best choice against him. Given the prophecy, it seems the answer is me. The entire issue here is that one of us will be the one to kill the other.

Lilly is a problem, too. Her strength surpassed Mom's long ago. As much as I hate it, sending Mom alone isn't a great idea. Perhaps I'll send her and Dad Jameson since I have to face Michael? The Tendu generals are another issue. Most of them have special abilities and it's been so long since we were allies that we no longer have reliable information on which ones and how many. I'm not a huge fan of guesswork, but life doesn't seem too keen on giving me another option. If they still have the standard five generals, my guess is that at least three have the special abilities I'm concerned about. That means one of them goes up against Dad Kai, another against Commander Luca, and we need to work out a third person from our ranks. We also need to figure out how we plan to force them into these matchups.

"Commander Luca," I begin, "is there another general you can recommend?"

He sighs. "That's a tough one. On our side, very few can hold their own against a special ability user from Tendu, especially if we don't have intel on what the ability will be. These bloodline abilities manifest in strange ways. There is no way of telling who will perform well, but if I had to name someone, my guess would be on General Shiva. He's a friend of mine and I spar with him frequently. Often, the matches end in a draw, so he's not lacking in ability. Although, it's worth noting he's a new general, assigned to his post within the last year. His lack of experience may outweigh his latent talent."

"He's a risk, then." I reply. "I'm a risk, an inexperienced leader running a wartime operation. Risky people have something to prove. I like it. Set up a meeting with him. We will bring him into our confidence, then leave the decision to him on whether he accepts the task."

Commander Luca smiles as he accepts the order. It seems he likes my willingness to take such risks as this. What I said is true. People who are untested will often yearn for an opportunity that will allow them to prove their worthiness. This General Shiva is no different. I can tell that much by the fact he spars with Luca. I wouldn't do that for fun. Hel, it would take a madman to do that. I won, but his heart also wasn't in the fight. I'm not sure I would win if he wanted to, and if I did, my body would hate me for it.

Michael

Having cut off Oceanica's supply line, we've weakened them in both strength and morale. Now is the time to go on the offensive, but it's too early to mobilize all our forces. No, instead, Lilly and I will just go light the carefully placed fuse we've created, the one that will set off the veritable war. They need to witness her choosing me. They need to plead for her to come home and watch her deny them. I need to erase every thought they have about reaching her or "helping her find herself again." As she's said before:

she could never be herself with them. My Seshen deserves to see them realize that her darkness existed long before I met her. I want her to see them realize all the ways they failed her.

Together, we head to the western border of Oceanica. I fly and she levitates beside me. With it just being the two of us, it's easier this way. Alone, she and I have ample power to shake them up and the ability to get out much faster than if we brought ships full of men. It takes little more than a few seconds for her to disarm their barrier, calling plenty of attention to our presence and ensuring her family comes. As the eyes of Oceanica gather, staring up at us, the murmuring begins. They believe we are here to kill them, but that isn't our goal. Not yet anyway. Leaping over the crowd, Callian arrives first. His trio of parents aren't far behind. Lilly's expression hardens when she sees them.

I wait a few moments, trying to gauge what will happen and how best to go about this. I hadn't given it as much thought as I should have. Believe it or not, my fear isn't that Lilly will betray me. It's that she'll—

An explosion of her spiritual power sends her mother flying back into the crowd. The massive collection of pissed people surrounding us makes it clear my fears weren't illogical or outlandish. "For years," she proclaims, "*Years*, mother, you made me bury myself as if every part of me that wasn't like you wasn't worth loving."

King Jameson moves to help his queen. Meanwhile, King Kai steps forward. "Stop this, Lilliana. You are being ridiculous."

She goes to attack him, too. It's powerful enough to kill him. Her little brother steps in and deflects it back at me, though. "You monster! What have you done to my sister?"

She bombards him with spirit bombs in my defense. "You spoiled brat! He didn't have to *do* anything. After the way they stifled me, all he had to do was not force me into a box!"

Callian glares at her. "Sister, what have you become?"

She howls a laugh. "I'm not your fucking sister, Callian. You are nothing but a hinderance to the life I've chosen for myself."

The iciness of her tone sends chills down my spine. It's hard to imagine what it's doing to them. Things are about to get intense. I'm already doubting my decision not to bring any men with us. Perhaps I should have at least brought Pythias. Protecting her will be no easy feat if we're outnumbered this much. I had planned to freak them out some, let them know we were coming so they wouldn't be able to find their feet again before I launched a full-scale attack.

It's too late for that, though. Before I can rein Seshen in, she's in all-out battle with the four of them and I have no choice but to step in and help her. I think fast on the strategy front. We're both strong. One-on-one, none of them would stand a chance, but we can't fight them all by ourselves. I need to change their focus, so I set my eyes on the civilian population while they're focused on her. Then I light my Helfire and let the flames consume them. That forces Callian and Jameson away because their water is the only thing that offers a chance to those burning. Helfire isn't as easy to douse as normal flames. Water, infused with angelic power, is much more likely to save them than if they ran into the ocean.

Knowing they don't stand a chance, King Kai and Queen Josella have no choice but to stand down. Otherwise, they risk dying and undercutting Oceanica's chances of winning in the long term. I put that hesitation to use and stop Lilly. "Seshen, we can't do this alone. Stand down, I promise you'll get your revenge, as will I, but not like this. We are just two people. They are four, not to mention their army is here, ours is not. Our time will come soon, but for today, we've accomplished our goal. We've stolen their hope of getting you back. They're off kilter and won't be able to strategize as well as we will in the war to come. We've thwarted their defenses on every front."

She sighs, knowing I'm right. "Fine, let's go."

We turn to leave, but before we can, Queen Josella comes out. "Wait!" Her voice sounds so weak and desperate. "Wait, Lilly. Don't do this."

Seshen turns around once more, looking at the woman she once revered. Callian joins the queen at her side, ever the loyal son. The sight of it leaves a bitter taste in my mouth as I recall my mother's death and how I could not stand at her side to protect her. It makes me hate these people even more. Lilly replies to her. "I am not doing this, mother. You did this to us. To me, to Oceanica, to the alliance, to our family, and to Michael, Johanna, Malachi, and Tendu. Every drop of this is your doing."

She watches as her words break her mother's heart. The queen is too emotional to defend herself, so her son speaks on her behalf. "That isn't fair, Lilly, and you know it isn't."

Lilly shakes her head. "I'm more concerned with truth than fairness these days, Cal."

THE FATE OF ANGELS AND DEMONS

***

I haul Lilly to the bedroom, foregoing telling others about our victory. They'll find out at some

point. Right now, I need her. I need the blackhearted queen I saw today. That display of hers enticed me. I'm going to drink from her like a soul in Hel being given his first sip in eons. I chuckle a bit at the thought. *Perhaps I can make Seshen squirt so much that she'll dehydrate as severely as that soul.*

I toss Lilly onto the bed, and she laughs like some sort of maniac at my urgency and desperation. Then I drop my knees to the floor and wait. That seems to settle her laughter, replacing it with intrigue she watches me bow to her. A cruel smirk twists her features, amusement sparked by the realization that her power over me is infallible.

She seems to enjoy just watching me for a moment before she yanks my head back by my hair, forcing eye contact. I can't be sure whether it's the force she uses or those stunning purple eyes of hers that cause me to gasp. "You want me to ruin you? You want me to take this monstrous demon and make him my little bitch boy?"

I quiver as arousal courses through my body, causing my cock to stiffen. "Yes, my queen. Make this vile little demon boy yours."

She pulls me to my feet and pushes my face down into the bed. On instinct, I push my rear out, offering it for her pleasure. Her grip as she feels it is nothing to sneeze at. I only wish my clothes were off so I could feel it skin to skin. Turning my head to the side so I can speak, I plead with her. "Please, Queen. Please. Let me strip for you."

Her hand comes hurling down on my ass so hard that I yelp. "I will order you to remove your clothing when I am ready."

She spanks me again, and again, and again, until I'm nothing more than a whimpering, submissive mess. My cock strains against my pants painfully as I sob. This is so fucking sexy. My Seshen knows exactly how to tame her tyrant. When she releases me, she barks the order I've been so eager for. "Strip, so I can put that worthless hole of yours to use."

I point at the trunk at the foot of my bed, so she knows where the piece is that I found just for her. I strip my tunic off, followed by every other scrap of clothing I have on. She strips as well, then attached the strap-on to herself. At first, I bend over again, but she stops me. "No, no. I want another position."

She lays back on the bed, then pats her hips. "Come ride on your queen's cock."

Excitement courses through me as I straddle her, aligning the tip of the strap-on with the rim of my asshole. She looks at me. "Do you want me to prep you first?"

I shake my head. "No."

I won't deny that I'm nervous about taking it without lubrication of any kind, but I want to. Something about her penetrating me and stretching me to my limits without lubrication appeals to me. It sounds like it's the most delightful morsel of pain a man could ask for, a delicacy only I will ever experience. With that, I push myself down until the tip breaks past my rim. I take a moment to adjust before taking another inch. My breathing becomes labored as I adjust to that one. It hurts like Hel, but in the best way ever. I whimper. "Do it."

She doesn't hesitate before she thrusts her hips up, ramming the other eight inches in, making for ten total. A cry tears through me as her daunting ten becomes buried inside me. Tears gather at the corner of my eyes, and she stops to check on me. "Are you still okay, or do you want to try again with lubrication?"

I understand why she feels concerned, but I wouldn't give this feeling up for anything. "No!" I beg, "No, please don't stop. I need it, Queen, I need more."

She nods. "Anything for you, my vile little beast. Go ahead, now. Use my cock to fuck yourself like the little whore you are."

I gulp, but I obey. At first, my movements are slow. I rise straight up to the tip and inch my way back down as I adjust to the size. Lustful moans leak from me as I pick up my pace. I find my hands cupping my muscular pectorals as if they are breasts. In part, I do it because it feels sexy, but also in part because it feels good. I relish in the way she moans as the strap-on stimulates her clit. "That's right, baby. You're doing so good. Ride that dick.

Show me what an obedient little bitch the demon king is."

It isn't long before she's thrusting upwards to meet me as I bounce on her. Each time she hits my prostate, I feel myself getting closer. I ride harder and her thrusts keep up with my increased pace. My dick bounces around even though it's harder than it's ever been. I try to warn her, but I end up too breathless to do so. "I'm gonna..."

It's too late. Seed pumps out of my cock onto her perfect, plump breasts as we orgasm together. Her sweet juices drench the bed until it spreads beneath my feet, leaving our mattress soaked in her scent. My legs shake as I lift myself up, removing the strap-on from my ass and collapsing down next to her. I rest my head on her chest, ignoring the cum all over it as it covers my cheek. She welcomes me into her arms. "Are you alright?"

"That was amazing." I reply.

"That's true," she says, "but that's not what I'm asking."

I can't help the smile that rises on my face. "Yes, Seshen, I'm alright. I just need to be in your arms for a bit while I recover."

She nods, holding my body against hers, rubbing my back. "I love you, Michael."

"I love you, too, Seshen. More than anything."

We lie there for about thirty minutes before we get up to clean ourselves. While we head to wash up, I order some servant to switch out the mattress so that one can get cleaned.

THE ART OF DECEPTION

CALLIAN

In the aftermath of Lilly and Michael's attack, I go around tending the injured. As I do, I hear cries coming from underneath some of the rubble. Someone got trapped down there. I call for help, knowing Dad Kai can move it quicker than I can. "Dad Kai! Help! There's someone trapped beneath all this!"

He's quick to respond, using the ground magic granted to him by his runes to manipulate the rubble out of the way so I can grab whoever lies beneath and get them to safety. Once he does, I grab the woman and get clear of the site so he can lower the pieces without worry. I waste no time before healing her crushed limbs, not wanting the injury to set before I get to it. "Are you alright, miss?"

It's not until the healing takes hold that the pain subsides enough for her to reply. With tear-stained cheeks, she replies, "I'm fine now. Thank you, Prince Callian."

She seems to be about my age. In Oceanica, most people live with their parents well into their twenties, taking their time to establish their finances before going out on their own, or waiting to be married, if they're nobility. We find this culture works well for our kingdom. Adult life is a big transition, and it works out better for the citizens if they can focus on building one piece at a time. Education, entering the workforce, building financial security, buying their own home, and then standing on their own two feet. "Good. Tell me who your family is. I'll send someone to find them."

"I'm the daughter of Marquis Revel." Her words, though drenched in agony still, remain filled with equal pride. I see why. The Revels are a noble family in Oceanica. It was my grandmother who named them nobility during her and my grandfather's reign, long before he discarded her for treasonous acts. Their family wasn't impacted much by that, though. Most people in Oceanica still think well of them, my family included. She loves her family and takes pride in carrying the Revel name. I like that in a woman. For all my complaints regarding my family, deep down, I feel unwavering love and loyalty toward them. Even now, with Lilly having betrayed us, it has changed nothing for me. I love her just as much as I did the day before she left. My wish is for her to come home. Should Michael be the one to kill me instead of I him, I will die hoping her grief will open her eyes and lead her to reunite with our parents and loved ones.

"I'll find him." The words are a whispered promise before I take off, knowing she'll be safe where she is in the meantime.

I scour the crowds of gawking citizens looking for a man who appears to be a marquis. Most nobles wear an insignia that helps people to identify them. Since noble titles in Oceanica come with a responsibility to the citizens, they do it so civilian populations recognize them and approach them for help when needed. From my years of study, I've memorized each of the insignias. The marquis' insignia is silver with the crest of the person's family. Dukes use gold and the royal family doesn't use them because we have crowns for that. Besides, our kingdom knows us by our faces since we are active in the community.

After searching for forty-five minutes, I come across a man with a silver insignia, crying. When he sees me approach, he sobs, throwing himself to the ground and begging for aid. "Please, help me, sire. I cannot find my daughter!"

I kneel, then lift his chin with a finger. "Your name, sir?"

"Marquis Revel, sire. My daughter's name is Mianora Revel."

Mianora... That's her name. "Come with me, sir. I know where your daughter is."

He hugs me in a moment of glee upon hearing my words. On any other day, it'd be wildly inappropriate to act so familiar with a royal, but today, I understand. The fear a father must feel upon realizing his beloved daughter is missing must be terrifying. I hug him back, reassuring him. "She's safe. Do not worry. I saw to it myself."

His sobs fade. "Thank you, sire."

I lead him to Mianora, who still rests where I left her. He runs to her side the moment he spots her. "Oh, my darling girl. I'm so glad you're okay."

The girl clings to her father. I make a point not to linger, not wanting them to feel indebted to praise me for my actions during their reunion. After retreating, I meet back up with my family and we walk home together. Right now, being with them feels important. Tomorrow, though, I hope to find time to check on Mianora again. She experienced trauma today and I want to be there for her in some small way, even if it's just to let her know I care enough to ask.

Experience has taught me an action that small can make a profound impact on the way someone's mind recovers after thinking their life was going to end. That's why following up seems important to me. I don't want to be the person who doesn't ask or doesn't think about it. Everyone deserves the respect of knowing people care about how trauma affects them. As a royal, I'd hate for my people to think I would ignore such a thing. As a man, though, I just don't want to be that guy who invalidates a woman that way. It'd be cold never to check on her again, so I will tomorrow.

Now, though, I have to attend briefing they have for me. I'm exhausted as I wander into the throne room to listen to it. Not so much physically, I'm more durable than that. It's the mental fatigue that weighs on me. As I listen to the briefing, it's one hit after another. Lilly has gone off the rails. It's worse than I imagined. For the first time, I wonder if she's too far gone. The thought alone breaks my heart. I didn't want it to come to this. I wanted to save my sister. It takes everything in me to fight back the tears. Every deed of evil they name, I feel just as responsible for it as I consider her to be. Seeing her in this light makes it feel like I'm every bit the villain she's become because I'm the one failing to stop it. Doesn't that make me the bad guy, too?

I retreat to my room right after the briefing, not wanting to give anyone time to inquire about my thoughts any further. If someone were to pry, I'm not sure I could hold it together. It's all just too much happening too fast. Every time I turn around, it feels like there's some new tragedy waiting for me. My mind begs me to stop blaming myself for it all, but that doesn't stop my heart from making me. I try to compartmentalize emotions from logical thoughts. After a while, though, I can no longer tell the difference between the two. No matter how much I grow, my inner turmoil always seems to bite me in the ass.

It shouldn't be surprising that I don't sleep well. Why would I sleep well, given the mental Hel I'm enduring? Depression is a bitch, especially when coupled with anxiety. I'll never understand its uncanny ability to make one feel simultaneously exhausted and wired.

The next morning, I head off toward the Revel estate early, since I'd given up on sleep by that point. I'm hoping Mianora's father wouldn't mind me stopping by to check on her. When I approach the get to the house, I'm met by a guard at the entryway. They recognize me and give me passage. He also orders a maid to inform the Marquis about my arrival. Minutes pass before he makes his way to the front of his large estate to welcome me. "Prince Callian, how may I help you this fine morning?"

I chuckle some at his formality. "No need. I merely came by to see how Mianora is doing after yesterday. May I speak with her?"

"Of course," he replies. "I think she'd like that. She's in her bed chamber recovering. Do you mind waiting for us to help her out? Your healing was powerful, but she still has some pain, you see."

I nod. "That makes sense. Angel stitching only repairs the damage and shortens the overall duration of the pain. I hate to cause the young lady any additional distress. Would you be comfortable with me entering her bed chamber under your supervision? It seems kinder than asking her to move and I don't mind you being present. I understand the need to protect one's daughter from men. Status of that man aside, it can be dangerous. I may not be a father, but I can see the need as clear as day."

He smiles, appreciating my politeness and understanding. "That sounds acceptable to me. Thank you for not taking offense to my caution around the matter."

I give him a reassuring look before he leads me to her room. He gives the door a light tap before cracking it open. "Sweetheart, someone is here to see you. Can we come in?"

She sounds groggy when she answers. "Yes, Papa. Come in."

I enter the room behind Marquis Revel to find Mianora laying beneath a pink blanket. She jerks upright when she sees me, trying to stand so she can curtsy. The movement sends a pain shooting through her and she cries out. I rush over to help her lie back down. "No, no, no. Don't you worry about such silliness right now. I just came to see how you were. Cause yourself no discomfort on my account."

Once the pain subsides again, she answers. "I'm well, thank you, Prince Callian. As you can see, movement is still challenging, but thanks to you, I will recover in time."

Her point is fair. She would have died or at least lived as a paralyzed woman if I wasn't there. I'm glad I could do that much for her, but I still hate to see her in such pain. I'd hate seeing anyone in such pain, but in her case, I find it even more disturbing. Such beauty should never endure such agony as this. "It's no trouble. I'm glad that my actions spared you the worst, and I hope your recovery is swift. It will be difficult to rest at night knowing your pain."

She smiles. "Pain that is lessened by your presence, sire."

The Marquis adds, "Perhaps after your recovery, Prince Callian will take you on a promenade to celebrate?"

I cut my eyes at him, but don't comment on the power grab. His care for his daughter seems to be sincere, but what better way to keep her safe than cornering the kind-hearted prince into courting her? Two birds; one stone, right? Increasing the family's status while also ensuring his daughter has a prospect that will treat her well and protect her. I don't like it one bit, but it isn't in Mianora's best interest for me to comment on it, so I let it go. The hope in her eyes gives me little choice in the matter, anyway. "Yes, a promenade sounds brilliant. I'd like nothing more than to give you a tour of the royal gardens in this season. The blossoms are so vibrant."

She wastes no time agreeing. "Yes! I'd love to promenade with you, sire. Looking forward to it will surely aid in my speedy recovery."

"Very well then. Send a messenger when you recover, and we will find a time. For now, you need rest. I should go; Commander Luca is expecting me soon."

We say our goodbyes and I head out to meet Luca at the barracks. Something about this promenade with Mianora gives me a bad feeling, but I can't go back on my word now. I don't think I have the strength to put heartbreak into those glittering emerald eyes of hers.

I arrive at the barracks in the nick of time. Promptly, the commander and I set out to repair and reinforce our barriers. Although, they are unlikely to do us much good, as Lilly showed us, none of us can keep her out if she wants in. Things are looking worse by the day and I'm worried about the outcome of this war. My life is neither here nor there. If I thought he'd stop at killing me, I'd let him. That's the beginning of his plans, though, not the end. I must fight. If only I saw a way to do so.

Of all the ways I've failed so far, I fear I have yet to fail in the way mattering most. My confidence is waning. At this rate, I'm even more probable to get tripped up by indecisiveness. That's a danger of a far more threatening level than the blunders I've stumbled into thus far. An indecisive leader may as well condemn those that follow him before the fighting even begins. I'm not sure why so many still believe in me after all this. Against my wishes and understanding, they place more and more faith in me. It feels more like a burden than I ever imagined it could. I understand now what Mom and Dads mean when they speak of the weight of the crown. It's heavier than any singular man can carry, even if that man is an angel.

Lilly

Back in Tendu, Pythias pulls us aside to tell us of something that has occurred in our absence. I suppose they saw an opportunity they didn't want to let slide and activated it before telling us. As long as it's not stupid, I don't think Michael will mind that part. It's well within Pythias' authority as a general to activate a plot without the king's consent when time is of the essence.

Michael stands with me, ready to hear what he has to say. "Tell me."

Pythias holds up a letter. "We got word that a noble in Oceanica has turned, a Marquis, to be more specific. He has a daughter, and he thinks he's in the position to get her close to Prince Callian."

Michael arches his eyebrow, suspicion marring the lines of his face. "And what, pray tell, does this Marquis want for his newfound fealty?"

Pythias shrugs. "Nothing we can't afford, sire. He asks that we spare the two of them if they feed us information. He thinks Oceanica is bound to lose this war. It's a barter to save himself and his daughter. I sent a preliminary acceptance to him because I thought you'd find the life of one marquis, who has made it clear he's a coward, and his daughter, a small price to pay for such intimate intelligence."

Michael looks at me as if he wants my opinion before answering. I answer his look with a nod, confirming that

I think this sounds solid. He looks at Pythias and replies, "You're right. This is good. Of course, we'll evaluate his information for ourselves as it's received to ensure its accuracy, but so long as we aren't being played for fools, this is acceptable."

Pythias seems relieved at Michael's acceptance of his plan. I suppose Michael is someone most find intimidating, even those he likes who like him in return hold a minimal level of fear toward him. This is the first time it's dawning on me, but I might be the only person in his life that feels no fear in his presence. I try to imagine the many ways one's self-image would be impacted by such reactions to their existence. The loneliness must be worse than any torture I've ever known him to inflict. Do people realize what they're doing to him? Or are they just blind to it because why would the demon king of Tendu ever have feelings? I'm not sure which answer is worse. Neither option settles right with me.

After he dismisses Pythias, Michael turns to me with a mischievous smile plastered on his face. "Come on, there's somewhere I want to take you."

He doesn't wait for my answer before grabbing my wrist and taking off. We run through the palace as our laughter rings throughout it. We make our way down and down until we are well below sea level. When we hit the lowest point of the palace, Michael points me toward a tunnel, meticulously carved and well lit. I'm confused about why he's leading me down here. "Where are we going?"

I admire his excitement as he answers. "You'll see. You're going to love it, I promise, Seshen."

We continue on for several minutes before emerging into a cavern made up of igneous rocks and I realize where we are. "My love, did you just bring me inside of a volcano?"

He laughs. "Yes, I did, Seshen. No need to worry, you're safe. My magic would allow me to hold back the lava flow if it erupted. I wouldn't risk your life for any adventure."

He takes my hand and leads me deeper inside. Once it comes into full view, I realize what we're standing on is the outer ring of a pool of lava. We take a seat near the edge of the magma, watching as it churns and bubbles. I'm tempted to touch it for whatever reason. Often, my curiosity overrides my brain function and urges me to do something stupid. I rarely act on such impulses, though.

I can't help falling in love with the sight of this. It's amazing. There's something hypnotizing about the way it looks. So beautiful, yet so deadly. Michael's bottom lip pokes out. "I wish you could swim in it with me."

I raise an eyebrow. "You wish I could swim in lava? Why did I not know you could swim in lava?"

He seems baffled. "Of course I can. I'm a demon. That's obvious."

I giggle. "No. I have never assumed that anyone could swim in lava."

He laughs, nudging me. "Wanna see?"

"Sure, I guess. Consider me intrigued."

I watch as he strips. His tunic is the first to go, exposing his sculpted muscular physique and runic markings. I stare at his pecs, probably looking as if I want to devour him. My eyes trace every hard line of his body until they reach the top of his breeches as he frees himself from them. His undergarments come off, too. I suppose that makes sense. Even if he's impervious to the lava, I doubt his tailors have the means to make his clothing so. Still, the sight of him is a marvel. I'd say he should be on display for all to bear witness to his beauty, but I don't want anyone else looking at him.

He dives in, careful to do it far enough that I won't get splashed. A few moments later, he rises back to the surface, laughing like a child going swimming for the first time. "So, what? Does it just feel like water to you?"

He shakes his head as he swims to the edge, crossing his arms on the ledge and resting his chin on top of them. "No, I wouldn't say that. It's different from water. Better, if you ask me. It's the perfect temperature for me. It's thicker, too. Kind of gooey. Perhaps about the texture of a thick honey."

My temptation to jump in there alongside him triples when I hear his description. I have to keep reminding myself that I'm not a demon and will die if I dive into a pool of lava. "Okay. Come on, my love. Get out of there. Come back up here and be with me so I don't lose my impulse control and dive in there."

He barks a laugh. "As you wish, Seshen."

I watch as he moves away from me before coming up. His biceps tense as he pushes himself up onto the ledge. I'm salivating like some feral beast as he stands, red hot magma dripping down his toned frame slow enough to hypnotize me. My tongue darts out of my mouth, running back and forth across my lower lip. "Careful, Seshen. If you keep looking at me that way, me and this lava will be all over you."

He says that as if it's supposed to be a deterrent. My voice sounds so seductive that I don't even recognize it. "Can't have that now, can we?"

The lava cooling on his body hardens bit by bit. I sense it as he uses his magic to keep it hot enough to drip, not wanting to deal with it attaching itself to him as rocks. He growls, leaning over me with enough caution to stop it from dripping on me. I know he doesn't want to burn me, but Hel, if some part of me doesn't wish he would. He's so damn sexy like this. It doesn't help at all when I notice the hot earthy liquid coats his erect cock as well. I sense him playing with his magic for a moment. It takes a minute to realize what he's doing. He's trying to find a point in which the lava is cool enough for me to touch, but still liquid. "Touch it, just with the tip of your finger. See if this works."

I do as he says, carefully dipping my fingertip into the lava coating his body. It's hot, for sure, but not hot enough to cause injury. It's slightly hotter than candle wax, tolerable to touch. I suppose that the lava should solidify at this temperature. It seems Michael's magic is more complex than I realized. He's not just controlling its temperature; he's also controlling the point at which it changes states. That's amazing and so fucking hot. "It feels nice. Can you hold that?"

He smirks. "Would I be your demon king if I couldn't?"

I wrap my hand around his balls, mushing around the lava covering the plump berries. "I don't suppose you would be."

He groans in pleasure, embracing the feeling of me using the warm liquid to tease him. With my grip firm on his sack, the free one moves to get his shaft in my hand. I pump it slowly, letting the lava splatter on my breasts, which peek out from beneath my half open miko. Michael's hips bulk, thrusting into my grip as he lets out several husky moans. I keep going, pumping his sculpted shaft in a perfect rhythm, pulling him closer and closer to the edge. "Ah, fuck! Seshen! I'm gonna—"

Then, just before he reaches his climax, I stop and squeeze the tip between my fingertips, robbing him of his orgasm. He pants and whimpers, pleading with me to start up again, but I wait until the waves of pleasure subside entirely. When I decide to start again, I don't go straight back into pumping him. I take my time teasing his taint with a finger dripping in lava. His knees wobble as his desperate sounds echo through the volcanic cavern. By the time I take hold of his dick again, he's crazed. I have to move slowly to keep him from ejaculating too quickly. I watch him try desperately to refrain. It's so pleasurable seeing him torture himself for my amusement.

Increasing my speed in small, measured increments, I work him back to the edge. He's in absolute agony when I once again ruin his orgasm. "Please! Please, Queen. It hurts so bad, like I'm going to explode. I'll do anything, just please let me cum."

Those sweet cries of his make me even more reluctant to give him what he wants, but he's earned it. After enjoying the sight of him begging for a few moments longer, I start up again, rubbing him from base to tip. "You're ready to cum for me, baby?"

"Yes." His voice is breathless and drenched in submission. "Yes, my queen. I'm ready to cum for you."

I pump harder, drawing him to the edge of orgasm once more. This time, though, I put my mouth to his tip and let him spill his enormous load into it. I hold it in my mouth as I rise to my feet. Swiping a finger beneath his chin, I beckon him closer. We exchange his cum between our mouths in a passionate kiss. He moans when he tastes himself on me. I love it.

THE SECRET TO SECRETS

MIANORA

The secret to keeping a secret is not telling anyone. If you share a secret, if you get too comfortable, they become like wildfire spreading to any and everyone that will spare the time to hear them. My secret is that the injuries Prince Callian saved me from were a setup to help me get close to him. A setup intended to disarm him and get him to tell me his secrets. Now, I am healed from them, and as agreed, he takes me on a promenade through the royal gardens. I can't deny that I admire the grand design, but to me, the awe is but another tool I can use.

I play at being innocent and taken by them, letting him be the gentleman to show me things I thought I'd never see. That look on his face tells me everything I need to know. He will fall hard and fast for me, consumed by my presence as I cast myself in the role of the innocent siren accidentally luring men to their deaths... Or just manipulating information out of them, in my case. I skip toward him with a handful of lilies I plucked, hoping the flower provokes some kind of visible response about his sister, the kind that might make it possible for me to ask questions about her, and subjects connected to her, like the war. It's a simple trick, but one I'm sure will be effective.

An uncomfortable smile rises from him, as if he's trying to be polite, but isn't happy at all. "Uh, thank you, Mianora. They're gorgeous and this is very sweet of you, but..."

I force my eyes to widen as if the realization just hit. "Oh my, I am so sorry, Prince Callian. I forgot. They were there, and they were just so pretty. I didn't even think about her."

"No, it's alright. I suppose I can't avoid lilies forever. They are pretty. Thank you for the kind gesture."

I give him the lilies. He's so polite. Anyone would have understood if he rejected them. It's sort of annoying that he'd make himself so uncomfortable for no reason. It makes my job easier, though, so I shouldn't complain. "Thank you for your patience. It was silly of me. It's sweet of you to accept them. Maybe I can listen to you? I know there must be many things you're feeling as you traverse our current political climate. Please vent to me. It may help."

He's hesitant for a moment, but then he talks. It doesn't seem like he means to. From what I can tell, it's like he can't hold it back. Perhaps I chose my moment even more ideally than I believed. He's so overwhelmed and has held back so much, the information I want just spills from him as he can no longer refrain from boiling over. The more he talks, the more he wants to keep talking. Soon, he's spilling out information I wouldn't trust even the most qualified with. How simple are men to be disarmed with such ease? A pretty face and a half-hearted act are all it takes for them to pour their souls out. Yet, they call women emotional.

As he vents, he falls deeper and deeper. I continue to plot his demise even while he lays in my lap crying. I will not let my father down by falling for this prince. After he's calmed, I head home, promising to see him again another time. It's nothing more than another lie, though. Tonight, when I write to Tendu, informing them of all I've learned, I'll be making myself a traitor. Thus, my father and I need to disappear. There's no way Callian won't figure out it was me who betrayed him once Tendu uses the information, which I'm confident they will do right away.

I update my father before writing the letter to Tendu. He had mentioned in passing that General Pythias gave specific instructions to ensure the sanctity of information, as well as the proper level of confidentiality to protect us all. I want to make sure I get it right, so I have him talk me through it.

"*To my venomous friend, a python to the west.*

I'm writing to inform you that our mutual distaste for the mountainous east is still treacherous as ever. Traversing the rocky front, it continues to taunt us as the ocean rams against its base. I am happy to say my father has prepared plans for our return home in two weeks' time. Please see that our home remains well kept until then.

Sincerely,

Your Devilish Best Friend, a Siren to the East."

I add our family seal to the page itself, but leave the envelope unmarked before giving it to my father to send by whatever nefarious means they've developed that requires no information. He heads off late into the night to send it. Meanwhile, I'm home, alone. I stay up packing and preparing for our escape. I hope General Pythias can keep his end of this bargain. Some part of me doubts it, though. I suppose if his word is good enough for my father; I'll have to accept it. It just seems unlikely. How could Tendu ever trust us if we offered to betray Oceanica so willingly?

It makes no sense to me, but I choose not to overthink it. I trust my father's judgement and there may be more to the story than I realize. If I had to guess, he only told me the bare minimum in case something went wrong. He's protecting me, as any good parent would. It wouldn't bother me so much if I weren't the type of person who's resistant to change. I've never liked it. It feels like being thrown off a cliff then having everyone around me act confused about why it scared me. It's unreasonable. I understand that there are people out there who cope with it better than I do, but from my experience, change is always for the worse.

Pythias

Within days of setting up this arrangement with the Revel's, I receive a letter from Mianora Revel, the daughter of the Marquis. I read it without delay. The information she found shocks me. The Alacrians are still in communication with Prince Callian. They still have an ally. We're in trouble and must act now.

I take off, running through the palace in search of my king and the lovely Lilly. I find them in their shared chamber and burst in announced. Lilly sits back on the bed with a seshen in her hair and the king's arm around her. Looking away, I speak. "My king, urgent news from the spy in Oceanica."

Without looking, I sense the irritation in his answer. I know he doesn't like his time with her interrupted, but it is urgent. As luck would have it, they're clothed. "What is it, Pythias?"

"Sire, I received word that the Alacrians have not abandoned Oceanica. We are short on time to act if we want to face them without allies."

The king's irritation is replaced with fury when he hears my explanation.

"Your orders, sire?" I ask, trying to gauge his reaction better because I'm not sure if he's mad at me, or the situation itself.

He looks at Lilly before answering. "From this moment forward, we are at war. Full scale. No more playing around or toying with them. At dawn, we crush them."

I gulp, knowing how serious he is. "As you wish, sire. I will spread the order and prepare our warriors."

My king nods, rising from beneath his sheets. "Go ahead." He waves me off, then looks to his future queen. "Come, Seshen. We must prepare ourselves for battle as well."

I leave, relief filling my chest when I realize he's not blaming me for this. It seems a strange fear, but many are in the habit of killing the messenger. My king just seems grateful for the intelligence. He's pissed, no doubt about that. Not at me, though, just at the fact that he must now act sooner than he intended. It doesn't affect our original plans by much. We will still win; it's a mild inconvenience at best. Although, if left to fester, it may have become more serious. He's making the right move by taking early action. I must say, I am proud of our young king. I believe his mother would be too. He's proven competent.

Lilly

After Pythias shuts the door, I rise from beneath the sheets. Now that it's decided that we'll attack at dawn, we have things to do beforehand. The generals will prep the troops plenty. We must, however, get word to those we have posted on other islands. They need to tighten up and prepare to squash any attempted rebellions because we won't be able to send them help if they lose control. We also need to be sure that they remain tight-lipped. We don't want anyone hearing war updates we don't intend. It creates a weakness that would be difficult to re-fortify.

As we go through the process of getting everything in place, the reality of things settles into my mind. By this time tomorrow, my entire family will be dead, if we succeed, which I'm sure we will. I'll also have killed Callian with my own two hands. I should feel sad, or something along those lines, but I don't. Instead, there's nothing but anticipation coursing through my veins as the prospect of such violence and bloodshed presents itself. I enjoy the feeling without remorse, embraced my whole self.

This feels like my true self in ways the nice Lilly never understood. This sadistic queen I've become is so free and I love it. I'm no longer bound by duty or trauma, and I never will be again. It's the most exciting, empowering, and extraordinary thing I've ever experienced. Nothing could make me go back to the girl I once was now that I've met the woman I can be. If the world doesn't like it, I'm sure the demon at my side will burn it down just for my entertainment. I can almost imagine myself cackling as I watched it turn to ash at my feet.

THE FATE OF ANGELS AND DEMONS

The image conjured in my mind pleases me more than any sane person would admit to. What a relief it is to no longer be sane. Sanity is mere conformity to an illusion of a shared reality that so few fit into at their core. If my choices are acceptance via obedience or freedom via craze, the latter will always be my choice. It's a choice that has proven to be correct.

Michael takes me into his firm arms, holding me fast against his chest as we finish our preparations. "No matter what, you stay close to me tomorrow, understood?"

I hug him back. "Yes, my love. I'll be with you."

"Seshen..." The nickname I've become so fond of comes out breathy and desperate. He's scared, not of battle, but of losing me to it. I share this fear; it's challenging, facing the prospect of losing him in battle. I hate the way it makes my heart clench up and my lungs constrict, as if I could die of nothing more than losing him. My mother has never made more sense to me than she does right now. I understand now why she couldn't let it go when Kai and Cal died. I also understand why Johanna couldn't when Malachi got taken from her, and why Michael can't now. It's funny when you think about it. The thing that once brought us all together is now reason to kill each other. Love. Love is controlling all of us and we are doing nothing but abiding by its whims. It controls us like puppets, and we submit to it so willingly. It's beautiful and disturbing in equal measure. If there's one thing I think we could all agree on, it's that no matter how it treats us, we wouldn't have it any other way.

The suffering of war is always worth it when the reward of winning it is the privilege of being in the arms of that person, or persons, whom you love more than any other. Knowing that, I know what reassurance my love needs. "Michael, I will be with you, win or lose. We will either win together or die together, because I cannot live a day without you in my life now that I know what it is to have you in it."

He smiles, brushing my hair out of my face some before cupping my cheek. "That fire of yours, Seshen. You are awesome. I'm lucky to have you in my life and at my side."

With that, we enjoyed our last night together in peace before unleashing Hel upon Oceanica in the morning. It was a night of bittersweet cuddling and fucking, trying to get it all in before the war began. As confident as we are that we'll win, there's no such thing as a guarantee that someone will survive a war.

In the early hours of the morning, we wake before the sunrises, hoping to beat it to Oceanica. Attacking them while they are sleeping will give us a head start before we have to face the powerhouses among them. For the sake of transporting vast numbers of troops, we take a battleship to their shores, ready to devastate them. The warriors in our command are in good spirits; energetic and prepared. We've taken enough victories up to this point that they feel confident. The morale they hold will serve them well today as they battle against a kingdom that must already feel boxed in, as if they are waiting to be slaughtered. The instability we've caused, and consistent thwarting of their plans, has left their people and their military uneasy. They know now that they cannot outwit us. Callian, though he shows potential, is not yet an experienced strategist. They'd have had much better luck if my parents hadn't put such faith in him.

As we sail, we take a few more hours of rest, but wake when we enter Oceanic waters. For all our planning, Michael still held concerns about them being alerted to our presence. Angelic and spiritual security spells can be tricky and hard to spot. Michael and I would recognize them much easier than the average man under our command. It takes years of special training to recognize such things, and even then, it's not an exact science. There are plenty of things even he and I may miss, but us being awake and scanning for anything that might alert Oceanica to our approach at least ensures that most possibilities get nullified. In that way, Michael's right to make this call.

The ship inches closer to their shores as we stand at the bow, nullifying anything suspicious before the boat touches it. Mom and I have a similar power type, so I just take control of them and disarm them the way she would as their maker. Michael's methods are much less discrete than my own. His demonic power essentially just causes the traps to malfunction to the point of explosion. Mine acts more like a true form of nullification. "Babe, stop. You blowing things up will draw attention. Just let me do it."

He smirks. "Okay, Seshen. Sorry, I didn't want you doing all the work."

I giggle just light enough for him to hear it. "I'm sure there will be plenty to do during the actual war, beloved."

He moves behind me, wrapping his arms around my waist and resting his chin on my shoulder. "Go ahead, gorgeous."

I continue nullifying Oceanica's defenses as he holds me. It's amazing how relaxed I am with his arms around me. I think his touch could unwind me, even in the worst situations imaginable. It's impossible to be stressed when he's near because I know nothing could happen to me. He'd never allow that. I believe that even if I were to face probable death in this war, he'd sooner use his own body as a shield than let me take the hit. It's who he is at his core. Most people may see a tyrant, a king, or a demon, but not me. I see nothing more than a loving man willing to do anything to protect the woman who matters most to him. If he has any flaws at all, I am blind to their existence because I see none.

When we arrive on the shores of Oceanica, several posted guards spot us. We slaughter them before they can sound any alarms. We whisper orders to the troops, having them spread out across the island. Our warning for them to stay as quiet as possible is strong. Our plan is to get everyone in position, then attack several targets at once. We hope it'll disorient the royals and make them scatter to different locations so we and our people can face them in more ideal circumstances.

Pythias takes his people and heads for the far side of the island. Michael and I head to the Revel estate. An attack here will lure Callian. Of course, he won't know that the Revel's will be on the ship safe and sound when he arrives. Another general takes some men to the barracks run by Commander Luca. I'm sure he and Callian have been working together, and I don't want him trying to come to Callian's aid. Then, a unit deploys to this shore and another to the village. This way, Dad Kai and Dad Jameson will have to split up to tackle them.

We wait for a long while, giving each unit plenty of time to maneuver to their assigned places undetected. They have orders to kill anyone who spots them in silence. We need to buy as much time as possible. No attacks will begin until the sun is on the horizon. Any earlier and we risk troops not being in place. The risk, though, is that waiting so long makes it difficult to remain undetected. Hiding so many men is no easy feat. Still, our well-trained generals should be up to the task.

Michael and I sit together under a tree. I use my power to give us as much cover as possible. I can't create illusions, per se, but I can distort my surroundings enough to hide myself and one other person. Spiritual power is just diluted light energy, so I essentially bend the light in a way that makes us difficult to see. Lucky for us, it doesn't take much light, so the glow of the stars is plenty enough to control. It seems like such a small thing, but its impact is significant. The power's usefulness is apparent in clandestine moments such as this.

Together, he and I lie in each other's arms, awaiting our moment. The anticipation of battle has us antsy, but we lose ourselves in the embrace and put off the excitement. As the hours pass, he and I wait and watch. No sign that our men have failed becomes visible. "Nothing" is a good sign right now. I suspect if any of them got into a situation they couldn't get out of, we'd see fire somewhere.

As the sun peaks over the horizon, Michael and I move into position. I stand back, letting Michael handle the opening salvo of battle himself. He eyes the size of the estate to get an idea of how big the flames will have to be to obliterate it. Meanwhile, Mianora and Marquis Revel make their way out. I direct them to the ship, threatening to kill them both if they draw attention to themselves. They quickly leave in silence, then Michael forms a fireball from his runic magic. It starts off small, but morphs in the blink of an eye, becoming massive enough to take out the entire estate, which I estimate is about fifty acres of land. He launches it at the main house, and we watch as it burns. Soon after, all our targets light up in flames.

NEAR DEATH

CALLIAN

I wake to the sounds of war and terror. Confusion and dread both knot in my stomach as I approach the window to see the havoc being reaped across my beloved Oceanica. Slow realization creeps into the back of my mind. They informed on us. Marquis Revel and Mianora have betrayed us all. Now, the people will suffer for it. How could I have been so stupid? I knew trusting that woman was a bad idea. I saw every sign and yet, I'd been so overwhelmed, and I just couldn't resist talking to someone who was on the outside of all this nonsense.

My emotions overrode my logic, and I failed my people. All that growth I thought I was making seems so irrelevant now. Here's yet another mistake that will be so ingrained in my memory that I'll never risk it again. Trust is a luxury I can no longer afford.

I note the fire burning the Revel estate as the guilt eats at me. It's a signal, one only I could understand. Michael and Lilly are giving me their location. They want to be the ones to fight me. I assume they hope to stop me themselves while the others end up divided across the kingdom, quelling other attacks.

The trap isn't one I mind falling into. I know my parents can handle the rest, but they could never do the one thing I can. If it comes down to it, I have to be the one to kill Lilly. Doing it themselves would destroy them, but not me. I love my sister. That love, however, is far less than that which I hold for this kingdom. I would kill any who sought to harm it, no matter how I felt about them. Steeling my heart against my sister, I throw on some pants and head off to meet her. One look at the estate as I approach is all it takes to see that there will be no survivors.

Michael and Lilly stand together on the ashes. I never glance his way. My eyes remain locked onto my sister's, staring her down in silent communication. They don't walk in my direction, attempting to psyche me out by making me come to them, as if either of them are true rulers. Michael holds his throne because Malachi is gone, not because he is dead. He is no king; a regent at best and an entitled princeling at most. My sister is even worse than he is. She could have been a queen, but she never wanted it. Now, she acts as if she always has. I don't even recognize her anymore.

The screams of the dying echo across my land and that ancient part of me that descends from Rettferd, angel of justice, stirs to life. I don't recognize the booming voice older than time itself as it comes from me. "You have brought suffering to the innocent and tears to the eyes of the blessed. Consider me the consequence of your crimes, for they are many."

My angelic power comes to me all the easier in my rage. The moisture in the island air heeds the call as my runic magic combines with the bloodline's ability in ways that seemed impossible before this moment. My fury will spell their demise. I know this because the look on my sister's face tells me she knows I am more powerful now than I ever have been before.

I make the first move in the fight between us. After having led them to believe I'm too focused on her to attack Michael, it's the perfect time to do the opposite of what they expect. Fast, I swipe a blade of water sharper than any holy sword straight across his body. He's fast, so the cut isn't deep because he'd already backed away some, but it's enough that his chest and stomach drip blood down the rest of him.

"Michael!" Lilly screams his name in panic, wasting no time trying to draw my attacks away from him by hurling her living barrier in my direction. "Your fight is with me, little brother."

The once affectionate phrase now sounds like an insult. While it wounds my soul, it doesn't distract me from avoiding her barrier. White, feathered wings sprout from my back, spanning ten feet. A singular, large beat of them propels me into the sky and out of the range of the barrier. I fly fast overhead, looping up, around, then landing once more behind her. Whispering into her ear, I issue my demand. "Fight me, then, sister."

I try to stab her, but I miss as she turns fast enough to counter the sharpened ice I wield in my right hand, pushing it down and away with her left palm. I raise my left hand in a fist with the white light of my angelic power swirling around it. She meets it head on with a fist of her own, packed with spiritual power. The clash of energies sends us both flying in opposite directions. All the air is knocked out of me when my back slams against the brick wall lining the ruins of the estate. Her state isn't much better when my vision clears enough to see her. Before I get on my feet, Michael hurls himself toward me, Helfire raging around his entire body as his black, feathered wings, equal to mine in size, quicken his movements.

I scream as his furious fire eats away at my flesh but force myself to remain calm enough to call up ice cold water to protect myself. It's not enough. Third-degree burns already cover my body. I activate my angel stitching techniques, trying to heal the dying flesh as I continue fighting. It's improbable that the technique can keep up with the damage at this rate. That unlikelihood confirms itself as I feel more burns searing every inch of my body. Fighting both of them is more difficult for me than I imagined. I need to come up with something fast if I want to survive this. The increased levels of power fueled by my motions aren't closing the gap as much as I'd hoped.

Struggling against Michael, I have to force the strength to push him off of me and get to my feet. It hurts so badly to stand, but I manage. He and Lilly move closer together. Something about the way they move in sync is alarming to me. They aren't communicating out loud, yet they seem to understand each other well enough that they don't need to. I realize they're going to launch a joint attack. I won't be able to defend against that at all. In a half-cocked attempt the prevent it, I shift into calling on just angelic power. I've never favored my bloodline ability over my runic magic, or vice versa. My whole life, I've used them in combination. Now, though, my best chance lies in my bloodline alone. If I stop trying to control both, I should be able to further amplify one.

I lean into it, throwing as much willpower as I can muster in to the light energy. The alignment of the universe shifts as I do. It's as if my ancestors and I are no longer different people of the same line, but one soul in one body. I can feel them all, even Rettferd, who still lives. His voice whispers into my mind. I don't know how I recognize it because I've never met him. Somehow, I do, though. *"We remain, my precious descendant. I cannot promise you won't die here, but I can promise you won't die alone. We shall not abandon you."*

As he speaks those words, the strength he and all the others give me leaves me hopeful that this is not how I die. I lunge, targeting Lilly, trying to separate her and Michael so they can't attack together. She and I are more evenly matched than Michael and I, so I'm better off trying to separate her. This power is more than my body can handle, though. Just as I'm about to connect with her, my body crumbles, too weak to handle the gift my ancestors granted me with such grace. I become a blight on everything they stood for, disgracing them as I crumble to my knees at Lilly's feet. It's over. There's nothing I can do besides sob from the pain as I wait for them to kill me. Pain from wounds, pain from shame, pain from knowing it's my sister who is about to end my life. It all just floods me, weakening me more with each passing second. I force myself to look her in her eyes. "I'm ready, sister."

There's a brief flash of something that looks like guilt in her eyes, but it's gone as fast is it came. She makes a light spear, then glances at Michael.

"Are you sure you want to be the one to do it, Seshen? It's okay, if not." He asks her.

She shakes her head as if she's trying to shake her hesitation away. "No, it has to be me. Stand back."

Michael steps away, giving her space. I can't help but respect the way he respects her decision, even when he disagrees. At least I know she didn't turn on us for someone who doesn't even love her well. It's nice to know their love is true. More true than whatever I felt for Mianora, anyway. During all of this, nothing is more clear to me that letting my emotions get the better of me in front of her is the reason this is happening to me. My death today will be on account of my lack of experience and poor decision-making. Even as I thought of all the reasons that venting was a mistake, I was too weak to hold back the tidal wave of pain that I'd been trying to bury for months. I never should have asked to take command. Even with all that's happened, and with what Lilly's about to do to me, I've never stopped wanting what's best for her. Although, admittedly, I wish it wasn't Michael. She looks down at me. "Close your eyes, Callian."

I don't know why, but I do as she says. Perhaps because there's a strange sort of comfort that comes from knowing she's the one taking my life, perhaps because I'm just too tired to fight anymore. Maybe it's a bit of both. There is but one thing I'm sure of in these moments before I die: I'm okay meeting my end this way. Killed by my sister as my ancestry stands with me in spirit doesn't sound like such a bad way to go. At least when I reach the Spirit Realm, I'll be able to say I died surrounded by family, even if it's not in the way I'm sure other spirits will imagine.

I brace myself for the final blow, sensing the energy as Lilly draws her arm back in preparation to strike my heart with the light spear. "I love you, Lil."

She doesn't answer, but I could swear I feel a teardrop hit my forehead. That might just be rain, though. It was cloudy. Just like that, I black out. Dead that quickly? Or maybe unconscious? That would be nice. At least unconscious, I may not feel the pain of my death.

Alexandria — Two Hours Before the Attack

"Father!" I holler at the stubborn bastard. "We're long past the time for thinking about it. People are going to die."

I can't believe he's being this difficult. It's not that big of an ask. It's also beside the point. If Michael is coming after Oceanica over our decision to take Malachi, there's every reason to believe he will come for us, too. Since, you know, we are the ones who did the actual taking. It's better to meet them where they are and fight with them as an ally before Tendu gets around to attacking Alacrium and hurting our citizens.

"Humans, Alexandria." He scoffs. "Humans and angels aren't demons. We rule over demons. Our duty is to protect demons. Explain to me how you think sending our demons to fight Tendu's demons is protecting any demon?"

I groan. "I knew I should have gone straight to Malachi! Those are his friends being killed by his son; he has a right to know."

"Don't you dare!" His rage is palpable as he snaps back. I know it's idle, though. My father would never hurt one of his own in earnest. He just uses the rage that simmers beneath his surface to intimidate us. It doesn't work on me. He seems to forget that I know him; unlike most of the people he scares into thinking he's anything more than an emotional, loving wreck of a man. It's one of my favorite things about him, in truth. I love knowing my father is a big, overprotective softie. "Telling him would be to risk his life. You know what happens if he leaves without my say so. The magic contract will kill him."

"And if I don't tell him, the grief will kill him anyway..."

He grunts, knowing what I say to be the truth. Malachi has a heart much like his own. He'd find out the truth in time, and he'd hate himself for not being there to stop it, even if it was out of his control. I can picture him withering away in the depression of it. There would be nothing my father or I could do. "I know, but I just don't see a way, Alexandria. Not one that doesn't compromise our duty as rulers."

"Dad, if the demons under our rule knew what was happening, do you believe they would ask us not to send help to Oceanica and the islands?"

Again, he knows I'm right. Even if there was a zero percent chance Michael would come after us next, which there isn't, not a single demon under our rule would ever consider letting others suffer for decisions we forced them into. In fact, they'd likely overthrow us if they ever found out we had been so irresponsible about dealing with the consequences our decisions imposed on others. I don't know about my father, but I don't want my head on a pike. I've seen it happen to royals before. It's not a pretty sight. I'll pass on that sort of brutal death.

"I concede that you have a point there. Ugh..." He contemplates for a moment. "Give me thirty minutes. I'll have an answer for you after doing a brief feasibility review."

That's fair. I already know how the results of that will turn out. Our fighters need to stay right where they are, but there's no reason he can't send Julius, Malachi, and me to handle this ourselves. I smile, hopeful this means he'll let me tell Malachi soon. "Of course, father. Thank you."

I leave the room and go find Julius. As always, he lingers nearby, awaiting the opportunity to serve me in whatever way I need. "Prepare," I tell him. "I think we'll be going to the islands soon. Tell no one until I speak to my father again, though. If he says yes, I suspect he'll have a short list of people allowed to know about it."

Julius nods. "As you command, my queen."

His demeanor shifts from kind as he addresses me to fearsome as he turns away. That's my butler. In times of war, he's scarier than any warrior I have at my command. He could have been a general, if he wished. The only reason he became a butler instead was because it kept him at my side. He was worried about threats to my life when I became queen. The title is beneath his ability, but the loyalty implied by it fits him like a glove.

I pace the halls, frantic for the thirty minutes to pass. About twenty of them do before I spot *him* sneaking around. What is he up to? *Malachi...*

Malachi — One Hour and Forty-Five Minutes Before the Attack

As she approaches, I realize she must know what I'm up to. She would have realized it the moment she saw me. I overheard enough of her conversation with Myrkr to know that my loved ones are in danger. It seems my son has some misconceptions about the reason for my absence. Imagine my surprise when I deduced my wife had misled him into blaming Josie, Jameson, Kai, and Callian for it. I always knew she would resent Josie for this, but I'd imagined she'd gotten over it at some point. It's hard to say for sure why things have ended up this way, but I don't think it matters. What matters now is that they need me. I must go to them.

"Malachi, what're you doing?" She inquires as if she doesn't already know, feigned ignorance if I've seen it.

"I don't think I need to tell you that."

She smirks. "Don't. You must trust me."

I glare at her. "As if I'd ever."

She levels me with a glare of her own. "Trust. Me. Malachi. My father will let us go. Just give me ten more minutes to prove it."

"Myrkr hasn't done a single selfless thing in the twenty goddess-damned years I've lived at his side. That's bullshit and you know it."

"No, Malachi. I don't. What's your plan, anyway? You'll never make it there. The magic that binds you to him will kill you the second you leave. You're being irrational. Just wait a few more minutes and I promise you, if he says no, I'll find a way that doesn't involve you dying."

I don't like it, but she's right. This magic isn't something I can break on willpower alone. "Ten fucking minutes..."

She nods.

"Fine, Alexandria."

We wait the ten minutes, pacing the halls together. Six hundred seconds and I feel every one of them like millennia. When I overheard her and Myrkr, it felt like my world came shattering to bits. All these years, I'd imagined them all together in my absence. It was the only thing that kept me going. I imagined Johanna, a loving mother, raising Michael alongside Josie's kids. I imagined them laughing and playing, not at war with each other. Whatever happened after I left must have been bad. This poison whispered into my child's ear has led him down a path I know only I can save him from. My family needs me, and whatever happens, I will show up for them. I don't care if it's the last thing I do.

When we enter the room to see Myrkr, there he stands. He looks at me, leveling me with his gaze. "I figured you overheard, my little protégé."

I snarl. "Tell me what you've decided."

He chuckles. "I don't have a choice, now, do I? If I say no, you'll kill yourself trying to get there. You won't be of any use to me dead."

"Your terms?" I ask, knowing there are some.

"Are simple." He replies. "I'll release you from the contract in totality. Your training is done; you have the strength to help me when the time comes. However, I ask for your word that you will come back when I need you. I've known you long enough now that I understand you're honorable enough to keep your word without magic bindings forcing you to. Promise me, and you can be free once more."

Well, I guess Alexandria was right. Myrkr does, in fact, have a heart. "I promise."

He nods, then approaches. Placing his hand over the sigil that has held me all this time, he burns it off. The pain is nothing compared to Myrkr's full power. Besides that, I have a pretty high tolerance for fire, given that I'm a demon. I feel nothing more than a light itch as it erodes. Once it's gone, Myrkr looks at Alexandria. "You, him, and Julius. That's all you get."

Her face contorts into a demonic smile as she drags her tongue over her bottom lip. "I think that's plenty, don't you, Malachi?"

I laugh. "More than enough."

She and I depart to meet Julius in the courtyard. Together, the three of us make our way to the tower. There, he opens the veil between worlds, and we return to Alacrium. We stop by the council room briefly to let them know they're in charge of the kingdom until we return. The council knows how to get to Myrkr if they need help while we're gone. Most of the council travels between the worlds with heavy frequency since they have family and friends in both. Alacrium gets treated more like a sub-kingdom to Hel. It's not a separate entity, just an extension of the original kingdom.

After Alexandria's finished relaying instructions, we make our way outside. Taking flight, heading straight for Oceanica. The three of us move through the sky at a speed unattainable for most beings. On a normal day, I don't fly this fast. I prefer to take my time, enjoying the scenery as I soar. There's nothing quite like seeing the world, any world, from the sky. The fresh air, architectural sights, natural beauty... It's all amplified from the sky. Today, though, there's just no time to be concerned about such things.

When we reach Oceanica at dawn, we see there are attacks already under way. Josie and the other royals are split up across the kingdom, forced to fight one-on-one. Tendu must have more powerful generals than ever before if they're holding their own against this kingdom. I wouldn't have thought it possible if I hadn't seen it with my own eyes. Alexandria, Julius, and I split up as well. Julius goes to help Kai, who is fighting for his life at present. Out of all the royals in Oceanica, I suppose Kai's the weakest. Not that it makes his power anything to sneeze at, but he doesn't have a bloodline ability to go with his runic magic. Meanwhile, Alexandria opts to help Josie. Between her and Jameson, Josie's situation looked worse.

I decide to take the location of Callian, Lilly, and my son when I realize Lilly isn't aligned with Callian and Oceanica, but with Michael and Tendu instead. Alexandria didn't have enough time to brief me in full, so I don't know how this happened, but here we are. I position myself in the sky above the two versus one battle between Michael, Lilly, and Callian. It doesn't take me long to realize Callian is about to die by Lilly's hand. I have but a moment to act, so I do.

FATHER AND SON, REUNITED

MICHAEL

Seshen draws back her arm, prepared to kill her brother. The force with which she thrusts the light spear toward his heart is lethal. Seconds before the spear pierces the boy, a massive force shoots down out of the sky, creating a wave of fire so powerful that it blasts all three of us in separate directions. When I land, I look around to find Seshen already standing. Callian is across the estate, unconscious from what I can gather.

In the center of the triangle the three of us create is a man, dark in complexion, not unlike me. His right fist is supporting the forward weight of his squatted body. I don't know his face, yet I know his name. It is a legend that has been the center of my life and the fuel for all the hate I've felt in it.

My father, Malachi; after all these years, he appears before my eyes. His choice for this momentous occasion? To help Callian. Not me; *him*. My hatred for him deepens tenfold as I watch him stand up. When he turns to face me, his face softens. "My boy..." I could swear there's a hint of sadness in his voice, but it's overshadowed by the disappointment. "How could you?"

I look at him, shocked that he's blaming me for this. Seshen seems to be stunned as well, albeit for a different reason, I'd imagine. The man she loved and admired so much has returned. I think she's conflicted. "Malachi?" Her sweet voice, once bright and full of life, has dimmed to nothing more than a weak whisper.

His manner is awkward as he lifts his arm, scratching the back of his head and laughing. "Yeah, I'm home, Lil. Care to explain what's going on here?"

She looks at me as if to communicate that she's leaving the decision on how to proceed up to me. I shake my head at her, steeling myself against the tsunami of emotions ripping me apart right now.

"We kill him!" I say. She doesn't hesitate to follow suit, circling up with me to attack him.

He groans as if he considers our decision to attack little more than an annoyance. "Have it your way, kiddies, but I warn you, this isn't the best decision-making."

I scoff, lunging inwards to attack him with my Helfire. "Maybe if I'd had a father, I'd have better judgement, asshole."

Josie

Alexandria lands beside me, her massive wings blowing away much of the venomous smog General Pythias produced. "Nice to see you, Alexandria."

She smiles. "Couldn't miss out on all the fun, you know? I take it you knew we were coming?"

"I sensed the three of you from miles away. Malachi's helping Callian, right?"

"Yes." She replies. "Now, who is this guy?"

"I'm General Pythias, most trusted by King Michael and his future bride, Lilliana." He butts in.

Alexandria smirks, but her annoyance is visible. She must not appreciate a man putting himself in the middle of a conversation between two queens. I share that sentiment. It's infuriating, as if they forget our power and rank when they see us. Even in a war, some modicum of respect is called for. "I see. Young Lilly went and found herself a demon all her own, did she?"

I roll my eyes at the intrigue in her voice. It doesn't matter who she loves as long as it's not someone trying to kill her whole family. I still don't understand how she got here. Once this is all over, I'll have a heart-to-heart with her. I want to understand more than anything. "I wouldn't mind as much if he weren't trying to kill my entire family at present."

She nods. "Understandable. Shall we resolve that, then?"

I chuckle. "Yes, let's dispose of this general so we can knock some sense into the young ones."

Alexandria's arm reaches out toward me, demonic energy pulsating around it. I reach mine back, combining my spiritual power with it. A massive ball of my purple auric power and her Helfire culminates in between us. Pythias knows better than to take this blast head on. He's not like the kids; he's powerful *and* battle-hardened, with years of experience and the blood of a noble demon coursing through his veins. No doubt he'll find some way to evade the attack. This is to terrify him before we kill him. No man would want to face two women who hold this much power. It'd kill their egos faster than it'd kill their bodies.

We launch the ball of our combined energies straight toward him and his men. He thinks fast, taking flight and getting his own body out of the way, up above his men. Then, he shoots a spherical dark barrier down, trying to protect them. As expected, the force of our attack is too great. It shatters the barrier. Even though it'd not stopped, it slows a considerable amount, buying his men time to put up more and more dark barriers. One after another they rise, protective walls of demonic energy. In the end, our attack kills one or two men at most.

It seems our match is more equal than that of Malachi. Michael and Lilly couldn't touch him. I sense his power clear as day. He's not the same Malachi that left us twenty years ago. It seems my brother-by-choice has outgrown me on the strength scale. I'm proud of him. Although, I can't deny that there's a flare of sibling rivalry as well. I'll catch up to him again, no doubt about it.

That thought fuels my determination all the more. I want to get through this so I can go see him. Irritated, I launch my specialty, an array of light spears that can kill hundreds of enemies in mere seconds. It's successful. I devastate Pythias' army, leaving about half their original number standing. Alexandria looks at him, trying to gauge his willingness to back down. I'm curious too. Will he choose to live and fight another day? Or is today the day he'll choose to die for his king and country?

Kai

I recognize Julius by his energy before he ever reaches me. Overwhelmed by an onslaught of attacks, I try to hold out until he makes it to me, but I feel my power waning more with each passing second. That little bastard, Michael, sent me a leech. A general with the demonic gift of neutralization is fighting me. It's a bloodline ability that neutralizes all forms of runic magic; mine is no exception. I'd say I'm holding up well considering that I can't use my power at all. This whole fight has been hand-to-hand combat. It's not my specialty, but if I choose my moments wisely, I can use my power to force him to neutralize his and land hits. It's keeping me alive until Julius lands.

At last, he arrives. That ends the fight faster than anything I'd hoped for. It turns out the general is a coward. The moment he sees Julius, he quakes. This type of neutralization is useless against another demon and the man won't stand against someone at their full strength. He tries to escape, but Julius has no interest in allowing that to happen. "Come now," He heads the man off. "Don't you want to play? You were so tough when fighting someone who couldn't fight back, weren't you?"

Demons have always looked down on someone who had to neutralize to fight an enemy. They see it as a weakness, a sign that someone has to rely on their enemy's weakness more than their own strength. Neutralizers were banned in Alacrium centuries ago. Most of them live in the wild now, but it seems some opted to remain in the open, fighting a shameful war that has torn our family apart in so many ways. I don't blame Julius for being pissed. He now had to fly all the way out here to kill a man who was barely beating the powerless version of me. It's pathetic, and a waste of time and resources.

The general pleads. "Please, sir. You don't understand. I'm a loyal subject of King Michael; I had to follow my king's orders, or I'd be..."

Julius snaps. "That child is no more a king than you are a demon. Tendu's true king still lives. You're a participant in a coup because you were too much of a coward to stand up to a princeling who has no right to attack Oceanica. I will not allow such a thing to go unpunished."

The general flinches as Julius speaks. It's over for him and he knows it. The honorable thing to do would be to accept it and die with dignity. Instead, he continues to beg for his life, like a petulant child upset about being made to eat vegetables. "End this," I say.

Julius nods, and just like that, the general's neck snaps. Julius wanders back over to me. "Damn, had to go ruin my fun."

I huff. "You need to get back to your queen, as must I get to mine."

He smiles, realizing it's my way of saying I want my husband and wife. These days, I prefer their company to most things. In my younger years, I longed for a good fight. I loved being the ruffian rebel, always brawling. Then, I discovered this thing called cuddling and I haven't looked back since. Far superior to fighting, in my not-so-humble opinion. Unlike most, I'm acutely aware of his feelings for his queen, Alexandria. So, when he huffs, I can't help but feel bad for him.

Their situation is... complicated. Their world seems to allow them to either be close physically or emotionally, but never both. I don't understand Alacrian politics in full, but I know it's much different from here on the islands. They have these strange social rules about who one is to love based on their rank. Here, we figure that if someone of a high rank loves someone of a lower rank, they must see something in that person deserving of the higher rank. So, we raise the rank of the lower ranked person. The logic is different there, though. The rules are stricter, more regimented.

We head back into the city the meet with the others. Jameson, Josie, and Alexandria sit, awaiting our arrival with patience. We all sense that Malachi hasn't finished yet. He doesn't seem to be in any trouble. I think he's just toying with his son a bit, trying to get a feel for where things are at. We all agree that it's best to just wait here for him and Callian. After all, if anyone can end this, it's Malachai. Maybe now that he's back, we can return to the way things once were. The islands united and at peace. That'd be my preference, but I'm not so sure anything can return us to that state. Things have changed in such a profound way. Johanna is dead. Trust between the kingdoms is no more alive than she is. I'm not even sure there will still be an alliance once we liberate the other kingdoms. They must feel abandoned since it's taken so long for us to come for them.

Michael

My attack hits him head on. It does nothing, though. He just stands there in the heat of my flames with one eyebrow raised, looking at me in confusion. He's not impressed with me and doesn't seem to mind letting me know it. "That's it? Twenty years of resentment and this is as hot as your flames get. Jeez, you need me around more than you think, kid."

The words are like a knife to the gut. I can't believe that after twenty years, that's all I get. He's disappointed my Helfire isn't hot enough to cause him true harm. That's the best he can do. How shallow...

The anger and resentment drive my power to new heights as I attack again. The flames within me rage. They're burning hotter than ever before as I bombard him with a series of attacks. Most of them miss as he dodges them. Fuck, he's fast. I land a blow, though, and that feels like a victory of its own. Even as we fight, I'm catching up to him. I've always learned fast. This time, there's visible damage to his seemingly impervious body. It's not much, just a surface burn. How much heat can he withstand? I suppose it's to be expected that he has more resistance than I do, but I didn't expect this big of a gap. Now, he responds. "That's more like it, son."

The enjoyment on his face pisses me off more. He's smug as Hel. That's it. I hate this man already. How dare he call himself my father? This pompous, arrogant, annoying ass prick is not my fucking father. He abandoned me for twenty years, left my mother to die in slow misery, shows up and takes the side of my enemies, and now has the nerve to call me 'son.' I've never witnessed something so damn ridiculous before.

Then it clicks to me. He had to know this reaction would tick me off. Something isn't right. Why is he egging me on? I don't understand what his goal is here. It makes no sense that he'd want me to attack him seriously. Poking to get a feel for each other's strength is one thing, but I don't think that's what he's doing here. No, there has to be a larger goal. I can't decide what's best. Attack for real so I don't appear weak or reserve my strength so he can't judge the severity of the threat I pose with clarity; it's difficult to tell which is the better choice at the moment.

I look at Lilly, hoping to see what she thinks, since she knows him better than I do. Her expression makes it clear he wasn't this strong last she saw him. Attacking is useless; we've already done considerable damage to Oceanica. If we retreat now, we win the day. If we stay, the tides may turn against us. She's right, it's better to wait. Take the minor victory and return for the larger one after we've strategized around Malachi's presence, as well as whoever the Hel those with him are. My next words grit out from between clenched teeth. "Don't bother coming back to Tendu. This isn't over."

With that, I sprout my wings and give Lilly a nod. She follows suit, using her power to levitate and propelling herself at my side. We signal our troops to retreat. They all follow suit, making their way back to the ship in droves. I'm not too worried about Oceanica chasing after us. They'll want to turn their attention to the wounded as soon as possible, so we take our time, getting a head count and waiting as long as we can for any stragglers. Once we set sail, I have the general's report, wanting as much information as they can provide as I turn my attentions toward strategizing for much more bloody battles in the weeks and months ahead. This war just became a long game that I intend to win.

As we fly, Pythias informs me that there were two more demons with my father, each of whom were equal to him in strength. I have an idea; something that might work to purge Oceanica's new demonic allies, but it will take time to prepare. Seshen, being a priestess, should be able to hold a purging ceremony to get rid of them. I have this old book of rituals that teaches it. I can't understand the damn thing because it's written in angelic tongue, a language lost to our kind since the fall. The reason I kept it all this time was to prevent it from falling into the hands of someone who might use it to get rid of me. Now, though, I may have found usefulness in it. She might understand it. Priestesses are beings of light; perhaps one could read the angelic tongue.

I run the idea by her as we sail home. She agrees the plan is worth trying. There's no harm in her looking at it. If she can read it, great; if not, we'll find another way. This is my first idea, but I have others, if they're needed. However, this would be the best path if it's truly available to us. Fighting, we have a shot, but with this ritual, we'd have a guarantee. There's nothing more pleasant in a war than a surefire path to victory. The queen who some in Tendu tried to reject might now be the reason so many more of them will live. A sort of ironic honor that brings the sweet taste of justice to the tip of my tongue. Oh, how they will beg to worship my queen one day. It's almost pitiable that I'll never allow them to worship her

THE FATE OF ANGELS AND DEMONS

in the more entertaining ways I do. My tribute to this woman is a bit more intimate than I would allow another man to give her. Still, I get some twisted sense of pleasure from knowing they'll want to.

Upon our arrival back in Tendu, we rest for a while, recuperating before we shove ancient angelic rituals down Seshen's throat. She needs to be at her best when we try this, anyway. Controlling these sorts of things might be tricky and we'll need her rested enough to judge her actions well. It's best if she doesn't accidentally kill half the island while she's reading.

The purging ritual is volatile. I hardly understand what it is or how one performs it. The general idea is the priestess will have power over all of demonkind, though the power is short-lived. The angels intended for it to be used to wipe out demonkind if they failed to get us back on the leash, but because of a weird ancestral love triangle, a temporary truce made by those with power came into place and nothing ever happened. By the time anyone who'd had an interest in using it resurfaced, we already stuffed the magic away in this library. No one was getting to that magic while Tendu was its guard. If things go as I hope, Lilly will use the ritual to kill specific demons rather than all of them. Namely, Malachi, Alexandria, Julius, and Myrkr—the ones who would actively prevent us from destroying the islands, as I hope to do. It could backfire, though, if Seshen can't control the magic as well as I hope. The caution I'm exerting is meant to protect the demons we don't want to suffer harm.

More important than the ritual, though, I wanted to be with her. I hate every moment she's not in my arms. Battle is necessary and I know we must fulfill our duties, but I feel a blazing fury when I consider how many seconds it keeps me from holding her. Being with her has become the primary reason for my existence. There's nothing more important in this life. I'm not sure how I ever survived a day without looking into those violet eyes. It's no wonder my life felt so hollow before I met her. Any existence that excludes her would be hollow by nature. I'm so in love with this woman that I damn near crumbled at the sight of her. It's not pathetic, though. I see no weakness in that. There is nothing more startlingly strong a man can do than allow a woman to become his weakness.

We hide ourselves away in the library with Ace. It's become her favorite room in the palace. Her subject of choice is less predictable than our location, though. "The nannies tell me the boy is doing well. You know, the one from Loft? Do you have any plans for him?"

I shrug, wrapping my arm around her waist and pulling her into my lap as Ace plays with his chew toy. "Nothing in particular, no. Why? Do you have some sort of opinion about what happens to him?"

She responds with a theatrical gasp. "Me? Have an opinion? When have I ever?"

I laugh, appreciating her sense of humor. "Come now, Seshen, you can't fool me with that act. Tell me what you think, beautiful. I'll always hear your thoughts on anything."

She nuzzles her face into the crook of my neck. "Let's adopt him, you and I."

I figured that's where she was going with this. What surprises me is that I'm not opposed to the idea. I find myself amenable to it, given certain conditions. Thus, I negotiate with my bride-to-be. "You must marry me first."

She chuckles. "Well, no shit. It makes no sense to claim the child before that."

Her reaction makes me happier than I could have ever dreamed possible. She still wants to marry me, even after all that's happened since she arrived. I feel honored to know she still wants to be my wife. It's the best I've felt in my entire life.

"Yes, Seshen. We will wed and adopt the brat. I like him, you know? He has fire. Willpower, like his, is always a good thing. We will raise him as our own."

She doesn't hide her joy. It's a contagious thing, infecting the deepest parts of me. I can't imagine not smiling when her face lights up this way. She's so fucking adorable. I wonder if my father ever looked at Mom this way. I wonder if this is how Queen Josella feels about her lovers. If so, I might understand a bit more why she thought it was worth the risk of going after them. I'd risk far more lives than she ever did on account of this woman beside me now. If every other being in the world dropped dead, I'd be content with it so long as I knew she was okay.

HOMECOMING

MALACHI

After Lilly and Michael make their escape, I wander over to check on Callian. He's still unconscious. There's not much I can do for him aside from getting him back to his parents. They'll be able to heal him, I'm sure. As I scoop the young boy up into my arms, looking at him, I think to myself, *"Josie and Jameson sure made themselves one hel of a kid."*

Making my way toward the others, sensing their energies to guide my way. For whatever reason, walking feels like the right move. Flying, as much as I love it, is fast. Right now, I need time. Any moment, I'll be face-to-face with them again. After all these years, the idea of seeing them makes me nervous. Josie, Jameson, and Kai were all so dear to me back in the day. I worry our bond will have withered, much like everything else, in my absence.

When I reach the center of the kingdom, I find the royals sitting with Alexandria and Julius on the lawn in front of the palace. Josie offers a cautious smile as I approach. "Welcome home. Thank you for helping our son."

I'm just as awkward as she is. "Of course, Jos. You know I'll always come when you need me."

Jameson leans over Callian's body as I sit him down. "Did he fight well?"

I look at him. "He did, cousin, for quite some time, it seemed. However, it looked as if he'd accepted his death by the time I intervened."

I watch as he and Josie tense up. The idea their son would resign himself to death in battle must frighten them. When I see the pain etched onto their features, I feel bad for them, but I'm also grateful that my son appears to be just as stubborn as his mother was. Someone as hard-headed as them will never accept death. I can't imagine how hard she must have fought in her last moments. It's hard, and it hurts, but I find solace in knowing that she died fighting with the same fierceness with which she lived. I'm not sure how I feel about this whole situation between Josie, Jameson, Michael, and Johanna still. My heart blames itself more than it blames any of them. I wasn't here, so I still don't know what happened. I want to ask, but now isn't the best time for that.

Instead, I focus my energies on helping Josie and Kai clean up the aftermath of the battles that took place across the kingdom. Meanwhile, Jameson attend to Callian's welfare. Alexandria and Julius focus on another task altogether. We need them to move straight into planning for whatever happens next. With our presence, this war will get drawn out. Michael won't attack thoughtlessly now that he knows Oceanica has us. In the long run, it'll be a fair exchange, I think. The people of the islands will suffer longer, but far fewer of them will die.

The damage to the kingdom is horrific. Already, so many people have lost homes and loved ones. Oceanica's protocols and wartime aid ensure they'll get the help they need, but it's not the same as returning to the comfort of your own home. Rather, they'll live in discomfort with four or five to a room filled with bunk beds until their homes get rebuilt. It's worse when you consider that this means the families not only lost their comfort, but those who lost loved ones, lost their ability to grieve in private. The cost of war never ceases to break my heart.

Once we get the kingdom to an acceptable state, we all retreat into the palace. There's plenty more planning to do, but not tonight. Tonight is a night for me to get caught up on everything that's happened, but also for me to enjoy being back on the islands with the people I love. There's so much I want to know, and just as much that I want to tell them. We need this. In times of war, there is the occasion that doing something that makes us happy is winning a battle few see. When we see light, it becomes easy to see the value of fighting the darkness. As a demon, a being of darkness, even I see the beauty that lies in contrast. There's a necessity to it that blinds many to the fact that it's not an eternal struggle, but an eternal balance instead.

Callian is awake now. Jameson says he's stable, but that he shouldn't drink for tonight. The boy doesn't seem to mind and encourages us all to indulge in the wine, content to enjoy our reunion with us while sipping water. The servants bring trays of food and bottles of wine as we share our stories from the last twenty years. One of the most exciting aspects for me is getting to know Callian. I'll be damned if he isn't a clone of them. He shares the same insecurity Jameson faced as a young man, as well as the same blindness to the enormity of his accomplishments. From what I understand, he's the one who drove my return. I wouldn't be free now, or be able to help them, if he hadn't first engaged and earned the respect of Alexandria and Julius. He says he's failed the islands, but that's so far from the truth.

After chatting with Callian, I take some time to catch up with Jameson, Josie, and Kai. The three of them seem so happy together. Their relationship is adorable. They're always playing with each other and goofing off. Something is off about the way it makes me feel. I love being back and seeing them all this way, but I hate feeling like I missed watching the lives of everyone I know and love. There's a sense of grief that comes with it. A part of me feels as if I no longer have a place among them and it hurts. Is this even still my home?

Jameson

Malachi wanders outside, and I get the sense that something is bothering him. I follow my cousin to find him leaning against the rail of the terrace. To break the ice some, I crack a small joke. "I wouldn't lean on that if I were you, cousin. You have no clue how many times we've railed against that railing."

He chuckles. "I suspect that if I wanted to avoid touching everything in this palace you three have railed on, I'd have to remain flying my entire stay."

I shrug. "You have a point. But seriously, what's up? Something's on your mind."

The smile fades from his face as he considers his answer. "I don't belong here anymore. Your lives are whole and complete without me in them."

What an idiot. "Malachi, you always belong here. Our lives can never be complete without you. We are happy together, yes, but that doesn't mean we don't feel your absence in every moment of that joy. There have been countless times where we've gone from smiling and laughing to bawling our eyes out because we wished you were there to smile and laugh with us. Your presence, or lack thereof, affects us just as much now as it did twenty years ago."

"That's bullshit." He proclaims. "That's bullshit and you know it! Months. Months I waited when Myrkr first took me. I spent twelve of them convinced that you all would come for me; that you'd find a way. None of you did. Not even Johanna, who supposedly died trying to avenge me. You all left me there. I suffered so much because of it. Myrkr wasn't cruel to me, but I suffered. Every day I had to live with the knowledge my son would never know his father's face. I had to accept that because of you, and Josie, and Kai, and Johanna. Each of you, who did nothing to save me after all I'd done for you. It's a betrayal of the highest order. Yet, I've blamed none of you. I made myself a martyr; this was my doing. My actions hurt my son and now I have to fix it. Don't get me wrong, I still love you guys, but I will trust none of you again."

His voice makes his pain all the clearer. Tears rise from the depths of my soul, overwhelming until they pour from my eyes. "Gods, cousin. Have you thought we gave up on you all these years? No. Oh, no." I grab him and pull him into a hug. "We tried to come for you over two-hundred times. Ten times per year for twenty years, we tried, each time with a different strategy, plan, and timeline. We failed. We failed you, but we *never* abandoned you."

He resists at first, but as I speak, he goes limp, burying his face in my shoulder. Moments after I finish, his arms wrap around me. I feel his tears as they wet my sleeve. "If you tried, you didn't fail me. I care for the efforts, not the success of them."

Now, we're just crying together. "I missed you, cousin."

"I missed you, too, Jameson."

For several minutes, we remain that way, desperate to feel that connection we've both felt deprived of for so long. He's home. My big cousin is home. I'm so glad he's back. So many times, I've wished for his wisdom and advice. For as much as I resented him growing up for always lecturing me, I've missed it more than I ever thought possible. I love him so much. Now, here we are once more, angel and demon, descendants of the Great Brothers, Rettferd and Myrkr, united, as family should be.

After embracing a moment longer, we head back inside, where we're greeted by Josie's glowing smile and Kai's prying smirk. "You guys alright?" He asks.

"Always," I answer.

Josie runs over and hugs me. "I'm so glad you're home, Malachi."

It's impossible to resist her, so I hug her back. She's always been like a sister to me, even before she fell for Jameson. Hel, even before Jameson and I found the relationship we have now. I cringe at the thought that I ever believed these people had abandoned me. Of course, Myrkr wouldn't have told me about their attempts. He wouldn't have wanted it to affect me or give me false hope. As much as I resent him, I can't say I don't understand. Our relationship got complicated when he took me, and we weren't close beforehand. I have a sort of begrudging affection for him and Alexandria. I wanted to hate them both, but that's easier said than done.

From across the room, she and Julius stand together, watching as my reunion with the others continues to unfold. I can see the regret etched into her features. It never settled well with her the way she and Myrkr took me from these people. On some level, I understand why they felt they had to. I suppose that's the part of me that was once king of Tendu. The ruler in me understands they were protecting their people from a threat that will one day come for us, just as it came for them. Still, the human part of me feels like they stole everything from me.

Some naïve part of me hopes now that I've returned, time will pass, and my feelings toward them will become less complex. One day, I hope I see them as family, just family; not family that forced me away from everything I love. If that happens, it won't be for a long time, I'm sure. I'm willing to wait out the resentment, though. Since my mind can understand what they did, my heart is bound to let it go one day. When that happens, we'll be normal.

They'll come visit me or vice versa; we'll stand together in times of danger. It'll be good. I know it will be.

Lilly

I sit in the palace with Pythias and Ace at my side. Michael is gone to Pallentine, trying to reign in yet another attempt at rebellion. I've taken on the role of regent in his absence, a task I'm not complaining about because it gives me time to make a few minor adjustments around the palace. Pythias snickers as he watches me direct the servants as they bring in some new furniture. "Are you trying to piss him off?"

My attempt to hide my amusement fails, resulting in a half-laugh, half-scoff as the smile takes over my face against my will. "He won't get mad at me. Come on, that couch was ancient, and gods, what a horrendous color it was."

Pythias looks at me, one of his thick eyebrows raised. "Lilly... Be nice. His mother chose the furniture."

I choke down a giggle. "I'm not mean. Besides, isn't that all the more reason to replace it? She allowed him to grow up feeling unloved. I want the stuff in our home to have loving memories and associations for us both."

He lets loose a deep breath. "That's true. Our late queen wasn't the kindest mother. She loved him, though, in her own way. He never felt it, but she did. I understand his side as well as I do hers. Love given in a way in which we cannot receive it may as well be absent altogether. You might be right about this. The best thing for the two of you is a home in which you can retreat into each other's love, erasing, or at least easing, the lack of it you've both felt prior."

I wince a little at his words. It's true, I didn't feel love prior to meeting Michael. I knew I had it, but I never felt like it was for me, if that makes sense. It felt like it was for parts of me, sectioned off into what was palpable for those loving me; a poor excuse for love if I've ever seen one. With Michael, he loves every part of me. He can't relate to the part that wants to skip through a field of flowers singing with woodland creatures surrounding me, but he adores it just as much as the twisted part of me he's able to relate to. I like that about him.

Pythias notices that he's upset me. "Lilly... I—"

I shake my head. "That's alright. Forget it." I turn back to the servants. "Take it back out. Bring the other one back in."

One servant replies, "Then, what do you want us to do with this one, milady?"

I scoff, unwittingly taking my anger out on him. "You have fire runes, don't you? Use them!"

I turn back toward Pythias. "Happy?"

With that, I run from the room in tears.

Pythias

As I chase after Lilly, I make it only a few steps before I find her just outside the door, face-to-face with a messenger from King Michael. "What's going on?"

She's the one who answers. "Michael sent orders for us. He wants us to signal for total lockdown across the islands. He suspects word of Malachi's return has leaked and that mass rebellion is cooking."

I ask her. "Can you be sure the message is honest?"

She nods. "I can." She holds up a blue lotus flower, a seshen. "The messenger brought this."

I take a deep breath. "On your order then, Lady Regent."

She pushes her shoulders back, making herself tall. "General Pythias, I order a total lockdown of the seized islands. From this moment forward, all acts of rebellion are to result in the immediate death of the perpetrators without trial. Further, I order suitable fail-safes placed to prevent liberation attempts from the outside. I task you, General, with carrying out these orders in their entirety. Keep me up to date on your progress."

I accept her order as I would King Michael's, but I wish it allowed for me to resolve the leftover hurt I caused her. I didn't mean to make her to feel this way. Now, though, I must focus on my duty, but I'll make a point of addressing this later. The last thing I'd ever wish for was to hurt her. I consider her a friend. I never wanted to betray that. For a moment, I look at her before steeling myself enough to walk away.

As I wander off, she calls out. "Pythias, wait!"

I turn back, looking at her. "It's alright," she says, "Don't worry about it. It's still hard for me, you know? Dealing with what my adoptive family did to me is challenging. I don't like to be reminded of it."

I can hear her becoming more distant from them with each passing day. She's gone from calling them her family to just her adoptive family. It's sad, but I understand why she feels that way. It must be impossible to see people who never saw you as if they're a genuine family. She has a right to that resentment. It's justified. I'm a firm believer that we shouldn't try to pressure people to overlook such things or 'get over it.' For them to heal, they must feel whatever they feel. It's healthy for them to be angry when someone wronged them. Our society tries to deny them that with such frequency that it blows my mind. "Of course, Lady Regent. You're justified in that. Please, never feel as though you must hide it in my presence. I'm loyal to you and King Michael; I wouldn't betray that trust or make you feel weak for showing your pain. King and soon-to-be queen, you may be, but you are human, just like the rest of us. Or... You are. Not him, I guess, but you know?"

She laughs. "Yes, I know what you mean. Well, go ahead. I didn't want to leave that unresolved is all. It's not too soon to be expecting your report tonight?"

I smile, glad to see her demeanor shift back to the cheery one I'm more accustomed to. It feels like I'm talking with Lilly again, not my regent. "Of course, Lilly. I'll get it done for you. Stay safe in my absence. Don't wander too far from Ace. That beast of yours can sniff out threats, you know?"

She waves goodbye. "Got it."

After I'm clear from her vision, I get down to business, putting on my much more serious, general-like demeanor before I address my subordinates and the other generals. I hold a special place among them. The other generals have the same rank only in technicality. In reality, I'm considered the highest ranking because of the proximity and trust I have with the king and Lilly. None of them would ever test the bond I share with the royals, so via status, I have more authority, and they obey it.

I hand out orders to the other generals first, then to my subordinates. One group is to go provide support in Nollent, since they, after Pallentine, are most probable to rise against us. The second is heading for Mallishrine. We're framing it as diplomacy since they claim to be our allies in this, but the truth is we don't trust them. They're snakes and need to be babysat to ensure they don't betray us at the first opportunity. Loft, as the most mild threat, doesn't get much of an addition to the forces already deployed, just a few of my men who I believe can keep them from trying anything stupid.

We set up a more efficient way to send and receive information once they reach their posts, so I'll be able to give Lilly a full report by tonight, as she requested. Everyone leaves, making their way to their new posts. Hours later, information trickles in like drops of rain from a leaky roof. My report comes together bit by bit until I have a sufficient amount of information to bring to Lilly. There's still time left before dinner when I've finished, so I decide to find her early, hoping to avoid discussing military matters during our meal. That would be poor form.

When I locate her, she's sitting in that chair in the library that she and Michael love, with Ace in her lap. It must be lonesome for her without him here. Mindless, she pets the beast as the other hand holds a book above him. It seems an uncomfortable position to read in, but that must be preferable to her than not having any company at all. Several moments pass before she notices my presence. "Oh, Pythias. Come in. What news do you have?."

She seems to perk up a bit as she welcomes me. I approach her, sitting on another chair nearby. "I have the report you requested."

She sits up, giving me her full attention. The creature in her lap gets fussy when she moves and scurries off to lie elsewhere. "Go on, then. I'm listening."

I give her a total rundown of my report from locations, support sent, threat assessments, and more. She listens, careful to absorb all the information. When I'm done, she has a few questions. "No, I don't like that. Send more to Loft. They're a bigger threat than you realize."

She must be able to tell by the look on my face that I disagree, even though I don't say it out loud, because she continues onto say. "Trust me, alright? Think about it. Oceanica knows we'd deem a kingdom with no magic to be of mild danger. If we treat them as such and send little support, we leave an opening. Queen Alexandria could send Julius there with a few of Oceanica's men;

they'd overthrow us. After that, Loft would become a staging ground to free Pallentine while Oceanica, under Queen Josella's command, freed Nollent from us. It's an invitation for them to get us fighting on two fronts and we're already outnumbered, as is."

You're right. It's too dangerous to leave the kingdom without more support. I'll send more there. Good call."

CALL OF FREEDOM

CHIEF OF PALLENTINE

I'm sick of this Hel. Time continues to pass as my people and I waste away, trapped on this island, and unable to help our allies. We've tried to free ourselves several times, but each attempt has failed. Now, Tendu is tightening security more, further hindering our chances of getting free. Something is happening; something that makes them want to tighten their grip on us. No matter how many times I go over it in my head, it can be but one thing causing this reaction. Oceanica has become a larger threat. They have help from the outside. It has to be from Alacrium. Otherwise, Tendu wouldn't be this scared.

Perhaps a change of perspective is in order now that I think about it. If they're trying this hard, it could be our likelihood of success has gone up, and they're trying to intimidate us into stopping our efforts for fear that they might work. That's a chance I'm willing to roll the dice on, especially if I can find a pair of loaded dice.

I think over those posted here, on my island. During the last few attempts at rebellion, I've gathered intelligence on the ones that have been here for a while. They're hotheads. I'd guess they're not taking well to support troops since it implies they're incapable of holding the island by themselves. Sowing discourse could be an option for us. It's not in line with the typical beliefs of our culture, so I've avoided it until this point, but even in our code of honor, it's worse to abandon friends than it is to use dishonorable means to help one. I have to run it by my people in secret, ask them how they feel about it. So far as I know, our means of communication remain undiscovered by those occupying our land. Therefore, getting a secret message to circulate should still be doable.

I whistle to the wind, using my runes in secret to code its message to my people. They whistle back, making a string of music that would sound to the untrained ear like a song we're whistling in boredom. Little do they know, we can hear the whispers in those whistles that tell us what the person sending them wants to say. A few minutes later, there's a consensus between us. One hundred percent of my people agree that it's time to place our bonds above our honor and turn to 'any means necessary' rebellion. With that, it begins. A three-day plan to free ourselves so we can help our friends across the islands. First, we create division within Tendu's forces. Whispers of agreement that sending support was disrespectful to those who have already posted here. Others whispering to the other side, the new troops, about how ridiculous and petty it is for the first to be mad about them coming to help.

It won't take long for this method to break down their internal cooperation and create division. I keep myself from taking part so as not to arouse suspicion that division is being manufactured intentionally. By the next day, we see the fractures we hope to exploit take hold. Cooperation is now non-existent between them. Fights are breaking out left and right. They're injuring each other, weakening themselves against us. This type of petty bickering is more than I could have hoped for. To my people, it's unimaginable to fight our own allies, but Tendu has lost its sense of self since Malachi left them. Under Johanna's rule, and now Michael's, they've become weak, dishonorable, and blind to their shortcomings.

With them fighting amongst themselves, their attentions are off us. We sneak those who are not warriors onto a ship, sending just enough of our strong to keep them safe as they sail for Oceanica. The ship escapes without Tendu's side noticing. It buys time for them to escape but also frees our strongest up to try a more reckless method of rebellion without having to split their attention on protecting our vulnerable. The next phase of our plan is the most dangerous, so it's a relief this one went off without a hitch. The time to shed some blood is upon us. My people are peaceful when they are content, but much like myself, they're among the most bloodthirsty group when someone makes an enemy of themselves. Tendu will soon regret its offenses against us.

We wake, rising before the sun and slaughter many of their troops in their sleep, never giving them the chance to defend themselves. When alarms get raised, it's in a single compound that houses the troops that have been here longer because, in their squabbling, they forget to create a method of mutual alerts. Chaos ensues. They try to make it out of the compound to alert the other, but we have them surrounded. They all die, and the compounds are too far apart for the other one to hear it.

When the other compound does, at last, realize what's happening, it's too late. We defeated the first compound and are already seizing this one. By the time we're done, not a single member of Tendu's army on this island is breathing. I send a small faction of men to follow the ship that escaped earlier to ensure they arrive safely in Oceanica. Meanwhile, I lead the fighters into another battle. My first instinct is to help Loft, but that's meaningless. If we go there, we won't have help as Loft has no magic to help us. These men are too tired as is. Our best bet is heading to a place where the people have magic to help us free them from within. I hate choosing between lives to save, but I'm forced to choose the path that presents better odds. So, I choose Nollent.

Josie

It starts with a single ship arriving on our shores, desperate and begging for help. They're in rough shape; hungry and wounded when they arrive. I can't believe it when I realize they're refugees. They've escaped Tendu's grasp and fled here. A plethora of questions floods my mind as it registers to me what their presence could mean, but they'll all have to wait until I help these people. Their health and safety must be the priority right now. Kai helps me unload them from the ship while Callian, Jameson, and Commander Luca focus on directing their aid. Julius and Alexandria join as soon as they realize what's happening.

Luca, Julius, and Alexandria distribute food and water while Callian and Jameson focus on healing. First, they tend to those in severe conditions, then work their way toward those with minor injuries. Altogether, the number is two-hundred refugees. As soon as the last one is off the ship, Kai and I turn our attention to finding families who will volunteer to house the refugees. We find space for half their number, then offer the other half rooms in the palace until we can make other arrangements.

Once they're all settled and taken care of, we get their story. I document it from start to finish, knowing that one day the world will need to hear it told. While I focus on documenting, Kai factors the information into our plans. "Wait, wait, wait..." He says, "You mean to tell us the Chief is free?"

The refugee nods. "I believe so. If he was successful in his plans, which I'm sure he was because of the song."

"Song?" I inquire.

"Yes," she answers. "The coded song. We all agreed. Our bylaws say allies over honor because there's more dishonor in abandoning a friend than there is in worrying about honor while your friends die."

Kai and I smile at each other. "You're right. I'm sure the Chief succeeded too. Don't you worry about him and the others, just focus on getting better. There's no way he would have failed if that's what your people agreed to."

She nods and lies back down as we make our way around, collecting more information and stories. Hours later, a second ship arrives on our shores. A third follows near after. By the day's end, a head count of two thousand have arrived. With them, a note that reads, "*We've liberated Nollent. Those with the strength to fight are sailing with us to liberate Loft. Guards interrogated by my men imply Mallishrine isn't being held; it's betrayed us. Do not go there. Stay where you are and take care of those we send to you. We will face Mallishrine and Tendu together upon my return.*"

Kai's relief upon hearing Nollent is once again free is amazing. He cries in joy, hugging me. I've never been so grateful for the Chief's loyalty as I am now. It's an amazing thing when two groups, cut off from each other, still maintain such a connection that they are working in each other's interests without being asked. Allies are indeed invaluable ties that can face down even a tyrant as fierce as Michael has proven himself to be. With Malachi's return and the liberation of Pallentine and Nollent, things are looking up for us and our people. Now more than ever, I'm sure that we can win this. There's still a long road ahead, but at least with this turn of events, I know we'll be walking it together.

After settling the last of the refugees, we recalculate our resource disbursements to ensure we have enough. It's tight, but we seem to have just enough to last us three months. At the end of that, we'll need to shake something loose. I'm hoping that the other islands will offer some of their resources since they have plenty and we are housing many of their people until the war passes and it's safe for them to return home. Once the Chief arrives, we'll be able to send mixed groups to defend the various islands. Ones made up of some of the best from each, mixing magic types to ensure there's always a way out of any predicament. Of course, that's my second choice. My first would be for this war not to drag on beyond that time, but even with the recent turns in our favor, that's improbable.

THE FATE OF ANGELS AND DEMONS

It turns out to be a busy and overwhelming day. By the end, I'm exhausted, and so is everyone else. Tomorrow, I'll think more about these matters, but right now I need rest. Calls like these are not ones to be made on a weary mind or body. Beneficial decisions get made after well-earned rest and ample self-care. I learned long ago not to decide matters of life and death when I'm not in the proper mental state to do so. That's what got us into this mess to begin with. They were lessons, but most assuredly the kind that I don't want to be retaught. Thus, I respect what they taught me, so fate sees no need to repeat them.

Returning to our bedchamber, Kai, Jameson, and I fall onto our big, comfortable bed and allow the stress to drain from our bodies as they intertwine. Affection makes for one Hel of a pain reliever on days like this. While I enjoy it, it backfires in a way. Every moment we spend together, there's this looming implication that while we're able to retreat into each other, so many people no longer have that because they lost their loved ones to a war that started because someone resents me. Survivor's guilt is a frightening thing, eating away at my conscious and telling me I don't deserve the joy that comes with the presence of Jameson and Kai. Every other moment that comes and passes, I must remind myself it isn't about deserving joy.

Happiness isn't something we must earn. It shouldn't get reduced to being a trophy we employ cutthroat methods trying to win. That's not how it works. The idea humans have that leads us to believe it's some kind of achievement is a silly notion we impose for no other reason than to torture ourselves. My mind understands this; yet my heart can't seem to accept it. The guilt pokes and pries at me so often that I fear it'll drive me insane, even as I lay in the safety of the ones I love most. They sense it, and Jameson is all too happy to go into brat mode. He's upset with me for giving my illogical guilt more attention than I am to him. "Hmph! Goddess, why are you ignoring me?"

The laughter that escapes me is free-spirited and genuine to its core. "Yes, my bad. I should know better than to entertain my thoughts when I have a needy little brat desperate for some love."

Kai smirks. "Don't blame him. You're the one that got us all addicted to you and shit. It's your fault we're fiends for you."

I roll my eyes, playful, but sort of serious. "Of course I'd get blamed for this." Feigned irritation rises in my voice. "Oh, alright. Come here, my little monsters. I got you."

I take them both into my arms, each of their heads lying on opposite breasts as mindless hands skim over my body. Their touch is so intoxicating that the guilt I felt just moments prior seems like a distant memory.

Alexandria

With Julius and Callian on either side of me, we wander the settlements on morning patrols. Builders are nearby, erecting more temporary housing to accommodate the influx of refugees who arrived so suddenly yesterday. Everyone is working overtime trying to accommodate the effects this war is having on people. I appreciate how much effort Oceanica puts into assuring the cost of war touches as few lives as possible, and into helping those that were touched by it. This choice hinders their actual ability to fight the war all out, but it's far more ethical. I'm always glad to help people who are at least trying to do the right thing. All things considered; mere effort is still far more than most ever give. It's shameful, really. Humans are so cold to one another over the most petty differences. Demons would never imagine such a thing. We get more than enough grief for existing to be compounding it by hating each other.

As the builder's work, debris flies my way. I don't notice it until Callian leaps into action, destroying it before it can hit me. "Huh?" I whip around to face him.

"Sorry," he replies. "I know it wouldn't hurt you, just acted on instinct. The intention wasn't to offend you or imply some stray debris could harm Alacrium's queen."

I shake my head. "No, I appreciate it. It wouldn't have hurt, but it would have been Hel to get out of my hair."

Julius scoffs. He always gets like this when I'm nice to other men. His jealousy is a fuse that's easy to light. It annoys me, but I'm still not sure I'd change it if I could. Some part of me enjoys knowing he wants me, even if I can never return the affection. I'm pretty sure he knows how I feel, but he'll always be insecure about it so long as I cannot speak it out loud. It doesn't matter, though.

I will have to marry one day soon. It will have to be with someone who isn't him. Most importantly, though, it should be with someone like Callian, who I at least like. Being unable to be with the man I love shouldn't be a condemnation to a miserable marriage. There's a space in between. With Callian, he's qualified to marry me, royal, just as I am. He's also a good man. I can at least picture us being friends who have sex once in a while. It's not the worst outcome a marriage could have by any means.

Callian looks at us. He's aware there's a weird tension. It's confusing him, which makes sense because I just planned a whole marriage to him without letting him know and Julius is blaming him for a problem he doesn't know exists. Wow, okay. We're both crazy and clearly, we're assholes too.

"Um... Did I say or do something wrong?"

Callian's words make me feel even worse. "No," I answer. "Not at all. Julius and I are just... complicated. It's not you, though. Never you."

That serves no purpose beyond irritating Julius more because Callian still seems awkward as Hel. I can't even blame either of them. As a queen, I'd never admit this out loud, but I have no clue what I'm doing and its reflection on me is getting worse with each attempt I make to figure it out. You know what? I'm just going to shut up and focus on the war. I'm better at war than I am at romance, or any form of socialization, for that matter.

Callian and Julius both keep their distance from me after that. They stay away from each other too. It sucks because they were getting along well prior to me getting into the mix. I feel like I just ruined a potential friendship between them. Keeping straight, I follow my path. Callian veers off, wandering right. Meaning, Julius slows down, trailing sluggishly behind me with his eyes glued to the ground. Dammit, he's like a moping puppy. Why does this always happen to me?

I walk along, focusing my efforts on ensuring the safety of these refugees, as well as the native Oceanic people. Everything seems fine around here, so the patrol doesn't take us long, and the three of us find ourselves standing around awkwardly. Callian excuses himself. He didn't need to talk to Commander Luca; I think that was just the best reason he could come up with for not walking back to the palace with Julius and me. He's not wrong. I would have made up a reason to ditch us, too.

Callian

What the Hel was that about? Destroying that debris before it hit her was a mistake, and I don't even know why. She didn't seem mad. Julius did. Then she just seemed awkward. I have no clue what happened anymore, but I feel as though I'm missing a lot of context. Alexandria and Julius are both people I like. I hope I didn't upset or offend them somehow. Commander Luca was a convenient excuse to get away from them. There's not some important reason I need to speak with him now. Although, I do want to speak with him, just to check in on him and his men. Things have been so hectic, I haven't done so in a little while. I don't want them to feel like I've forgotten them.

I make my way from the refugee settlement to the nearby barracks. When I arrive, I head straight in. Commander Luca and his men were relaxed but snapped into attention when I entered. I wave my hand. "Relax, boys. I've just come to say hello. I'm not on official business."

The commander gives them a nod of his head, confirming that they're permitted to go about whatever they were doing prior. His attention drifts back to me. "How have you been?"

I shrug. "More worried about you guys than myself, in truth."

He grunts. "That's what makes me worried about you. You're always worried about everyone, never yourself. Besides, you were just betrayed. That has to hurt. You can talk to me about it, you know?"

I tense at the mention of Mianora Revel's betrayal. Even if he didn't say her name, it stings just the same. "I'm not ready, Commander." I force my body to untense. "When I am, though, you will be the first person I come to. I hope you don't mind, but I see you as a friend. Maybe even a best friend, or an only friend."

Luca smiles. "No, that's alright. I feel close to you, too. I have from the start. There's an intense feeling of kinship you provoke in me. It's not just now that I want to work alongside you, not just for the duration of this war. The men and I have talked about it. We want to stick with you for the long haul. We feel our family is incomplete without you. I hope you share our feelings and will have us."

"Of course I will." I blurt it out, not even bothering to act diplomatic or like I need time to consider my answer. The answer is obvious. These men are my family. I will keep them at my side now, and for the duration of my time as a royal. Luca is my brother; they have all become my brothers.

CHAPTER Twenty Three

ALLIES RISING

CALLIAN

My confidence once again spikes as I'm reassured that Luca and the men haven't abandoned me. So many still have faith in me, so I must continue having faith in myself. Otherwise, I will have abandoned those who believe in me. I could never do such a thing to them. With that said, I go back to the drawing board as I search for a new way to approach this war. This time, I propose a strategy we haven't yet considered until now because it wasn't possible. Our allies had fallen. Now, though, we have a shot at a large-scale joint attack on Tendu.

I create a plan to firm up support across the islands via an underground network we once used for classified information. We stopped using it long ago because more efficient means of communication arose, the kind that allowed us to communicate more specific information, but I plan to reactivate it because of the state of emergency we're in. It's the best way to communicate without any substantial risk of Tendu intercepting or messages. I hadn't even thought about it until now. It's such an outdated system, but if we can confirm a large enough number of people in other kingdoms willing and able to fight, this option will be viable and I'll bring it to my parents, as well as Malachi, Alexandria, and Julius. To do this, Commander Luca and I will have to go to the old tunnels ourselves. It will be alone, at night, and in total secrecy.

We both go about our days as if we've plotted nothing. I return to the palace and act as if I'm still distraught and unsure of myself. As planned, everyone believes me, keeping their distance and disrupting only when necessary. This gives me plenty of time to work on the activation method and targets. I want my call to reach those on each island that I'm sure won't betray us. My lesson about trusting those I don't know on a profound level got carved into my heart by Mianora. Who do I know best? Royals. Those who I've interacted with the most for diplomatic purposes. The royals of the islands are by far some of the best people I know. Except for Tendu, who took a turn toward fascism so long ago that I've never known them as anything else.

By the time night falls, I'm ready. I meet Commander Luca at the edge of the palace near the gate. We sneak across the kingdom from there, escaping into the tunnels. They're easy to access since Dad Kai had a meltdown there not too long ago. Once we're down there, I call on my angelic power to create light around us. The bright, white shimmer of it creates a contrast with the pitch-black cave that might be alluring if we had the time to focus on it. Luca stays close as we search for the spot we need to locate. It proves challenging to find. There's a lot of ground to cover and we don't have an exact image of what it looks like. I'm working under the assumption I'd recognize it by its energy.

Three hours passes and we must have run our hands over every rock and grain of soil in this stupid tunnel and found nothing. Frustration laces Luca's voice as he asks me, "Are you sure this is the right tunnel?"

I can't blame him for questioning it. I would too if I weren't as sure as I am. "No, that's the problem. There's no doubt in my mind that this is it."

He groans. "Then, why? Something isn't right about this. We've searched every square inch of this stupid place."

I shrug. "I don't know, Luca."

He paces, thinking. "No, wait. Your dad comes down here, right? King Kai?"

"Yes, once in a while. It's a retreat for him."

"Does he often use his magic for stress relief?"

I nod. "Yes, every magic user does. What's your point?"

Luca smiles as the pieces fall together in his mind. "Your father uses ground type runes, Prince Callian. The landscape of this place has changed from its original form."

My eyes widen when I realize what he's implying. "Start digging!"

My command is one I follow, just as he does. I may not have ground runes, but I can use my magic to dig if I freeze my water, sharpen it, and spin it like a drill. Luca does the same, although he doesn't work half as fast. It takes the two of us no longer than ten minutes to find it after we begin. Excitement brews in my soul when I see it there. A small crystal imbued with more magic than I could have hoped for. I don't pick it up. This is no normal crystal. It only works down here in the privacy of the tunnels. Its power will caress the runes of my allies. They won't hear or see each word, but they'll feel it, perceive it, and know I call to them. I leave it where it is and start talking to it, trusting it to carry my words to ears that remain loyal. "Tell them for me, crystal. Tell them I need my friends and allies to let me know that's still who they are. Call on them to rally at my side."

The crystal's magic flickers in response, almost as if it's happy with my message. It wants to be used. Is this thing sentient? I look at Luca to confirm that he saw it, too. Otherwise, I'm crazy and that's not a convenient thing to be at the moment. His response does indeed confirm what I saw when his face twists with curiosity. I tilt my head and look back at the crystal. "Do you understand the messages your magic conveys?"

It flickers yet again. I glance back at Luca. "You think it means yes?"

He laughs. "I don't know. Maybe, or maybe it just flickers like that every time it's spoken to."

Three more flickers in quick succession come from the crystal. I chuckle. "I think you offended it."

He tries to hide his amusement. "I suppose I did. There we have it. The freaky magic rock is sentient."

I pinch my lips together. "Yes. Well, I'm not complaining. We can tell everyone we have a new ally. No need to specify that the ally is, in fact, a sentient rock with magic."

We continue joking about the crystal, and it seems to enjoy the attention as we wait for a return message from our friends on the other islands. It takes some time, but next thing we know, confirmations flood us. It's more than we could have hoped for. Pallentine, Nollent, and Loft are all still on our side in full. They seem grateful that we've stretched ourselves so thin to accommodate their refugees and are eager to help us do so. I figured Pallentine would be, but Loft and Nollent are a bit of a surprise. They haven't been as active in holding together the alliance, so I thought they'd be passive allies at best. Yet, I'm proven wrong. They're all willing to fight with us. Tendu and Mallishrine are the only ones truly acting against the alliance, and I suspect one because of callous cowardice more than malice.

Luca

Using the crystal's power, Prince Callian and I convey messages for nights to come to communicate our plans to the allies. In our own kingdom, we prepare as well. Attacking Tendu head-on is a major move, but it makes the statement that we're not to be antagonized. Until now, everything has unfolded on the soil of Oceanica or its friends; taking the fight to their soil will intimidate them. At a minimum, it will make them think twice about what they've done. The cost of war always seems small to those who don't bear that cost on their own backs. Some, such as Callian and our native royals, know this is a privilege they have and work to offset that cost for the lower class, who are most often victims of it. Others, such as Michael, choose to remain oblivious to the harm their actions cause until they're forced to see it day in and day out as their people resent them for allowing it.

I appreciate the idea of opening his eyes to it, but I also regret the harm we'll have to cause to do so. Our war isn't against the people of Tendu, just its ruler. It'll touch their lives just the same, though. That's the guarantee that comes with war; its sole promise to the people waging it: *I will come, and I will destroy lives.* It's not a comforting promise, but it's true.

The philosophical implications of this action continue to haunt me, even knowing that they're by far preferable to the alternatives. It may be a good sign that it bothers me. Empathy is what most separates us from those like Michael, who cannot see beyond their pain well enough to acknowledge the pain they cause others. Some call empathy a weakness; I'd say otherwise. I'd even call it a strength. It's an ability, like I said, a skill that takes time and commitment to develop.

Knock. Knock. The sound coming from the other side of the door snaps me away from my musings. "Who is it?"

"Julius," the voice on the other side answers. I'm surprised he's come here to speak to me. It makes sense, I guess. We are collaborating, but until now it's been through Callian and Alexandria. For the sake of efficiency, we should at least have an icebreaker conversation. At some point, he and I are going to have to work together in a more direct manner.

"Come in." He opens the door when he hears my words. Not knowing what to say, I go for something as base level as possible. "Welcome."

He shifts his weight, appearing anxious. "Oh, thanks. So, we should like..." his voice trails off.

I pick up, trying to help him. "Spar or something." That seems much less challenging than speaking at the moment. I think it counts as a bonding activity, anyway.

He presses his lips together in an uncomfortable, forced smile. "Yeah."

I stand up and lead him back outside toward the training grounds my men and I use without a word. He follows, but in silence. The situation is weird enough, but after Callian mentioned his behavior the other day, I'm not sure what to make of him. I'd prefer not to work with him at all, but that doesn't seem to be an option at the moment. Brushing him off risks offending Queen Alexandria and I'd rather not be responsible for a diplomatic incident that alienates a key ally in the middle of a war.

Once we're on the training grounds, the tension fades as we turn our attentions to the sparring match. If nothing else, it'll be good training for us both. I'm keen to see his fighting style and willing to bet there's a reason Queen Alexandria relies on his service so much. I activate my runes, causing the markings on my body to light up, glowing light blue as they await my command. For now, I don't give them one. Instead, I wait to call on the magic until I see what he does.

He observes me for a moment before calling on his demonic power. The weight of it in the atmosphere causes my knees to tremble, threatening to buckle. How is he this powerful? Even Michael and Callian couldn't do this. It shouldn't be possible. Whatever fuels him must be deep: love, loyalty, hatred, a deep, burning passion. Demonic and angelic power, unlike runes, is infinite. They're limited by nothing but the emotions one feeds them with. He just takes it to a level I've never seen. I'd forfeit at the sight of him if I didn't think it'd put Prince Callian to shame for choosing to place so much faith in me.

With a growl rumbling from my chest, I roll the dice and say he's a long-range fighter, then make my move to get close to put him at a disadvantage. Getting creative, I call up water from the ground to surround him, trying to cut off any fire he tries to sling as I dart across the field to get near him. It works. For a moment, I'm right under his nose. My magic responds, swirling viciously around my hand, an idea I gained the other day when Callian and I were in the tunnels using our magic to drill. I recreate the same motion around my fist and swing, landing an uppercut to Julius' jaw. The impact of it did little to pierce the durable skin his demonic body affords him, but I caused some pain by displacing his jaw.

He shows his sharp teeth in a dangerous smile, with blood dripping from his jaw. "Interesting. I didn't think you'd be able to do this much damage. I see why Callian likes you now. Even in a losing battle, you make damn sure it's closer than it should be."

He grabs my head from behind and slams it down on his knee, not even using magic or bloodline abilities. Sheer strength is all this man needs. "*Gah!*" I collapse to the ground, but I'm not ready to give up yet. With blood trickling down from my forehead, I swipe low with a kick enhanced by my magic straight to his kneecap, trying to make it buckle. It failed at everything but causing him to laugh harder as he grabs me and throws me back to the side of the field I started on. I grunt when I hit the ground.

He approaches in slow, measured steps. "Are you ready to admit defeat?"

My voice shakes. I try to remind my body that he's an ally and won't cause me any actual harm, but that doesn't stop the fear from taking hold. Sobbing, I cry out. "Yes! Yes! I'm done; you win."

His response is immediate when he deactivates his magic and rushes over to help me. "Shit, did I go too hard? I didn't mean to hurt you. I thought I was holding back enough to make it fair."

He's crazy. How was that holding back? I try to laugh at the absurdity of it, but it hurts, and I end up groaning instead. Julius gasps and I wave him off. "No, it's okay. I'm just glad we're not enemies."

He barks a laugh as he offers me his hand to help me up. I take it, and just like that, I don't mind his presence anymore. Everything that was weird about it prior feels fine now. I'd even say that I don't think he meant to set Callian off. It seems to me he's just an instinctual guy. His response to what happened might have been a primal reaction more than it was a genuine threat to Callian. He cares more for his queen than he lets on, if I'm not mistaken. The image of another man getting close to her would put him on edge, even if he likes the guy.

He helps me to the nearest healer and sits with me while she tends to me. The woman uses more traditional methods of healing that Callian or King Jameson, so it takes a while. Julius' singular wound seems to have healed this fast on its own. Accelerated healing is a gift in battle. I'll never cease to be amazed at the way angels and demons differ from us mere mortals. No wonder they live such long lives by comparison. I've never heard of one dying before the age of two hundred. We have no clue how old the eldest of them are, though. Rettferd and Myrkr are vague about such things, according to the rumors.

Callian

I wait for Alexandria in the halls of the palace. She and I are supposed to be going to meet with the Chief and other leaders before our plans get set into motion. There are things we must provide for them to carry out the parts they're assigned. Alexandria arrives wearing a full body suit. It's plain and black, inconspicuous, but she looks great wearing it. I don't think this woman would look bad in anything, though, so that might be called stating the obvious more than it is praise.

She and I haven't spoken since that odd moment the other day on patrol. It's unsettling to see her again. She must get the sense that I'm still uncomfortable because she tries to address it. "I'm sorry about that. It must have been—"

"No, please. It's fine. Don't bother." I say, realizing afterward that it created more tension than it resolved, which it contrary to what I was hoping to do. She tenses and goes silent for a few moments. Then, I correct my mistake. "I didn't mean that to sound harsh. It's just not that big of a deal. We're fine. I would like to know what you and Julius were thinking at that moment, though. It's likely to differ from what I perceived is all. Better for us all if I don't make assumptions."

Her expression relaxes some and we walk together toward the palace exit. Our pace is slow since we're in no rush to get there and feel we have matters to discuss before arriving. "Julius and I have a complicated relationship, you see." She explains, "There's a tradition in Alacrian society, particularly among royals and nobles. It's a choosing ceremony where those of high rank select other children of a similar age to act as their friends, but also as their servants. It's meant to cultivate loyalty over our lifespans with other powerful demons so we can appoint them to our councils later in life."

I nod. "And Julius was one of those you selected?"

"The only one I selected, actually. I met all my other council members later in life. From that first day, he and I were thick as thieves. I remember it like it was yesterday, with a clarity that puts any diamond to shame. One of the other children brought to me for selection was obnoxious. He was older than I and often tried to bully me. Julius caught him pushing me into the mud one day and stood up for me. It wasn't because I was a princess, either. It wasn't because I was a girl. He just did what he thought was right on instinct. I know that because there was no way he could have known it was me in the mud. I was face down and dressed in leisure clothes, which don't vary by rank like our formal wear does. It could have been any of the kids who roamed the palace."

Listening to her, I sense her sincerity. She thinks the world of him. I can't help the tinge of jealousy that sparks. I've spent my whole life wishing someone would care for me that way. Pushing that aside, I continue listening to her without interruption. "Ever since then, our friendship is infallible. We've done everything together. Over many years, we became attracted to each other. Physically, yes, but also on another level; the kind that's all-encompassing. My mind, heart, and soul belong to that man. He's not eligible to marry me, though. I was going to make him a general, but he didn't want to go fight wars. He wanted to be at my side, even if it meant assuming a title that was beneath him."

This is getting to be heart-wrenching. They're in love but can't be together. My mind can't help but wander to the way it would have destroyed my parents if such restrictions kept them apart. It must be agony for Julius and Alexandria. "Anyway, this still leaves a glaring issue. I'm a queen. As such, part of my duty is to continue the bloodline. I have to marry and produce an heir, which means Julius and I both know that we'll get torn apart someday."

His reaction is making more sense now. I'm a prince. Not just any prince, either. No, I'm a highly eligible, respected prince and the sole heir to the throne. She could marry me. I'm a threat. He doesn't dislike me at all. He just doesn't want Alexandria and me being any closer than we have to be. I can understand that. It's sweet when I think about it. It brings me an odd sort of peace to know love like theirs exists, even if that peace gets tainted by my personal experiences with love. Not to say that I was in love with Mianora, but it wasn't a great venture into the idea of romance entering my life. "I'm sorry you and Julius have such barriers between you, Alexandria. I hope it works out for you."

The exhaustion and lack of certainty I hear lace her tone are unmistakable. "Someway, somehow; I'm sure it will."

She says those hopeful words, but I can hear the doubt behind them. I wish there were some way I could help them. There's not anything I can do, though. These matters are complex and the best I can think of is to be there for them, always ready to listen. It sounds like a platitude, but it feels like a resolution to me; a silent promise I'm making to my friends.

With that resolution in mind, as we enter the meeting place, I feel strong. The other leaders walk through plans with us, and we give them the things they'll need to carry them out. Each of them gets spelled crystals that connect back to the one in our tunnel to make the communication more efficient. This way, it will convey things in real time. I also give them charms that will help to complement their runes based on the specific type they use. It took forever to make them, but I'm sure they'll come in handy. They're made with a fusion of angelic and demonic power from Alexandria and me. It was her idea. Her creativity has proven invaluable in the planning process.

CHAPTER Twenty Four

A BITTERSWEET SYMPHONY

ALEXANDRIA

Ever since opening up to Callian the other day about the situation between Julius and me, I've wanted to be around him more. Somehow, his presence makes it all feel a little less terrible. He continues to keep me at a distance, though. I can imagine several reasons he's doing this and I'm not sure which one it is. Maybe he's trying to respect my relationship with

Julius? Is he scared to be close to any woman right now? Is his mind preoccupied with matters of war? All the above, perhaps? I can't say. It's too much. I just want him to stop doing it. Julius and I will never be together, and neither will he and Mianora, so I want him to stop ignoring me and acknowledge that we click too well for us to let factors that will never change force us to ignore it.

I try to catch him during the lull, but every time I approach, he suddenly has some urgent matter to attend to. It's getting to be ridiculous. So, I track him down once more. This time he's in the garden. I can tell matters are weighing on his mind when I spot him, but I don't care right now. He has to talk to me. Just as I walk over, though, Julius approaches from the opposite direction. Since I was coming from behind, Callian spots Julius without seeing me, but Julius' face lets me know he sees me because it twists. He may as well have glued a question mark to it. Of course, Callian notices his confusion and turns to see me.

Moments don't get weirder than this. Julius and I haven't spoken. When we have, it's been of official matters. He doesn't yet know of my plans to pursue Callian. What's more is the fact that Callian seems to have been expecting Julius, which means the two of them have talked behind my back and I have no clue what about. All I know is that none of us seem to know what to do right now, so we're just looking back and forth at each other. It's like some sort of challenge to see who makes the first move. Not knowing what to do, I lift my hand

and press my finger to my nose. My hope is the playful gesture signaling 'not it' sparks something.

They both smile, Julius rolling his eyes and Callian chuckling as they race to get their fingers to their own noses. Callian beats out Julius. I can hear him gasp across the distance when he realizes he lost. He sprouts his wings and takes flight, trying to escape. Callian and I do the same, chasing after him. All three of us are laughing hysterically. We can't even take ourselves seriously at this point. There's little else to do with the pathetic display besides enjoy it at this point.

When Callian and I catch up to Julius, Callian tackles him and they both come tumbling into me, which causes us all to crash land on the beach. The laughter keeps coming for several more minutes. It only ends when it hurts, then fades away until we're all just lying there in the sand, looking up at the clouds. Too afraid to speak for fear it would ruin this moment have together, we remain silent. The unspoken feelings haunting each of us are too much to bear, but we tolerate them regardless. Not one of them is worth losing this other feeling; the one of serenity and freedom we know we can only share now. When this ends, so to do those simple pleasures. So, we make them last as long as we can, which is nowhere near long enough. My heart shatters when Julius finally assumes the mantle he got burdened with when he lost our little game. "We're fucked, aren't we?"

Callian shrugs, a hint of sarcasm leaking into his words. "If only. The stimulation would feel better than the truth."

We all giggle, but it has more to do with keeping ourselves from crying than it does the small bit of humor in Callian's words. In the back of my mind, I wonder if this means what I think. I might not need to tell either of them anything, nor do they need to tell me or each other anything. All there is to say, we all already know. Vocalization would serve no purpose besides wrenching the metaphorical knife deeper into each of our already damaged souls. Hurting one another that way isn't what we want.

Forced to get up as a voice approaches, we rise. "Prince Callian," someone calls out, "are you alright? I saw you in the sky. What's happening?"

Callian groans. "We're fine, Luca. Nothing has happened." I see the pain etched on his face before he continues. "We were just celebrating. I found a way for Alexandria and Julius to be together. The purpose of her marriage to another royal, politically, would be to offer an alliance to Alacrium, strengthening them against their enemies." He turns to look at me, but it's unclear who he's actually talking to. "As I was explaining to her, I think we can accomplish that without an arranged marriage. I know she turned down alliance with the islands in the past, but as the heir, it's within my authority to create alliances outside of a marriage pact. I'll pledge to her the support a king would to his queen, and that she should free up her future."

Shock moves through me as I freeze. He's sacrificing so much to ensure I get my happy ending with Julius. I know why. We all know why. Hel, even Luca, knows why our happiness matters so much to him. None of us say anything. Julius and I just accept it, knowing Callian has likely already written to my father about this proposal and got an affirmative reply. We'll be together, but... just not with him. He'll be our friend. Our good friend and ally. That's okay. Luca agrees with a measure of reluctance. "Very well, I'll leave. I just wanted to ensure your safety."

Callian stops him. "Wait, don't go. You can escort us back to the palace."

Luca obeys the order, but Julius and I are both irritated by it. Callian doesn't want to be alone with us. Nothing has happened, and as much as he hates it, he won't let anything happen. Callian will place blockades between the three of us at every turn. In part, it's to protect us all from the disaster that is our urge to grow closer. The rest, though, has become too complicated to explain. I suspect things between us will always remain this complicated, but at least he's ensured the two of us can live with those complexities. I hope one day he finds someone who helps him live with them, too.

Josie

My loves and I have been apart so much as of late. In my heart, I feel their absence like a mortal wound on my soul. Our duties to Oceanica and the allies have kept us so busy that our only time together has been at night when we're too tired to enjoy each other's company. During the days, I'm off at the refugee settlement helping those who fled here. If only my spiritual power allowed for me to grow extra limbs, I might do enough to ease my conscience for a few moments. It doesn't. What little it does hasn't scratched the surface of the guilt which has made its way so deep into my psyche.

Meanwhile, across the island, Kai works to set up more permanent housing solutions for the citizens who had their homes destroyed. We hope they'll be safer on the far side. He has his work cut out for him, though. The refugees from Nollent are runeless. The small force the Chief found when he freed Nollent must keep their attentions committed to the wartime plans. This leaves Kai to handle most of the construction on his own, since only he has the rune type to do it. Some builders and architects are with him, but he handles the heavy lifting. They advise and handle more menial tasks.

Jameson has a task, too, of course. His work keeps him at the palace, alone. He occupies the throne room, spending his days handling council members and hearing concerns. So many times, each day, he must ask how he can help and so few does anyone ask him how they can. Thus is the job of a royal, but oh how that burden multiplies when the three of us aren't side-by-side. It must be exhausting to hear all their burdens alone, and work to resolve them without the input of the partners you rely on most. Imagining how difficult this must be for him breaks my heart.

My worry for my husbands and how their duties affect them multiplies my guilt by factors so far out of my control. Soon, the product grows so substantial that all my education seems useless because I can't solve this problem anymore. I'm such a terrible ruler for worrying about my loved ones while my citizens suffer, but if I worry for the citizens instead, I'd become an unsuitable wife. That isn't something I can afford to be. It's like no matter which way I turn, I'm wrong because I'm just me. I'm but a singular queen. Strong as I might be, I carry the burdens of many people. Can't they see? I'm losing it, just as I lost my daughter, and just as I'll lose my son if I can't figure out how to get us free.

Twenty years ago, when Lilly first told me of this fate, it was of a prophecy, which the Chief confirmed. Twenty years we spent preparing for this, even though we hoped it would never come. I never imagined that Michael would render those preparations so useless. Some dark part of me, the part that always knew Lilly held a darkness not so unsimilar, wonders if she always knew they'd be useless, since they centered on her power. Could she have foreseen her own betrayal? It couldn't be, but what if it was? I hate to think about it, but I don't think there's any way to avoid it anymore.

If it's true, she must have struggled far longer than I realized. Under my nose, my daughter may have hidden the betrayal she foresaw for fear we wouldn't understand and stand by her to help her change that fate. I would have stood by her. How did she not know that I would? Her hiding it might be what dragged her further into that darkness and created the circumstances that drove her to this. She must have disassociated her mind and divided her soul so many times that she lost sight of who she was altogether. I missed it all. I failed my daughter.

Now, because I failed my daughter, I'm also failing my kingdom, my friends, and the two men I deign to call my husbands. For a woman once known for her greatness, it's quite the fall. How blind I must have been not to see this. I'll never forgive myself for it, but I can't wallow in the self-pity either. My mind might, but my body can't. Doing something is the only way I can atone, so I keep moving. I keep trying to help. Every waking moment I spend here, carrying pales of water, helping to catch more fish, comforting and healing people the best I can. No matter what it costs me, it's a price I must pay. My only regret is that my loved ones must also pay for all the ways I failed them.

After another long day, I lumber myself home to the palace. Its grandiosity feels burdensome as I enter, covered in muck and grime. The sight of me is anything but regal, I'm sure. I make my way to the bath. There's nothing like soaking after a strenuous day. Nothing except for the sound of my beloveds as they wander in to greet me. As I lie in the warm water, a sense of awe lightens both their faces. With that much ease, they erase the tensions of my day. "How are you, goddess?" Jameson asks.

Kai doesn't give me a moment to answer before he collapses at the side of the tub, draping his hand over it to touch my thigh. "We're tired, King Hubby. Take care of us."

Jameson's slow smile is everything we need. "King... Hubby? That does it. I'll never be accepting any other term of endearment again."

I giggle. "Now look what you've done, Kai."

Kai's smiles. "Yeah, guess I should've known better."

By the gods and goddesses of all the realms, what is it with these two? Mere moments ago, I was on the verge. The moment they come in, though, I can't even remember why I spent all day beating myself up. I let out a grunt as my mind goes quiet. Jameson sits at the edge of the tub with Kai. I'd ask them to get in with me since the tub is big enough for it, but the time it'd take for them to undress and climb in feels too long after days of distance between us.

Malachi

I'm alone. It seems I'm always alone these days. Josie, Kai, and Jameson are busy helping their kingdom and getting lost in each other every time they get a chance. My son and Lilly, who I was once close to, are plotting against everything I hold dear because of poison my now dead wife spent twenty years whispering into his ear. Alexandria, Julius, and Callian are—I'm not entirely sure what those three are doing, but they're doing it with each other. So far as I can tell, Commander Luca is the only one who has the slightest clue what's been happening between them. Although he doesn't speak on it, my judgement of him tells me he has their best interests at heart, so it makes no sense for me to get involved.

Given everything that's happening, I wonder if I wasn't better off with Myrkr. Despite the resentment I held toward him for binding me to begin with, he and I had grown close. There was a sort of understanding between us. He's the one I have most common ground with. Even before I was bound, I was more like him than I ever realized. He was the villain in my mind for so long, the ancestor I tried my damnedest not to be like. After I got to know him, though, I learned he was always just as misunderstood as I am.

I meant what I said to Jameson on the terrace that day. I have forgiven them all. That doesn't wholly erase the difficulties of my return, though. I still feel like there's no longer a place for me here. Not just in Oceanica, but in the islands. I'm not sure what I expected for my return, but it wasn't this. Never have I been so naïve to think the second my son saw me we'd overcome twenty years of resentment, but I hadn't expected for him to want to kill me. It makes sense that he'd feel like I abandoned him, but this goes deeper than that. It's hard to say what all Johanna told him to make him cling to the resentment, but I wonder if there isn't a piece to the puzzle we're all missing. I might bring it up to Josie next we speak. She has to be aware there are still things we don't know about why our children want to kill us, so maybe if we talk, we can understand a little better where they're coming from.

I still don't know what our actual plan is for them. We win the war and then what? Do we kill our own children? No. Detain them and hold them captive until they like us again? No. I'm not sure any of us know what happens next. There's no clear path forward, and it makes me question everything. I've never been in a situation that makes right and wrong so murky before. It's like floating in a grey area as large as the oceans that lead to whatever lies beyond our islands.

In the meantime, I sit in my loneliness day after day. I help when I can, but my skill set isn't very useful until the fighting starts back up. Waiting has become the bane of my existence, since I'm not even sure what it is I'm waiting for. More bloodshed, more war against my heir, more lives lost, more energy wasted on a fight I'm not sure has a meaning. There are more outcomes, but none of them are good. If there's a light at the end of this tunnel, it isn't reaching me. At least the others have tasks to distract them, but I have no choice but to wallow in the sorrow and self-pity. It's pathetic, the most useless I've ever felt.

My attempts at finding something useful to do all fall flat. Soon enough, I find myself in the room Josie has me staying in. The depression takes hold, and I lie there in the dark, hopeless. Allowed to rampage, the wallowing turns to sobbing, and the loneliness turns to abandonment and insecurity. My mind wanders back to the days of my youth. I wonder if this nagging sense of inadequacy is how I once made Jameson feel. If so, maybe I deserve this? I never meant for my strength to make him feel like less. He should have never thought he had to be as strong as me to feel loved. My existence caused all those feelings, and when it came down to it, Josie was the one to help him heal. I didn't even shoulder the responsibility for the damage my existence inflicted on my cousin. There's no doubt that I deserve to go through this. He deserves to know I understand how he felt. I can accept that I deserve this extreme suffering I'm enduring.

Failure. Worthless. Useless. Unloved. Empty. Demon. Evil. Destructive. You are nothing. My subconscious rages. I don't even know how many days have passed since I've been lying in this bed listening to it berate me for deigning to exist on the same plane as people, such amazing people as Jameson, Josie, Kai, and Callian. *You should let your son kill you. Michael is only trying to rectify the many wrongs you commit by continuing to live.* I should...

I wail; half cry, half scream, desperate for an end to this. There is no end. It keeps coming, flooding me in waves until I haven't just lost track of the days, but my identity altogether.

Knock. Knock. The sound disrupts my suffering. I'm not as grateful for it as I thought I would be. Somehow, being pulled out of it feels like an even crueler form of torture. "I don't want to be bothered. Leave."

Josie opens the door and wanders in. She looks like Hel. The exhaustion on her face ages her more than the twenty years apart did. "That might have worked better if you weren't in my palace."

She draws back the curtains, letting the sunlight in. It blinds me. The headache is instantaneous, so I bury my face in my pillow. "Out!"

"No!" Her tone mimics mine, mocking me as if I'm dramatic. "What's going on with you? The servants tell me you've holed up in here for days, refusing meals."

I groan. "Josie, butt out. This has nothing to do with you."

She laughs. "Oh, you mean the way you always butt out of my problems when they don't pertain to you. Hm, wait. I'll just proceed with my butting in, then."

I look up at her just so she can see my eyes roll. "You're an asshole."

"So, I've been told. You know what I haven't been told? What's wrong with you—that's what."

"Nothing is wrong with me, Josella. I'm just dealing with the consequences of my life."

Her face scrunches. "Consequences, huh? Yes, those happen sometimes. Care to elaborate?"

I sit up and shake my head at her. "No."

"Fine, then. I'll talk; you listen. This shit sucks for all of us, Malachi. You don't think Jameson, Kai, and I would rather hangout with you than deal with this mess? Of course we would. We just can't, just like you can't lie around evading all these problems."

"Getting up is easier said than done, Josie."

"I know that. That's why I'm here to help you do it, Malachi. I don't blame you for feeling this way, but I won't let you waste away because it's understandable that you'd want to. Get the Hel up out of the bed and let's deal with this shit so we can do all the things we want to do."

"How? Josie, how are we going to deal with it?"

She shrugs. "Together, Malachi. We've dealt with far worse threats than our pissed off children together."

I chuckle. It's not funny, but there's humor buried beneath the truth of it. She shoots just as straight as ever. Her candor is something I've always loved about her. "Fine, fine. I'm getting up. I'll be out in thirty, I promise."

She huffs, a slight smiling curling beneath it. "You better be, or I'm fighting you."

"You never change, Jos. Bossy ass, violent, adorable little sister."

"Yeah, yeah, yeah."

I throw a pillow at her as she walks out the door. She made me feel better. The feeling of depression still weighs on me, but it's lighter now. As I rise from the bed, I have more confidence that I can overcome it. She's right. Before she met Jameson, or Kai, or Cal, and before I was on good terms with Jameson or knew Johanna, it was just me and Josie on a boat. She and I have been together since the beginning. She's my sister in every way that matters. It's underselling our bond to think that she can't drag me out of this mess.

CHAPTER Twenty Five

DERANGED, DEBAUCHED, DEPRAVED

LILLY

Michael was right. I can read this. Who knew I understood angelic tongues? Dad Jameson had a ton of books written in them, but I never bothered looking at them because I just assumed it'd look like gibberish to me. Of course, the damn purging ritual is so complicated that I don't have a clue what it's talking about even if I can read it. It says that for a mortal to perform it, they must first rise, then fall, so they can find the true medium. Those terms, when used by angels and demons, usually refer to either rising to the level of an angel or falling to that of a demon. I can do neither of which because I'm a damn human, being a priestess doesn't change that.

There must be something here that I'm not getting. Maybe that's not what those terms mean in this context. I toss the idea out to Michael. "It says I must first rise, then fall. Any idea what that could mean aside from becoming an angel, then falling to demonhood?"

He raises an eyebrow. "But the spell is for priests and priestesses. That's not biologically possible."

"I know. That's why I'm asking for a potential alternate meaning."

"There isn't one, Seshen. There's no other context those specific words could refer to. In angelic and demonic culture, they have no other meaning. That's actually where the mortal phrase 'falling in love' comes from. When Myrkr loved Linola, he fell from angelhood to demonhood. Many angels now believe romantic love to be the mark of a demon, which I find illogical. They seem to just skip the fact that Rettferd also loved Linola, and he didn't fall from angelhood. It's a superstition at best."

I enjoy hearing him discuss his thoughts on the culture of angels. My education was more one-sided than I realized. I don't think my parents ever realized that their views on demonkind were bigoted. To them, they loved

Malachi, so how could they see demons through an unkind lens? That's sort of the issue, though. They see Malachi as being good despite his demonhood, which implies demonic nature is inherently evil. I grew up with the belief that demons were bad but could overcome it if they wanted to.

Being with Michael has taught me otherwise. Now, I see that the things angels and humans consider 'bad' about demons are just reactions to a system that has repeatedly made them out to be monstrous. They have every right to be angry about centuries of oppression and hate being directed at them. In fact, I'd say it's a natural reaction to have. The world is wrong to make it out to be some great evil.

I look at Michael as he stands across the room. He's gorgeous. It doesn't matter to me what anyone else sees. I love him and I know in my heart that he's not evil. All I see when I look at this man is how wonderful he is. Part of it is physical attraction, sure. His flawless, dark skin, glowing red eyes, and the hard lines of his muscles are all enticing. Some part of me just wants to trace each of his bulging veins with my tongue, working my way down his body. The other part, though, is just the way he loves me. For everything he's done, he's always treated me like the most precious thing in existence.

I consider other demons that I've met. Alexandria, Myrkr, Pythias, and Malachi; aside from that guy who got out of line when I first arrived, I've yet to meet one I'd consider evil. With that thought in mind, I address

Michael again. "It's really, really shitty for the angels to treat you and the other demons that way. I'm sorry."

He gives me a reluctant smile in return. "It's hard for me not to blame them, but in the end, it's not their fault. Just like humans are just repeating what they learned from angels, angels are just repeating what they learned from their masters. When you boil it down, the primary source of discrimination against demons is the gods, particularly the one who created Myrkr and Rettferd."

I yawn, closing the book I'd been using to study the ritual. "I think it's time for a break."

Michael agrees, if for no other reason than because he would rather us indulge one another than continue discussing multidimensional cultural politics that always lead to his kind being screwed over. I get up and wander across the room toward him. The sight of my approach causes him to open up. His broad shoulders draw back and light flickers in his eyes. This man's instinct is to come to life at the mere idea of being nearer to me. There's nothing casual about the way he loves. It's the opposite. The magnetic pull between us offers such an unheard-of level of intensity that it sends us both into a frenzy.

I make a point of keeping my steps slow so I can observe the changes in him as I get closer. Each time my shoeless feet take a step; it elicits a reaction from him. I'm not even sure he knows it's happening. The rise and fall of his chest speeds up, his breaths becomes labored and desperate. His throat bobs and his eyes grow even wider. Both of his fists clench as if he's trying to keep himself from rushing to me because, as bad as he wants to, he wants to enjoy the sight of me coming to him for just a few moments longer.

I love how needy he is. It's adorable, but still somehow sexy. His cock is already hard, straining against the fabric of his trousers. I crave more from him, so I provoke more. "Is my little whore of a demon king so easily driven to the brink by my approach? Hm, I thought you were stronger."

His eyes shoot up from my hips to my eyes, then they soften. "Stronger than many men, yes, but no man is stronger than the influence of the woman he loves, especially if she is as mesmerizing as you."

Michael

"Prove it, then. Show me how strong my influence over you really is." Seshen takes a step back and I swear it feels like she's tearing my soul out in the sweetest form of torture I've ever had the luxury of tasting. "Come to me."

I step toward her, longing to please her. She steps back again, though. "No, no. You get on your knees and crawl to your queen."

I gulp, feeling my dick grow even harder. Something about the way she makes me humiliate myself to earn her drives me wild. I lower myself to my hands and knees, licking my lips as I crawl toward her. She steps back each time I near, making me whimper and beg. The sweet sound of her cruel laughter is reason enough for me to continue. When she at last lets me near her, it's after she takes a seat. Her foot lifts from the ground and she rests it against my face. "Worship."

The singular word acts as a binding command that I dare not ignore. It's an honor to worship any part of this woman. I sit back with my legs beneath me and take hold of her ankle, letting it rest in my hands so I can place a soft kiss on the bottom of her foot. A shaky moan makes its way out of me as I creep up the sole of her foot to her toes, careful to give each the attention it deserves. She relaxes. Her composure remains intact as she watches me, but I can tell she's enjoying this just by the way her eyes stay locked on mine. When I'm sure she's satisfied with my work, I move to the other foot, giving it the same treatment.

Seshen gestures for me to come closer when I finish. As she spreads her legs and leans forward, I move between them and look up at her. She curls a finger beneath my chin, tilting it up a bit more. "Good demon. You serve me so well."

The gentle kiss she places on my forehead causes an excitement I can't explain. I love the way she can be dominant and tender at the same time. It's the perfect balance. She continues. "Do you want me to fuck you? Or do you want me to dominate you while you fuck me?"

I gulp. Both options sound amazing right now. I don't know how to answer, so I let her decide. "I love both, Seshen. Whatever you decide, I will obey."

She nods, laying back and spreading her legs further. I take her cue and incinerate my clothes and her dress. Having her around has taught me how to use my fire without harming her while still accomplishing my task. It turns out I can choose exactly what the fire burns if I pay enough attention. It just never mattered enough for me to try before now.

As soon as we're nude, I lean forward, aligning myself to her entrance. She reaches her hand up around my throat and squeezes, yanking me forward as she grinds her hips up, forcing me into that tight, wet hole. Her soft whispers drift into my ear. "You better be grateful for this pussy."

"Mhm." My gargled answer gets pushed out as I struggle for air, becoming lightheaded.

She moves her hips beneath me, swirling my cock around inside her. "And you're going to show it by fucking me properly, aren't you?"

I nod, unable to get the sound out by this point. She releases my throat, and I gasp for air. Even through the pain, I'm loving it. I thrust into her over and over before I could even catch my breath, powerless to resist the feel of her wrapped around me. Her moans fill the room, mixing with her heinous laughter as she observes my pathetic, helpless display. I moan and grunt, echoing her passion as I pull out and sink into her time and time again. "Yes, good. Good demon boy. Use your cock to please me."

I plea with breathless words. "Yes, my queen. My Seshen. My cock is worthless if it doesn't please you."

I could nut inside of her right now. I feel it moving up my shaft, ready to explode, but I try to hold it back until she orgasms. She needs to cum on my cock. I want so badly to be granted the feelings of her unraveling around me. She knows this, and just to torment me she holds out, denying me that pleasure until I can't hold out any longer and I'm forced to cum alone. The shame eats at me as I collapse forward, holding her tight. Still, I love the way it torments me as my dark queen holds me.

"You can still earn your reward, you know?"

I perk up. "How? How can I earn my reward?"

I wince at the sound of my own words, realizing just how needy I sound. This deranged woman in all her debouched glory has turned me into her depraved little bitch. Her hand glides down my back until it reaches my ass, giving it a firm squeeze. "You asked me to choose; I chose both."

I tremble. After being buried inside her, the idea of more pleasure is so overwhelming that my body can't stand the thought, yet I agree anyway. I know I can say no. She'd stop in a heartbeat if I didn't want to. That doesn't make me want to stop, though. It makes me want to push the boundary and find out how much more I can take. If it's too much, I can just call it off then. There's no point in not trying now. So, I bend my ass over and display myself to her as I wait for her to get the strap. A few minutes pass before she approaches, dawning the harness. She circles me a few times before moving to my back. Part of it was just to tease me, but the other part was her giving me a bit of a break before she tears into me.

Lilly

With both hands, I spread Michael's ass wide. I take a minute to watch the greedy way his ass puckers before I spit on it. With my thumb, I rub it around his rim for a moment, prepping him. Sometimes, he doesn't want or need prep, but right now I think it'd be too much not to do it. So, unless he tells me otherwise, I will. He doesn't tell me otherwise. I continue circling his hole for a few moments before pushing a finger inside. Then, I add a second once he's relaxed. I see his cock getting hard again as I take my time making sure he's ready to take me. "Fuck, Seshen. The way your fingers feel inside me is mind-blowing."

I massage his prostate a bit. His moans become frantic and wild. "Oh, shi— Oh, shit! Please fuck me."

Once I have him begging for it, I give him exactly what he's asking for. Bringing my strap-on to his hole, I push against it. I only put the tip in, making him even more crazed. "Go ahead," I prompt him. "Finish shoving it up your ass."

He moves a few times, prying himself open more and working his way down onto the strap. It takes a few attempts. I watch him bringing it out to the tip and leaning back into it before he can take it all. I set my hand on his back, pushing it low so his ass pokes out before

I take hold of his hips. At first, I move gently as I push and pull the strap, guiding his hips and help him. Then, my thrust become harsher. I keep pace, increasing the force of the thrusts without increasing the speed, making damn sure each stroke hits perfectly. It isn't long before we find our rhythm.

For each time I drive the strap-on into him, he throws himself back with equal force. The stimulation of it rubbing on my clit drives me wild. We're both moaning and crazed, losing ourselves in each other as I fuck him senseless. It's wild and unhinged, but we relish in each moment of our unadulterated bliss, not thinking once of the judgmental glares we'd have shot at us if anyone saw us like this. My orgasm builds rapidly, and I can tell he's close to the edge, too. He shifts all his weight to one hand and starts massaging his cock, working the load up. "Ah! Seshen!" He pants. "Please let me cum, Seshen!"

I moan back. "Yes, cum for me, baby. I'll cum with you, don't worry."

And there we both go, toppling over the edge. The orgasm is so intense I swear my knees are going to buckle as it squirts down my legs. I have to lean forward into him more to keep myself standing. That juices the last of the pleasure from us both. Once the stars fade, I pull out of him, stumbling back a bit. He falls forward, curling into a ball on the chair he was bent over. I remove the strap-on and wander over to him, sitting on the edge of the chair. "Can I touch you?"

I ask, so I know he's not too overstimulated for it. He whispers his reply. "Yes."

I rest my hand on his side, caressing him just enough to help him come down. It takes a few minutes for him to become grounded again. Even when we enjoy the play, I understand that its intensity warrants needing aftercare. He's made it known that he appreciates that before. It's important to me that our games stay games. I never want my beloved to forget how much I love and respect him. I'm glad this helps him with separating the two.

After a while, I help him up. He ends up taking the cloth that covers the ornament display in this room. He wraps himself in it, then leaves to go get our clothes. As soon as he gets back, I get dressed and we clean up, not wanting to leave this kind of mess for the servants to deal with. Once the room is clean, we head back to our own and climb into bed, just wanting to lie together and chat for a few.

We get comfortable. He lies flat and I rest my head on his chest with his arm around me. "I figured it out, y'know? While we were fucking."

He raises an eyebrow. "Figured what out, Seshen?"

"The rise and fall thing. I can do it."

He smiles. "You can do the ritual?"

I nod. "Yes. I'll gather all I need tomorrow."

"Okay. Sounds good. You can tell me all about it in the morning. Right now, let's just focus on me and you, okay?"

I like that answer. I love that no matter what, he and I come first. Our relationship is so important that not even a war can overtake it. The next day, I go gather the materials and begin the process and planning. We have to be careful because we don't want the ritual to go wrong and end up purging any of the demons on our side, so we plan carefully. It takes time to make sure we consider every factor and possibility. In between it all, we steal moments together, each of them precious memories.

One day, we drink ourselves into oblivion and goof off together. Another, we indulge in a torture session with some captives brought to us by a general who found stragglers on our shores. We assume that they're spies posing as betrayers to Oceanica and have decided it's best to torture them for what information we can get, then kill them. Besides, torturing people together is so hot. I'm not as hesitant about it anymore as I was that first time. There's nothing holding me back and Michael definitely enjoys seeing me delve so deep into the darkness we share.

Every time, we fuck afterwards. He always laughs when it's all over and says, "I love you, Seshen."

I love him, too, and I make damn sure he knows it. It's hard for me to imagine a time when I didn't love it when he called me Seshen. I can't believe I ever saw him as an enemy or someone I had to stop. I'd never wish for that now. Watching him grow and achieve his goals at my side means everything to me. I enjoy the chaos and malice we bring to this world. That's what the world needs. After everything they've put us through, they deserve whatever Hel we unleash upon them.

May they suffer our wrath and feel our rage each day that we wage war against them.

I hope we haunt their every waking thought like a plague of their own making.

May we cause every nightmare and be the root of every fear.

Together, Michael and I will bring down everything they hold dear.

Death and destruction at our hands be all that awaits them. Between the two of us, we will lead Pythias and the other men to absolute victory as we reclaim the joy that was stolen from us. Our love is our will. We will avenge every wrong done to one another.

Maniacal laughter comes from us both as we rejoice, for our plans are coming together. I haul off and stab the man. "I want him for the sacrifice."

Michael burns away his flesh slowly, drawing out screams of agony. "I'll make sure the bones are good and clean for you, Seshen."

The smell of burning flesh fills the room as I watch the spy endure the dreadful death by Michael's hand. By the time it's over, Michael has fulfilled that promise. There's nothing left on the bones, not even a single drop of fluid. If Michael hadn't purposefully prevented the fire from affecting the bones, those would be gone, too.

Now, though, they're safe. A quick rinse to clean off the residue and they'll be suitable for my purposes.

Michael has a guard take them to be washed. The man gets strict instructions to make sure they're spotless. I wouldn't want them tainting the ritual instead of helping it, after all. Immediately, I run up to Michael and leap into his arms, giggling. "That was so much fun! Can we do it again sometime?"

He chuckles, rubbing his nose to mine. "Do you have other rituals you need bones for, Seshen?"

I shake my head. "No, I just want to."

He kisses my forehead and nods. "Well, can't be telling you not to do things you want to do. I'd look like an inadequate lover if I did. Of course, we can do this anytime you like, Seshen. You know, I'd love it if you pleasured yourself while I tortured someone."

My smile must be so wide as I pictured it. "That sounds so hot."

He kisses me as we fantasize about our future explorations. If there's one thing I know for sure, it's that this man is perfect for me. Nothing could ever tear us apart. As our war rages on, that singular truth is all the reassurance we need to know it will end in our victory.

A SHIFT IN PERSPECTIVE

PYTHIAS

From the beginning, I've watched as Lilly's relationship with King Michael has grown. I am of the opinion she'll be a fine queen for Tendu. Further, I believe she will be a fine wife to him. Their happiness is something I've seldom witnessed in other couples, my marriage not excluded. The love between them is more true than any I have witnessed. Just the other day, I spotted them in each other's arms with Ace lying at their feet; the peace in their features spoke volumes to their comfort with one another. There are, of course, other instances where I've seen the undying elation they've brought to one another.

One instance is when they visit the child from Loft. The boy was understandably cautious of them at first. Given time, though, he observed their tenderness with him and has become more open. They plan to wait until he can see for sure that they have no intention of harming him to ask him if he wants to be adopted. They also hired a tutor to teach him demonic history. That way, he might come to understand why the attack on Loft occurred. I think it's a wise call on their part. Otherwise, the child might end up damaged, like they both are, and resenting them for how his life unfolds.

I'm excited about the wedding, and for the coronation that will follow. Michael hasn't received his coronation yet, since the transition of power was so sudden. He wants to hold off on it so he and Lilly will get crowned together. His position is safe anyway. The coronation is just a formality. I'd slaughter any usurper before they ever had a chance at stealing the crown. As their most trusted and most loyal, I will protect them until my dying breath, which I'm sure will be many, many years from now. Even with the likes of former King Malachi returning, they are safe so long as I am with them.

In the meantime, I watch them from the sidelines, happy to bear witness to the progression of their relationship. I admire it more with each passing day. They never hesitate to explore each other's darkness, yet, for all their relishing, their love remains as pure as the waters that filter through our native volcanos. This brings endless hope to me, as well as to others. The citizens, who once opposed the war and the separation from the alliance, are now in favor of it as they witness the greatness and prosperity Lilly and Michael are building together. Tendu will flourish for generations because of them. The people have never loved the royal family so much.

It's an honor, of sorts, when I consider my privilege of being able to watch it unfold from the front row. It feels like watching history before it becomes history. A rare pleasure, indeed, and one that lightens the load of my role. The dreadful part only comes at night, when I return to the icy atmosphere of my home. My wife has grown to hate me. We don't speak most days. When we do, it's only to argue. She has become less and less content with the royals over the years, calling them tyrants. My loyalty to them has led her to see me as a bad person. I disagree, though. I think they are wonderful and my loyalty to them is honorable. Thus, our relationship faces moral differences I'm not sure it can overcome. Whatever love we once shared died out years ago. "Pythias," she says, "Don't forget that I need money to buy Isa clothes for her coming-of-age."

I'm shocked that the woman spoke to me. Usually, she just leaves a note. I read it and sit money on top of it for whatever expenses she listed. Our daughters' coming-of-age is a special occasion, though. She deserves for her parents to set their differences aside, even if it's just for one day. My instinct is to recommend using the palace seamstress, which we wouldn't have to pay for since King Michael allows his generals to access her services on the palaces tab. I don't want to start another fight, though. "That's fine. Twenty gold pieces? Fifty? I'm not sure."

Liza seems to do some mental math. "Fifty is plenty. If there's any left, I'll bring it back to you."

I shake my head. "Just take what's left to get your own dress. You're her mother. You should look the part."

With that, I hand her seventy pieces. Her expression softens just enough to let me know she actually appreciates the gesture. "Thank you, Pythias."

We don't speak any further. She goes to our room, and I sleep on the couch. The next morning, I head to the palace for the day before she wakes. As always, I spend my day guarding Lilly. As I do, I hope Isa will grow up to be like her. Over the last weeks and months, I've seen Lilly at her best, and at her worst, and I don't think there's anyone who shines brighter. She even puts our king to shame.

I would call Lilly the prime example of the ways those most shrouded in darkness have an equal contrast of light. One side couldn't exist if the other didn't. After all, people don't hate that which they did not first love, nor do they care about rejections if they did not want to be accepted. All her traditionally 'evil' traits are just reactions to what this world has done to her. I can understand that. The world is wrong to treat people so horribly and then blame them for reacting to it.

What a beautiful thing they've done to help each other find something so pure, even as Hel breaks loose around them. "To the King, and to his Future Queen..."

Luca

My life was empty. My only family was the one I led on the battlefields. Home was the barracks where I slept alongside those I would take pride in dying for. My wife left me long ago and my daughter left with her. There was no hope beyond those walls. It wasn't just my life that was empty; it was me. Then he came. The man that threatened me with the life of the daughter I haven't seen in years. Our estrangement didn't matter. I'm her father and my role will always be to protect her, even if she doesn't know how much I love her.

I gave into his blackmail for her sake, knowing it would make myself and my men treasonous. From the start, I prepared for it to end in my death. By the grace of a young angel with more character in his pinky finger than I have in my whole body, that didn't come to fruition. It's sensible that I return that kindness by swearing to him the life that he spared. Many call swearing an oath to a boy a death sentence, but I call swearing an oath to this boy a gift.

His name is Callian, son of Queen Josella and the Kings Jameson and Kai, Crown Prince of Oceanica. I've watched him and stood at his side for many days now. His insecurities are many, but there are none that I've seen to be true. Where he thinks he is incompetent because of a lack of experience, I think he shows great competence in his decision. Where he would call himself soft, I see nothing but the level of empathy anyone who deigns to call himself a royal should display. Callian is not some young boy that will lead me to my death without proper consideration. He's my friend, and the person I trust most in this life.

Over these months of partnership between us, I've watched him grow into the king I always knew he'd be. When it comes time for his parents to step down, I have full confidence that Oceanica will be in excellent hands. To ensure that his birthright remains protected, I must not allow Michael to continue his invasions across the islands. Michael is a dangerous man who passes the poison his mother fed him along to all he reaches, even to the point of corrupting Lilliana. I must ensure he's not allowed to harm Callian either by physical body, or by reputation.

With that goal in mind, I will fight this war by Callian's side. He will come out victorious because that is the only path I see to protect my daughter, my ex-wife, my men, and my country. I like Malachi, but if I have to kill his son to protect them all, I will. If he wants to take vengeance on me after that, I will fight him and die by his hand, but it will not change what I must do. So long as I am with him, Prince Callian is safe. I suppose Alexandria and Julius are, too. The three of them probably haven't realized it yet, but they have a rather powerful attachment between the three of them.

I didn't even see it at first. Their communications just seemed confusing and semi-hostile, but as I've observed more, I don't think that's the case at all. It seems more likely that they're just getting mad at each other for an attraction that's beyond them all. Ages aside, they're all inexperienced with romance, from what I gather. Moreover, Callian was impacted more by Mianora's betrayal than he says. He has trust issues. So, they lash out and behave ridiculously because they don't understand their own emotions, which makes them fearful of those emotions. They might be mature in many aspects of their lives, but not in this one. I'm confident they'll find their way, though.

Until then, I'll just look out for them from the sidelines. I don't mind watching over them. The three of them might have something even more special than what the queen and her kings do. It could be a sign of great things to come if they have the space to continue building upon the unspoken bond that's already in place. It'll be fun to watch; one of the few bright sides to the chaos that has taken over our land. In times of darkness, it always helps to find some silver lining to help us get through the bloodshed and hatred being perpetuated around us. Love and acceptance are the best deterrents to evil.

My plan is to protect it until they can do so themselves. I hope this will allow Callian the opportunity to heal and give love another chance. He deserves more than he's received in his experiences with it. If his connection with the Alacrian demons helps him get there, I see nothing wrong with it. Alacrium has already made themselves clear: They don't intend to fight us, ever, which I believe because there's been whispers of them fighting on another front. If my suspicions are correct, they do, in fact, have bigger fish to fry. If we survive this, I know they'll ask us to help them do so.

Who knows? By the time this is all said and done, they may be a greater ally to Oceanica than even Pallentine has been. It's a shocking thought, but one that's becoming more plausible by the day. The inklings of greater wars to come lead me to believe that their enemies are our enemies, too. In the long run, I think things will work out. I'll make sure they do. Callian, Alexandria, and Julius are the future, not just this land, but the entire world, from where I stand. It makes sense that I'd back them all. My decision to stand by them above all others is for the best.

Alone in the barracks, I take a moment to myself, not to grieve the negative, but to hope that better will follow. "May the new generation lead us to a better world; one where all the wars have passed and peace reigns as the supreme mark of the era."

Johanna

Hours blend to days, which blend into weeks, and then months. It doesn't take long for me to lose track of time in the Spirit Realm altogether. It's always night here. With no sun, no warmth, but no cold either. It's sheer nothingness in the Spirit Realm. Before things went south between us, I'd always admired Josie's connection to the Spirit Realm. I'd wondered if perhaps it was a world better than our own, from the way she spoke of her visits here. Wherever I am, though, is not the place she described. None of the vibrancy she depicted in her long-winded rants about this realm is present. It's just me, alone, in the darkness. Yet another reason to hate my former best friend.

I walk, if only so I don't cry. There's no way to go, no way out. The emptiness becomes so overwhelming that I lose myself to it, finally collapsing and letting the despair take hold. I wail. My instinct to reach for my runes takes over as the sadness and rage merges into a cauldron of unchecked fury, but they've evaporated from my body. I'm powerless here, just a soul like any other. I'd never put much effort into my physical strength because my magic was all I needed to make my enemies tremble before me. It's impossible to word the many ways in which that bites me in my ass now.

I lie flat on my stomach and bury my face in the ground. Imagine my surprise when I playful chuckle approaches me; one I recognize well. "Are you done, or should I allot more time for your tantrum?"

Cal... Not Callian, but Cal, the one whose name is now carried by the prince of Oceanica. I look up. "Cal! It's really you."

He smirks, answering my shock with a bit of that playful banter Josie so loved about him. "I had no clue. Here, I thought I was some other dead person impersonating me."

I smile, truly smile, for the first time in so long. The familiarity of the friendship he and I once shared flaring back to life. Then, it hits me. He doesn't know who I am now, or how things have changed in the Living Realm. There's no way he could.

I stop to think for a moment about what to do. Should I tell him? Should I just omit it? I'm inclined to think it'd be more beneficial to hide it. He could be helpful. He's been here a long time now. Maybe he can show me how things work. How to get to the place Josie described. I stuff away every ounce of feeling I once had for him and immediately commit to making him help me. I'll have to play at being his friend and lie to him until he can get me what I need. Standing up, I smirk. "Same old smart ass."

He rolls his eyes in return. "Same old bitch."

I scoff, then he hugs me. "Good to see you, Johanna."

My laughter is almost authentic. "You, too, Cal."

"Come on, I'll take you to my place. You can stay with me until you learn the ropes."

I nod, relieved that it's working, as I follow him to wherever his place is. As I tag along beside him, he seems troubled. "I don't know what it is lately. Usually, souls get dropped straight into the village. Recently, though, they've been getting dropped further and further from it. I think the realms are unstable."

That's something I don't have to lie about. I have no clue what could have caused such a thing. It gives me an idea, though. "Hm, that's odd. It would take an enormous amount of force to destabilize the realms, wouldn't it?"

Cal agrees as I walk alongside him. "It would."

He doesn't say much else as we walk, but I can tell he's concerned by it. It sounds like an opportunity to me, though. If the divide is weakening, doesn't that make it more plausible for us to get back to the Living Realm? I don't know how we'd do it without our runes, but with time, I think we could find a way.

Our walk continues for quite some time before we reach the village. My eyes widen in awe as I see the marvelous place Josie once told me about. It's exactly how she described it. The vibrant colors and the smell of candied strawberries demand the attention of my senses, forcing me to realize how hungry I am. Spirits can get hungry, apparently. I wonder what else still functions in the Spirit Realm. Do I still have to use the bathroom, bathe, and sleep too? What happens if I don't? Can I have a second death? If so, where do I go? So many questions flood my mind even as I'm consumed by the sights all around me.

There's so much joy here that it's kind of amazing. I might even set aside my plotting if I didn't think the revenge plans my son undoubtedly has would benefit from my return. I know his enemies well. They won't be easy foes to face. I imagine the tides of that war will turn several times before he succeeds. With my support, though, I think he'd succeed much sooner. Michael is strong and competent, but so are those he faces. He'll be cautious as he plans, as I raised him to be.

In time, Cal and I arrive at a home. The structure is that of an A-frame, presumably because the style conserves space, which might be beneficial in a place that needs to hold every soul that dies. He opens the door, and we go inside. The atmosphere is cozy. His interior design choices favor comfort over luxury. Such things wouldn't matter as much here, I suppose. It is surprising, though, considering his aristocratic background in the mortal realm.

I follow behind him, listening closely as he shows me around. "This is the kitchen. Down the hall is the guestroom, where you'll be staying, and a bathroom. The linen closet is there, too. The living space is just over there. Upstairs, the whole second floor is my bedroom. I hadn't felt the need to add a door because it's just me, so just yell to make sure I'm decent before coming up."

I nod along as he loads some food onto a plate for me. "Here you go, eat up. There's plenty here. I remember how hungry I was when I got here. It'll fade overtime, as your spirit adjusts to not needing food to survive. Soon, food will just be something you eat for nostalgia or enjoyment."

Ah, that's how it works. I see. "Okay, that makes more sense. The same applies to the bathroom, I presume. Spirits just do it to maintain a sense of normalcy and connection to their mortal lives?"

He agrees. "Yeah. Some get past it eventually and just embrace the change, but many prefer to do it. There're no rules or guidelines. Do whatever makes you most comfortable."

After that, I spend the next few days learning more about my surroundings. There is one thing that seems very prominent. Everyone is very clear that we should not wander beyond the village. Out there, in the nothingness I wandered upon my arrival, is where the evil spirits get held. Priests and priestesses apparently guard the evil souls to ensure they don't escape. I'm glad I wasn't evil enough to get marked as one of them. I take it as a confirmation that I was as justified as I thought I was in my actions. The pure souls are disgusting, not even relenting in their duties after death. No one can navigate it until they're like Josie, a priest, or priestess. That might be the key to getting free, though. I imagine that if one can navigate the realm, they can also find a way out.

As I learn more, I form a plan. Assuming Cal knows where Kimble is, we can ask her to help us navigate. She's a natural spirit, not a mortal that died and became one. That's why she was compatible with Josie as a familiar way back when. I'm sure she could guide us. I think she'd go for it if we asked. She and Cal would both see it as an opportunity to get home to Josie and the others. They don't need to know that my son and I would kill them all upon my return. I'll keep that bit to myself. Now, I just need to figure out how to broach the subject with Cal, which is difficult because I'm not sure how to say it without rousing questions.

Eventually, I decide to just go for it. If he asks too many questions, I'll just drop it and shut down, then come back to the subject another time with a better plan. "Hey, Cal. Can I ask you something?"

"Of course," he answers.

"I just wanted to ask if we could go back or try to find a way."

He raises an eyebrow. "That's a risky move, Johanna. I'd be open to it in theory, but in actuality, it's not that simple. Even if we had someone who could navigate outside the village, we'd still have to spend a very long time searching. Then, we'd also be risking screwing up the balance even more, or allowing a less kind spirit to follow us."

"Oh," I reply. "Well, if we do, Josie could help us fix it once we're on the other side."

His facial expression changes at the mention of her name. He's considering it. With the seed planted, my plan is now in motion.

Maria Levato is a BIPOC woman and disabled veteran. She has written two books, ***The Islands of Rune*** (2023) and ***Journey to Rallem*** (2025). Maria also writes/hosts the Nerdology 101 blog on her website.

Outside of her writing, Maria serves the writing community in other ways. She's the chair of the PRO Advisory Committee for the Romance Writers of America and an ambassador for the Washington, D.C. chapter of The Authors Guild.

www.ingramcontent.com/pod-product-compliance
Lightning Source LLC
LaVergne TN
LVHW010148070526
838199LV00062B/4289